I0619437

THE RAVEN'S REVENGE

GINA BLACK

 GreatBird
Books

Copyright © 2011 Gina Black
All rights reserved.
ISBN: 0615472923
ISBN-13: 978-0615472928

Published by GreatBird Books
Contact: info@greatbirdbooks.com
www.greatbirdbooks.com

Cover art by Hot Damn Designs
www.hotdamndesigns.com

This is a work of fiction. Names, characters, places, and incidents are either the product of the author's imagination or are used fictitiously.

This is a revised version of the story originally published by The Wild Rose Press in 2007

10 9 8 7 6 5 4 3 2 1

Published in the United States of America

DEDICATION

To Elise, who helped me start it; Bobbi and Jerri, who set me on the road; and Lisa, without whose steadfast encouragement I might never have finished it. And to Sara, Theo, and Taylor for being there every step of the way.

CHAPTER ONE

Dorsetshire, England
Autumn, 1663

Nicholas Edward Henry Philip Montford, Seventh Earl of Ashton, struggled through the dense foliage, clutching his shirtsleeve to staunch the blood streaming down his left arm. His head throbbed. He'd looked back but a moment, to see if he'd lost his pursuers, and suffered a mighty whack from a low hanging branch as a result. That was when he'd parted company with his horse, an indifferent beast, rented from the inn, with no sense of loyalty to a somewhat incapacitated rider.

Now the pain, as relentless as a blacksmith's hammer, helped keep away the fatigue. But not for much longer. Nicholas could feel his life force drain away with each heartbeat.

Without warning, his boot slipped on the bracken. He went down, bracing himself against the fall with both hands. Pure agony shot through his wounded arm. His head felt like it split in two. He groaned a deep feral sound, more animal than man.

Rolling onto his back, eyes clenched against the pain stabbing at his temples, Nicholas took a great breath of the cold night air. The ripe smell of decaying leaves filled his lungs. He opened his eyes to see the full globe of the moon shining down through the branches. The stars twinkled like old friends happy to see him after a long absence.

Sudden crashing in the underbrush alerted him to danger. Snorts and grunts announced a new enemy. Nicholas raised his aching head. From across the clearing, the eyes of a wild boar gleamed in the moonlight.

He repressed a chuckle. What irony it would be to come to his end gored on the tusks of a swine.

But he had not survived the seamy streets of Amsterdam, the slave markets in Algiers, and endless days and nights floating adrift on the stormy Mediterranean to die here. It was not his time. At least he hoped not. He had yet to honor the promise he'd made to his father.

Rising awkwardly, Nicholas reached inside his cloak and pulled the flintlock pistol from his waistband. The weapon felt cold and reassuring in his hand.

They faced each other, wounded man and wild beast, quiet and still in the moonlight. Then the creature looked away. For a moment, Nicholas thought it might leave, but it turned toward him, and with a loud snort, it charged.

Swearing and praying at the same time, Nicholas pulled the gun's hammer from half to full cock. He aimed between the glittering eyes, adjusted to compensate for the pistol's tendency to shoot to the right, and squeezed hard on the trigger.

The gun's recoil threw him back. Pain throbbed through his head, echoing in his wounded arm. He struggled to remain standing. Sparks flashed brilliantly, then all went black. The loud explosion sealed his ears against sound. The foul stench of the powder invaded his nose and mouth, making it hard to breathe.

Had he hit the beast?

Nicholas strained against the night, trying to see through the murky air. With a pop, his ears cleared. All was quiet, save for the pounding of his heart and his own harsh breath. Finally, the darkness took shape.

Ten feet away lay the motionless boar.

Nicholas shivered. It wouldn't be long before another predator discovered him. Weakened and one-armed, he could not reload. He would simply have to keep going.

Gritting his teeth, he stuffed the still-hot firearm into his waistband and set forth once again. For what seemed an eternity, he heard only the sounds of his own boots crunching the fallen leaves.

He pushed on until he could go no farther.

Fighting against his own weakness, he braced himself against a tree to keep upright. The hot flush of fever crept through bones that now ached as much as his head. Nicholas rubbed his brow to clear the grogginess. Perhaps he could reach Ashfield before he died. Then they could bury him beside his mother. He'd like that. More likely, he'd be strung from a gibbet as a lesson to others.

But they'd have to catch him first.

A grim smile tugged at his lips. He staggered forward with new determination.

Then up ahead he saw Witches' Rock. Like a familiar scent packed away with clothes in an old trunk, a memory wafted through his muddled mind, and he remembered where safety lay. With sudden certainty, Nicholas knew it was not his fate to die this night. He had come home.

His steps took on new sureness as he skirted the large boulder. Another twenty feet or so brought him to a squat freestone structure. Pushing open the wooden door, he fell forward, collapsing onto the hard dirt floor.

"As you know, on your brother's death, this fifteen-month past, you became heiress to this great estate." Father's words echoed through the high-ceilinged room like a death knell.

As the morning chill eased into her bones, Katherine Welles tucked a strand of hair into her white cap, preparing herself for her father's usual lament.

Gray skies outside cast dim illumination through the tall mullioned windows behind her. Grandfather sat stiff-backed behind a great expanse of table, bare but for his open Geneva

Bible. Standing beside him, her father puffed out his chest as he prepared to continue.

"In that one moment, the fortunes of our family changed. It seemed my plans had been for naught." Gerald Welles shook his head. "I then steeled myself to make the best of the betrothal we had arranged for you with John Perkins, though it was no longer to our advantage. 'Twas your mother's wish for you to marry him, yet her ill health prevented it."

A wave of sadness washed over Katherine. "Yes, Father, I know this."

"Do not interrupt me, daughter," he barked.

Katherine's jaw tightened. She ached to get back to work and away from Father's offhand references to the loss of those she held dear, but there would be no hurrying him, not even on washday. Katherine bit the inside of her cheek to keep her expression blank and her thoughts to herself.

Gerald ambled around the table. "Now 'tis time to see you settled, with a husband to guide you and run this estate when I am gone." He clasped his hands below his rounded belly. "When your mother departed this life, I wrote to John's father. Robert apprised me of his desire to remove his family from England. The political climate—"

"Since that libertine Charles Stuart assumed the crown," Grandfather Wilfred broke in, wagging an ominous forefinger, "it is no longer safe to worship."

Gerald coughed and turned back to her. "The Perkins family will journey to Massachusetts Colony in the spring."

Katherine blinked. The New World? Leave Ashfield? A sudden lightness lifted her heart.

"Robert Perkins is a fair man. Massachusetts Colony is a great distance, and there is much danger in the passage. As you are now my heir, he has offered to release you from our agreement."

Katherine gripped her hands together behind her back to keep them from shaking as the hope, which had risen so suddenly, was dashed just as fast.

"It is now official. The papers arrived two days ago. We have set aside the prior arrangement."

Not marry John?

Not escape Ashfield?

Katherine bowed her head in a submissive gesture that covered her agitation. Short nails bit into her palms. Father had signed the contract three years ago. She had thought it ironclad. A great foreboding hit her. She did not want to hear his next words.

"In keeping with your status as heiress," Gerald rocked back on his heels, "we now seek a more favorable alliance."

Katherine's stomach tightened into a hard knot.

"To my gratification, our neighbor, Richard Finch, has offered to take you as wife. We concluded our negotiations last eve. You will say your espousals in a week."

Hot bile rose in Katherine's throat. Her head shot up. "It c-cannot be true."

"And why is that, daughter?"

"I cannot marry him. I do not even like him."

Gerald frowned. "That was precisely how your mother felt when we married, but it made no matter. She brought a good dowry, which I turned to my advantage by purchasing this fine property when Cromwell made the offer." He made a gesture meant to encompass all of Ashfield. "The purpose of marriage is to form alliances, join bloodlines, unite properties."

Grandfather spoke. "A daughter's duty is to obey her father."

Katherine was aware of her duties, as well as the usefulness of daughters. Yet, betrothed to John Perkins, she had felt safe from her father's ambitions. She would have been content with John, a sweet boy, with a native kindness. She might have even grown to love him. She would have welcomed a life in the New World, a rugged new land with limitless possibilities.

"You cannot ask this of me, Father."

"I am not asking." His eyes, now flinty, mirrored those of her grandfather. "I am telling you."

Katherine's breath caught. Turning away to hide the alarm she could no longer mask, she dragged in a mouthful of air. Her thoughts cascaded in a frantic search for a protest that might have some influence. "There has not been a proper mourning period since my mother's death. Nor since Sarah Finch's passing."

"'Tis sufficient," Grandfather interjected in his thin reedy voice. "A man has needs a wife must see to."

Katherine's stomach lurched, as panic rose like sickness in her belly.

Gerald rapped his knuckles on the tabletop. "His daughter is needing a mother. And he is needing a son."

Sarah Finch had worked earnestly to provide one. After two stillborn babes, a girl had survived. But the birth of this daughter had proved Sarah's undoing. She died a scant week later from childbed fever.

Katherine had attended the dying woman, noting that Richard Finch showed more disappointment over the birth of a daughter than the death of a wife. In truth, the man had always discomfited her. His ice-cold gaze sent shivers through her whenever they met. As one of Cromwell's magistrates, he had been merciless to anyone caught breaking the Sabbath, meting out punishment with a zealousness that bordered on cruelty.

"I will not marry him." Unbidden, the words spilled out.

"Look at me, daughter." Pudgy fingers grasped her chin. Nearsighted eyes drilled into her. "You will marry Finch because I say so. We shall unite our properties. In that, something good will come from your brother's death." His face grew red from the force of his words. "You will not defy me!"

"Nothing good will ever come from Edward's death."

Regret flashed in his eyes before they shuttered. He let go of her chin and drew back his hand. She knew what was coming, but she would not give him the satisfaction of flinching or cowering. Refusing to drop her gaze, she met his furor, eye-to-eye as his open palm struck her unprotected cheek.

"Hear me well, daughter, I give you a sennight to change your heart."

Shaking and blinking back tears, Katherine slipped out the

washroom door and stepped free of the imposing limestone and flint structure that held her future captive. She tread past the bare roses her mother had lovingly tended, making her way through the gardens, then the stables and finally across the back lawn.

At the shelter of the wood's edge, she heaved a ragged breath. The rich mulch of compost filled her lungs, but did not provide the inner calm she needed. Leaves danced in wavy circles at her feet. A sudden gust of wind pulled off her hood, tugging at the lock of hair that always escaped her cap. Dark storm clouds rolled in, but they did not deter her. She must get away.

Oh, to have the courage to flee—not just for this afternoon, but truly and forever. To leave this betrothal behind and the sorrow that permeated Ashfield, to make her own choices, dream her own dreams, and find her own life.

Would that she had been born a man, or that she had another brother who would inherit, or that Ashfield had been entailed. With a lesser dowry, she would not be as appealing. But as a woman of property she was prey to the schemes of greedy men. Father's avarice was shackling her to a lifetime with Richard Finch, to being ruled by a man with ice-cold eyes.

Like Sarah Finch, would she sicken and die?

Katherine's outer calm crumpled. She gave in to the tears she had been holding back. With them, the clouds opened, releasing cool raindrops. They fell lightly at first, soothing the place on her cheek still burning from her father's slap. She hadn't cried then. Now the tears wouldn't stop.

Neither did the rain. Big hearty drops splashed down on her, seeping through her heavy woolen cloak and the seams of her practical leather shoes.

In the distance, a jagged spear of lightning rent the sky followed a long moment later by the boom of thunder.

As her crying eased, a sense of wild expectancy ran through her. She wanted to scream with the wind loud enough to be heard in the treetops. To run and dance and sing. To defy the peril of the storm, and the peril of being the daughter of the ambitious man who ruled her. To shake off the Puritan strictures she had been raised by.

Instead, Katherine wiped her face and continued her walk through the undergrowth, ignoring the cold and wet. A branch snapped back, drenching parts of her that weren't already soaked. She slipped on the slick leaves but managed to stay upright.

As the lightning came closer, she could almost feel the earth shake with each crash of thunder. The weather seemed to mirror the wild thoughts infusing her soul. In truth, there had been a surprising number of thunderstorms in recent years. Grandfather said they were a sign of God's displeasure at the return of the monarchy and the general licentiousness of Charles II, but Katherine didn't think the same God that made her herbs grow would be so vengeful as to punish them all for the sins of just one.

Was it God's will she should marry Richard Finch? She turned her face up to the sky. Cold water pelted down in a harsh baptism. If lightning struck her, would it be God's judgment on her disobedience, or simply because she was a foolish girl who'd run into the arms of a thunderstorm?

She shook her head and plunged deeper into the cover of the woods. Her sodden cloak flapped about her ankles. She stumbled, grabbing onto a nearby tree to keep from falling to the rich loamy earth. Icy water ran inside her clothing. More likely she would catch an ague from this drenching.

Katherine shivered and pulled the hood back over her head. Even under the cover of the trees, she was soaked. She should turn back, return to Ashfield, to the warmth of a roaring fire and dry clothing. But her feet paid her thoughts no mind and continued to take her further and further away.

Then Katherine realized her destination.

The cottage.

Edward had been the first to find it. With each visit, they had braved the spirits said to inhabit Witches' Rock. If spirits there were, they had left her and Edward alone, and kept away everyone else. A perfect place to seek safety from the storm.

Pushing through low-hanging branches, Katherine burst out of the woods to the clearing. The full impact of the storm hit her. Holding her cloak against the deluge, she forded swollen puddles, scurried past the large rock, and came to a halt.

The door stood open.

Katherine hovered at the threshold until a sudden crash of thunder sent her inside the dark room. Raising a hand to her chest, she worked to quiet her unease. All was still, yet she sensed she was not alone.

A flash of lightning illuminated the small space. Not three steps away, a man lay sprawled across the floor. Katherine sucked in her breath. She peered into the shadows, her senses straining. Thunder boomed outside. As her eyes adjusted, his form separated from the gloom.

She waited and watched from the doorway. Could he be dead? Her nose would have told her so. Perhaps he slept, a vagrant having found a dry spot, as she had, to wait out the storm—or even a drunkard in a sodden stupor.

Katherine took a cautious step toward him. He rested on his back, one leg bent at the knee, the other stretched almost to the wall. She knelt down and sniffed. He did not smell of spirits, but of something foreign and aromatic, like an exotic spice. Gingerly she placed a hand on his chest.

He groaned and turned to face her.

She snatched her hand away and stepped back. Her heart pounded as the storm raged behind her. She waited but he made no further movement. His eyes remained closed.

Could he be ill?

The small pox?

Plague?

Was she safer outside, braving the elements, or inside with him?

As the rain pounded on the roof, a new question formed. If he was in need of aid, could she leave him?

Katherine heaved a sigh. No, she could not go without a fair effort to provide help.

Who was he? Dark hair lightened on one side by a streak of gray—or was it white?—framed a tall forehead over a pronounced aristocratic nose. A strong jaw, with perhaps a day's growth of beard, held a wide full-lipped mouth and a cleft chin.

Not a handsome face, really, but a distinctive one, and not one she recognized.

Perhaps he was a nobleman who had been set upon by outlaws. Dressed in unrelieved black, he wore no jewels. Might he be a Puritan?

She trailed her fingertips across the heated skin covering his cheekbone, brushing away strands of hair and revealing dried blood crusted at his temple. Matted hair clung to his ear.

Katherine frowned. Head wounds could be serious, sometimes stealing a man's wits. Although she tended the minor ailments of the Ashfield tenants, it was possible this man required a surgeon.

Ruing the lack of light, Katherine probed the wounded area.

His eyes popped open. Her heart jumped. He grabbed her hand, holding it in a powerful grip. The raging storm faded. All she could feel was the heat radiating from his fingers. He spoke, but his words were drowned out by a crack of thunder. His eyes were dark, glassy, and unfocused. Katherine doubted he saw her. She leaned closer.

He shifted position but did not release her. Unbalanced, she grabbed his shoulder to keep from falling. He bellowed and jerked away, relinquishing her hand. Katherine rocked back on her heels.

"Will not die. Get it back for you," he said to the darkness behind her.

Katherine tossed a quick look to see if someone was there, but saw only the rain pouring down outside the open door.

The man thrashed about again, and she stroked his forehead as if quieting a babe. Gradually he stilled, and Katherine stopped.

His eyes popped open. "Mother?"

The word was plaintive, a boy's cry, not that of a man full grown. A rush of sadness overwhelmed her along with an overpowering urge to comfort him. She touched his brow again.

"Hot...so hot...Hell?"

His eyes, focused now, looked straight into hers. Katherine felt a jolt of connection.

"Angel..." His lips curved, and he sighed. "Heaven." His eyes closed, releasing her.

As the intensity of the moment faded, some of Katherine's tension eased. The man breathed evenly and lay still.

Katherine eyed his shoulder. There was not enough light for her to make anything out so she used her hands to explore his arm for clues. The fabric was rough and hard. Even without illumination, dark stains stood out on his hands. Blood? She ran her fingers lightly over his upper body pulling back the heavy wool cloak.

The highly polished metal of a gun glinted from the waistband of his breeches. Her heart dropped.

Perhaps he was an outlaw. And perhaps she should know more about him before she ran off to get help. He must carry identifying papers or other items.

Awkwardly, and with full knowledge that she transgressed against a helpless man, Katherine began her search.

His finely stitched linen shirt revealed no information besides its obvious quality. An inside pocket attached to his cloak contained a powder horn, a pouch of bullets, coins of various denominations—some foreign, and an odd cylindrical item, wider at one end than the other, with glass at both ends. She'd never seen anything like it.

Was he foreign like his money? He'd spoken without an accent.

Katherine's eyes lit on a piece of shiny, black satin tucked next to the pistol in his waistband. She tugged it out, almost dropping it when she realized it was a cowl.

Realization hit her like a shot.

The Raven!

He'd robbed three coaches in as many weeks, causing a furor of gossip and speculation by stealing clothes off the backs of gentlemen, and sending their coaches off without them. He apologized to the ladies for "exposing them to the company they keep," and told the affected men, "Now you can be seen for who you really are." Her neighbors had been outraged, yet Katherine had silently approved the Raven's choice of victims, thus far all sanctimonious prigs.

Had that been by design? Or by chance?

She shook her head. Either way, she could not understand why anyone would behave as the Raven did. Was it perversity? And even if it was, could she leave him wounded and alone?

She sighed. For certain, if she went for help, his whereabouts would become known. She might as well turn him in to the King's justice. That meant Richard Finch.

Katherine brushed aside a lock of hair on the man's forehead.

His frown eased at her touch.

Her heart softened. Criminal or no, she could not let him die. Not if it was possible to save him.

She placed a quavering hand over his chest, and began a silent prayer. Not a Puritan prayer, as practiced in secret by father and grandfather. Nor the kind publicly professed by Charles II, or even the kind, it was said, he practiced in private. Katherine did not know if the man before her was Roundhead or Royalist, Protestant or Catholic. In the months since the death of her brother, she had come to doubt God favored one over the other, so she made a devout and impassioned plea for strength, and for guidance to save this man's life.

CHAPTER TWO

The rain stopped as suddenly as it began.

Katherine returned to Ashfield chilled, soggy, and determined. She might have a week before acquiescing to her father's wishes, but she had mere hours to save a man's life.

Heedless of the water trailing in her wake, she crossed the stone floor of the great hall into the antechamber containing their meager library. Pausing before the bookshelves, she noted the accumulation of dust and added another item to the mental list of tasks requiring her direct supervision. Cobwebs hung from the corners. A mouse had breakfasted on the spine of Edward's Latin primer.

Removing her sodden cloak, she laid it on the stone window-seat. The heavy tome she needed perched on the top shelf. Written by a French surgeon, it had been useful when she'd treated tenants with injuries beyond her skill. Fortunately, it was in the King's English and not Latin, of which she had only rudimentary knowledge.

Rising on tiptoe, she reached for the book.

"You are certain you shot him?"

Katherine fell back on her heels at the sound of her father's voice and the approaching footsteps. The small room offered no place to hide. She wished she could disappear into the floor.

"Indeed." She heard the smug satisfaction in Richard Finch's voice. "I winged the Raven on the Melbury road."

"What of the rest of his gang?" Asked her father just outside the doorway.

Katherine shrank back.

"Gang?" Finch cleared his throat. "Cowards all. As soon as I shot the leader they ran off."

Deserted him? Left him to die? Or did they go for help?

Katherine frowned and tucked a strand of hair back into her cap. Why did they not take him with them? And how would they find him now? He lay a good distance from the Melbury road.

Finch spoke again. "Quite foolish for him to attempt a holdup on a full moon. I could see him quite clearly. Although with that cowl I could not get a look at his face. Nevertheless, I expect he shall trouble us no further."

Gerald coughed.

"I have Jakes searching for him," Finch said. "Better I had killed the blackguard, but likely he will die from the wound."

He will not, Katherine vowed. *I will not let him.*

A vision of the man came to her. Even wounded and in pain, he had seemed strong and vital. But bullets carried noxious humors that were often fatal. She must get back to him and remove it before the poison spread.

"Mistress Welles," Richard Finch's voice pierced her thoughts. "What a surprise to find you here." He looked her up and down boldly. She ran her hands over the damp folds of her fustian skirt and wondered if Father's slap showed. Taking a deep breath, she raised her chin to meet Finch's gaze while her stomach tightened.

A perfectly coifed brown periwig sat above a handsome face. Refined, if diminutive, features joined with cheeks and chin as finely chiseled as a marble statue. But his appearance held no attraction for her. Lips—perhaps a shade too thin—fell into their usual sneer, the straight nose tilted up too high, and cold blue eyes stared back at her.

Katherine suppressed a shiver.

"I was concerned to hear you had gone out in such dangerous

weather." Finch extended an elegant hand. "'Twas most imprudent of you, Katherine. But I shall not chide you now, instead I shall rejoice with you on this happy day."

His well-manicured fingers hung in midair but Katherine did not take them. A very un-Puritan ruffle ran along his cuff. Like so many others, had he shifted his religion with the return of the King?

"Knowing your father apprised you of our betrothal this morn, I but awaited the storm's end to join you." Finch stepped forward, reaching for her hand. Katherine stepped back and pressed herself flat against the bookshelves.

Gerald stood across the small room, holding a sheet of paper close before his face. He paid no mind to their interplay.

Finch moved forward again. Eyes glinting, a smug smile played across his mouth. He pulled her fist from its hiding place in the folds of her skirt, and raised her knuckles to his dry lips. His nails bit into her fingers.

Katherine clenched her teeth, restraining the urge to grab her hand and flee.

Finch lowered his grasp, but did not release her or ease his grip. A challenge flickered in his eyes, and she knew he dared her to resist.

If she did, would he stop, or would he hurt her all the more? With vivid clarity, Katherine realized that marriage to him would consist of endless moments like this until he broke her will entirely.

But she would not scrap with him now. She must hasten back to the cottage to the man Finch had tried to kill. She had no time to waste. The outlaw's need was urgent.

"I pray you will excuse me. I shall catch my death unless I seek my maid," she said in what she hoped was her most lady-of-the-manor voice.

Finch smiled, squeezed her fingers cruelly, and let them drop. "But of course. I await your return."

Katherine clasped her hands behind her back. "Then you shall abide overlong."

"Look to yourself, girl," Father said, waving her off, a

petulant scowl marring his countenance. He brandished the paper at Finch. "We will see her soon enough. For now, we have business to attend. I believe this jointure is less than we agreed."

As the two men fell into a heated discussion, Katherine snatched her cloak from the stone bench and slipped from the room. With determined strides, she crossed the great hall and took the stairs to the first floor, moving at a rapid pace until she arrived at her mother's room. Once inside, she began to tremble. She hugged her cloak to her chest as shivers wracked her frame and a sob rose up her throat. The fear she had held at bay through the confrontation with Finch now hit her full force. She felt ill with reaction.

Dropping her cloak on the bed, she stepped to the casement window and pulled back the heavy drape. The storm had returned in all its fury. Rain poured off the eaves in a steady stream. The sky was dark and ominous. Her teeth chattered. Drawing in a shuddering breath, she rubbed her fingers where Finch had so cruelly clutched them.

Her mother's familiar and comforting scent of rose still hung on the air. Katherine leaned against the cold windowpane as her heart ached anew.

A flash of light reflected off the glass. At first, she thought it was lightning, but there had been no warning thunder. She turned to see her maid entering the room. The girl held a candle.

Katherine's hand came to rest on her pounding heart, and she heaved in a sigh. She had no wish to attend to some trifling domestic crisis right now. The kitchen staff should be able to complete washday without her. Or perhaps Lucy was here to tell her Finch would be an overnight guest because of the storm.

Despairing over that possibility, Katherine shuddered and turned back to the window.

As Lucy approached and the flickering light grew stronger, a face appeared on the glass. At first, Katherine didn't recognize herself. How could she? There were no mirrors at Ashfield; mirrors encouraged vanity. But it was not vanity she felt as she viewed her own likeness.

The face looking back at her carried such sadness she found it shocking. Below the white cap, the skin was pale and colorless. The eyes held a dull misery. The mouth seemed to have lost the ability to smile. The face was undoubtedly her own, but Katherine felt no kinship to it.

Perhaps she merely wished none.

Instead, she longed for a face that showed joy and happiness. A pretty face, and, dare she think it, a pretty dress made of a colorful shimmering fabric. The black dress she now wore disappeared into the shadows, hiding her body as effectively as it was intended.

Thunder cracked. A moment later lightning rent the sky, obscuring her likeness and taking with it her fanciful thoughts. Then her reflection returned along with that of Lucy who now stood behind her.

Katherine turned to her maid, noticing that something was moving in the fold of her apron.

"What have you there, Lucy?"

"Ah, mistress." The maid scooped a hand into her apron and pulled out a small ball of fur that wiggled. She held it out to Katherine. "I looked for you first in your room. Then I thought you might be here. 'Tis a wee cat I've found. In the garden. Cook sent me for sage and I found it instead, all wet, so I brought it inside. Cook was angry I forgot the sage. An' she said I should put the cat back. But I dried the wee thing off, ye see. I know'd I caint keep it. But, I thought…?"

As Katherine took it in her hands, the fur ball developed legs, a tail, and several very sharp teeth. "Ouch! 'Tis not a kitten you have found but a hellcat!"

She raised it up to her face. In the dim light, she could see it was gray with black stripes and white paws. Short white whiskers sprang from a white muzzle. The kitten stopped teething on her thumb long enough to look back. Its dark eyes twinkled as it sniffed her. Then it raised a paw and batted at her nose.

Katherine pulled it from her face and stroked behind its ears with her finger. Loud purring burst forth from the small kitty.

"It likes you, mistress," said Lucy. "You wiln't make me put it back in the rain?"

"No," said Katherine. Today was her day to rescue outlaws and orphans. "It shall stay with me." As the kitten stretched and snuggled, relaxing into her hand, her heart swelled. It would be so nice to have something to love again. She cradled it against her shoulder, and it melted into her warmth.

Lucy smiled at her. "Can I tell cook to give me some food for it?"

Katherine nodded. Since her mother's death, cook had become altogether too autocratic. "Tell her *I* wish it."

Lucy bobbed a curtsey and left, taking the candle with her.

With the warm kitten at her shoulder, Katherine did not feel so miserable. Gazing out the window, she saw the sky grow lighter. The storm appeared to have spent its wrath, and the rain had reduced to a drizzle.

The kitten yawned and began to purr again. Katherine scratched one of its little ears. "What to call you?" Should she name it in honor of her mother or brother? She didn't even know if it was a boy or a girl so she tried to pull the kitten from her shoulder, but it clung tight to her dress with its little claws.

"Well never mind then, it matters not—at least not yet. In any case, I shall give you a strong name." She let it snuggle back into her shoulder. "A man's name, I think. Even if you are female, 'twill serve to make you strong. What shall it be?"

The little cat purred instead of answering.

"Mayhap a big name, because you are so small. A name to grow into." Katherine leaned her forehead on the cold window and looked down into the courtyard. There were several big mud puddles on the ground below. She prayed Finch would leave soon so she could tend the wounded man. If he still lived.

He must live.

But she must get to him soon. Time was passing. Now that the rain had stopped, she should go, even if Finch did not leave. Even without the book. The kitten mewed in Katherine's ear as if in agreement. Her eyes scanned the room, finding her cloak where she'd left it on the bed.

That's when she thought of what to call the kitten.

"Montford," she said. "I shall name you after the family who lived here, the family who owned the book I need. They owned most everything we have, probably at least one of your ancestors as well. 'Tis a good and noble name, and it belongs here, even if they do not."

A sudden flurry of activity below grabbed her attention. The Finch coach rolled into view and stopped. The coachman jumped down just as Richard Finch appeared. Right before attaining the coach, he misjudged his step and landed in a big puddle.

Katherine smiled.

Montford purred in her hands.

Gray clouds leftover from the storm hung low in the sky. Mullein and verbena, burnt for purification, scented the air inside the cottage. To Katherine's great relief, the man's condition had not worsened during her absence.

He lay like a pagan offering within a circle of candles. Their amber light cast his face in high relief. Katherine again noted his noble countenance, prominent cheekbones, and full, generous mouth.

"Who are you, my lord outlaw? Displaced royalist turned highwayman?"

Of course, he didn't answer.

She laid out her supplies, taking some confidence as she lined them up. She had already decided to treat his head wound first, saving the most difficult task for last.

Dipping a cloth into a bowl of water, she bathed his forehead to cool the fever and cleaned a smudge of dirt away. Working carefully, she softened the encrusted area at his temple, pulling away long strands of black hair to reveal a dark ugly bruise.

"Ah." She lifted a candle to see it better. "'Tis not so big but very bloody. Still, I fear the pain will be fierce when you wake."

Would he wake with his wits, or would this injury leave him simple like Peter, the tanner's son, after he'd been kicked in the head by a horse?

Katherine lifted the Raven's head and cradled it in her lap. Upside down, his face lost its regal bearing; in fact, he looked rather amusing. She traced a finger over his broad forehead, down one cheek to linger on his lips before she realized the liberty she took and yanked her hand away.

What had come over her?

Shaking off her fancies, she wrapped his head twice with a long linen bandage and made a perfunctory knot before placing his head back on the floor.

In the flickering light, she opened the old medical journal and again studied the passage describing the treatment for a lodged-ball wound. Then, releasing a long sigh, she closed the cover and eased the book to the ground. Be it torture or succor, she must do it.

"I shall try not to hurt you, but I fear 'twill get worse before it gets better," she murmured.

Picking up her scissors, Katherine cut the sleeve of his shirt in such a way that it could be reattached later. Dried blood affixed the fabric to the wound. She wetted the material, peeling it away bit by bit.

She gasped as she pulled off the sleeve to reveal an angry red welt, puffy around the hole where the bullet had entered. Dried blood crusted his skin all the way to his fingertips. She washed his arm, while her body ached in sympathy.

"I am sorry," she whispered. "I wish I knew more of what I am doing, Sir Outlaw."

As if he agreed with her, his full mouth pulled into a grimace. She sighed again and wiped her hands on her apron.

Gritting her teeth, she inserted her finger into the wound. Warm red blood welled up onto her hand. Her stomach lurched. She tried not to gag.

The Raven shifted, murmuring incoherencies. She tightened her grip on his arm while she pressed forward until she felt something solid that moved when she tested it. It must be the bullet.

A great shudder ran through him.

Katherine's heart dropped. Bile rose in her throat as her

fingers, slippery with his blood, inserted tweezers into the wound.

The outlaw groaned and pulled away, but she held his arm firmly with one hand while probing with the other.

She could not tell if hours, minutes, or mere seconds passed before she grasped the slug, drew it out, and dropped it on the floor. Blood gushed out the hole, bringing with it a sense of urgency and desperation.

Would she kill the man while trying to save him?

She held his arm tight, pressing on the wound until her fingers felt they would fall off. At last the bleeding stopped.

Katherine raised a shaking hand to tuck a strand of hair back into her cap. Now to purify the wound. For this, she'd brought a mixture of comfrey and alcohol distilled this past summer.

Uncorking the bottle, she carefully poured a drop into the hole.

His arm jerked up, and his hand hit her in the jaw. Hard.

At this unexpected attack, Katherine reeled back. The bottle slipped from her fingers. She grabbed for it, but almost half her precious potion spilled. "See what you have done!"

But he didn't. He lay quiet and still, as if nothing had happened.

Katherine rubbed her jaw with a bloodstained hand and heaved a sigh of frustration. She didn't wish to risk further injury, but she must continue else the wound could putrefy.

Then an idea came to her. Holding the vial aloft, she sat on his chest. Pinning his arm at the elbow with her right knee, she poured the rest of the tincture into the wound.

He let out an outraged bellow and bucked.

Suddenly she lay flat on her back, winded and pinioned beneath him.

He squinted at her, breathing hard, a leg draped over her thighs. He balanced himself on the elbow of his good arm.

Frightening though the situation was, and as powerless as she felt, Katherine found herself peering into his eyes to determine their color.

Blue. But not like ice. A clear azure blue, like the sky on a sunny cloudless day.

"Who are you?" he asked in a deep commanding voice.

She swallowed hard. "K-K-Katherine Welles."

CHAPTER THREE

The heiress!

Nicholas peered at her intently, finally able to bring the two images of her together. He could feel her tremble as she stared up at him with big brown eyes.

She was not pretty. In fact, her face was rather plain, although her skin looked as soft as fine China silk. Her hair, a dull brown, was pulled tautly back into a stiff white cap. A dark smudge adorned her forehead and appeared to be her only decoration. The collar of her severe black dress hugged her neck.

A drab, psalm-reading Puritan, he realized with disappointment. But he had known that would be the case.

What the devil was she doing here? More importantly, what was he doing here? And where was he anyway?

The last thing he remembered was his rash attempt to waylay Dickon Finch. Nicholas shook his head to clear the fuzziness, but that only aggravated the pounding ache and did nothing to fill-in the gap in his memory.

"You should not have moved. You are bleeding again." She struggled to rise, but he did not let her. Trapped beneath him, she looked very frightened, and felt...well, nicely rounded, and soft. Like a woman.

"I have no more of the tincture," she said. He must have

looked at her stupidly because she added, with an edge of impatience, "It was in the bottle."

The soothing aroma of lavender filled his senses, reminding him of the angel in his dream.

"Let me up," she demanded. "Please?"

Nicholas had never been one to disappoint a lady if he could help it, and he disliked terrorizing innocents no matter their religious persuasion. Moreover, he realized if he did not lie down, he would soon fall down. Although she might cushion his descent, he did not think she would care for the impact.

He rolled off her, jarring both his injured arm and head. Wincing, he lifted a hand to his forehead and discovered it bound by a band of cloth. A turban? How could that be?

The woman scrambled to her feet and brushed herself off with just the hint of a sniff. Her white apron was covered in blood—his blood, he realized—as were the hands she gripped together. Her lips were drawn into a severe line. Eyebrows perched above disapproving eyes frowned down at him.

He felt like a small child about to be dressed down by a stern nursemaid. He closed his eyes and let out a sigh. His head throbbed, his arm ached, and he was very tired.

"I would like to finish," she said.

He grunted assent, not having a clear idea of what she meant but not wishing to gainsay her in any event.

"First, you must agree to cause no further insult to my person."

This time Nicholas grunted twice for good measure.

"Furthermore—"

Nicholas opened his eyes and groaned. "I dislike the word 'furthermore'. Nothing agreeable ever follows."

She ignored him. "Furthermore, I have no wish to tend to one so foolhardy as to cause himself additional injury."

Nicholas grimaced. Foolhardy. That was the crux of it.

"In other words," she continued with emphasis, "you must behave."

Nicholas had the urge to laugh but did not want to wound her dignity, or cause his head to ache further. "Yes, good K-

Katherine," he said, pronouncing her name exactly as she had and in the solemnest tone he could muster. "I would rejoice should you be so kind as to continue your ministrations despite the offense I have perpetrated against your person—an inexcusable lapse to be sure." He raised his good arm to doff his hat and realized the tightness around his head was not a hat or a turban but a bandage. Whatever had happened to make his head pound must have also addled his brain. Why else would he make such a silly speech to a Puritan lass who clearly had no appreciation for the courtly arts? It had not even raised the hint of a smile.

She looked away for what seemed to be a very long time. Then, as if she'd made up her mind, she let out a slow sigh and knelt beside him. Her blood-covered fingers trembled as they took up a cloth and dipped it in a basin of water. Avoiding his gaze, she began to dab at his arm. His wound throbbed like blazes, but her touch was feather-light, her motions soothing.

He closed his eyes. All at once, he realized the oddness of their situation. Did she know who he was?

He cracked an eye open. "What are you doing here?"

"Cleaning your wound."

"This I know. But why?"

Her fingers tightened on his arm as she gazed off, worrying her lower lip with her teeth. On another woman, he would have thought the gesture flirtatious, a calculated effort to draw his attention to her mouth, but he could tell she was unaware of it.

Her voice, when she finally answered, was almost too quiet for him to hear. "If I had left you to die, I would be as wicked as he who tried to kill you."

"No one tried to kill me," he scoffed. "'Twas an accident."

"'Tis not what I heard." She shook her head and went back to work on his arm. "My neighbor, Richard Finch, said he shot the Raven."

"What has that to do with me?"

"Are you not the Raven?" She frowned down at him.

"Do I look to be a bird?"

She ignored his attempt to parry. "The Raven I speak of is an outlaw."

"Do I look like an outlaw?" He gave her his most sincere and noble look.

She studied him. "Indeed you do. But if you are not the Raven, then I apologize."

He laughed. It made his head hurt, but the rest of him felt better. "If I am the Raven, why would a good Puritan lass like you tend to me?"

"I am not a Puritan." She picked up a clean piece of bandage.

"No, of course not. I remember now. You're one of our dear King's ladyloves. We were introduced when last I was at Whitehall. The injury to my head must have confused me."

She eyed him doubtfully and pressed cool fingers to his cheek.

Nicholas caught her hand in his good one and willed her to look directly at him. Her fingers were long and delicate, her eyes apprehensive.

"'Twas a jest," he said, unable to keep the exasperation from his voice. "Meant to make you laugh." She didn't look like she'd laughed at anything for a very long time.

He let go of her hand and sighed, rubbing the bridge of his nose between his thumb and forefinger. Good lord, he was tired. "Coffee," he said more to himself than to her.

"Kaw-fee? Is that not the sound a raven makes?"

Nicholas looked up at her but she was not smiling. Clearly she had not meant to be witty.

"Coffee is a drink from Turkey," he said. "When imbibed it gives clarity to the mind."

He closed his eyes as weariness overcame him. He was beginning to see double again. Perhaps what he really needed was sleep.

Gentle fingers spread tender warmth on his aching limb. Peacefulness wrapped around him. Then she applied a poultice of some evil smelling substance to his arm. Prompted by his nose, his eyes drifted open. His unfocused gaze came to rest on her. Limned by candlelight, Katherine sat within a halo—an angel keeping him safe.

Seemingly from a long distance, he heard her speak. "Your name, Sir Outlaw? What is your name?"

"Nicholas. Nicholas Ed—" he frowned and felt the bandage across his forehead tighten. No, he did not want her to know that. "Eddington," he finished.

His mouth pulled into a smile. His eyes slowly shut.

Ed-Eddington. A fitting acquaintance for a K-Katherine.

It was the last conscious thought he had before he floated into oblivion.

Several days later, Katherine was working in the garden piling soil high around the base of a bare rose bush. She shivered in the light breeze. The November sun provided scant warmth, but helped dry the soil. Even though there had been no rain for two days, the ground was still wet.

She wiped her hands on her smock and picked up a ball of twine.

A gray kitten appeared out of nowhere and attacked the end of string that dangled free.

"Montford!" she scolded, pulling the twine aloft. The kitten leapt high, and then fell almost onto its back, flipping over just in time to land on all fours.

Katherine gazed at the barren garden, marveling at how different it would appear next summer when the thorny branches would be covered by green leaves and richly colored flowers, their soft petals holding a sweet, exotic perfume. She had always helped her mother prepare the roses for their winter sleep. This year, she could have had Tom, the gardener, assist her, but working alone, she could feel her mother's calm presence, and it helped to ease the ache in her heart.

Her mother would not have allowed this marriage to Finch.

Katherine unwound and cut a length of twine. As she twisted it around the rose branches to bind them safely against the winter winds, she could almost hear her mother's advice: *Go to Cousin Alicia. She will help.*

Alicia Pemberton had visited several times while Katherine's mother ailed. At their last good-byes, Alicia had cordially bid Katherine come see them in London. With offspring ranging from eighteen months to eight years, Katherine knew she could make herself useful. Surely Cousin Alicia meant the invitation?

If anyone could keep her safe from her father's plans, it was Alicia—or more precisely Alicia's husband, James, a successful barrister. He would be able to protect her from this marriage. Her father did not have the legal right to force her to marry Finch, even though here in Dorsetshire, he could make her do it anyway. In London, she would be able to seek the protection of the law. While she did not have the right to choose whom she *would* marry, she did have the right to choose whom she would *not*.

So, she must leave Ashfield and make her way to London. Perhaps she had known this the afternoon she'd run into the storm, the same afternoon Mr. Eddington had made his propitious arrival. Had he been heaven-sent to help her escape?

Such a fanciful thought! Katherine shook her head. It seemed unlikely an outlaw—and an injured one at that—would provide any sort of deliverance. Most likely, he would offer peril rather than protection.

He had slept a good part of four days, waking for broth and bread. For the last two, he had been without fever. Blessedly, none of his band of hooligans had appeared. Soon he would need to move on.

Since she must also travel, it made sense to find out if he would be going to London.

Katherine rescued the ball of twine as Montford tried to bat it away.

How dangerous would it be to travel with him? Surely, the man was no gentleman. Still, since their initial encounter, his behavior had been above reproach. Of course, that could be because he had slept through most of her visits.

Yet, how else was she to get to London? A woman traveling alone and unprotected would be prey to both man and beast.

Katherine shivered and tied the twine into a knot. She eyed

the bush critically and discovered she had missed a branch. Her mind had not fully been on the task; she would have to do it again.

"Good Katherine," Richard Finch's voice came from behind.

Katherine rose with a start. She had been so preoccupied, she had not heard his approach. She had even missed the sounds of his coach coming down the drive and arriving at the front of the manse.

Finch's smile did not reach his eyes. "I have come to tell you we will say our espousals and exchange gifts before witnesses tomorrow."

So soon? "I-I am not ready." She looked away to mask her rising panic and took a step back. Her skirt caught on the thorns of the errant branch.

"I think you will be." He took a step toward her.

She shook her head. "Three more days. Father said 'twould be a sennight for me to—"

"Your father and I agree. It is time." Finch reached for her hand, but, seeing her fingers covered with dirt, did not take them. His nose wrinkled. "I have learned you do much walking in the woods of late. 'Tis not prudent."

Katherine tugged on her skirt to free it. The rosebush held tight.

"You may be aware there is a bandit loose in this area. I shot him when he attempted a holdup." Finch gloated. "Since then, none have come across him, dead or alive. He is dangerous, Katherine, and I would not see you come to harm."

She looked back at him, at the cruel smile that played on the corners of his mouth. He simply did not want her hurt by anyone else.

"Thank you for informing me," she said stiffly.

"Just this day I have offered a reward for his capture. Five gold sovereigns will inspire much interest in his arrest."

That much money would lure many to scour the forest. Even the most superstitious would brave Witches' Rock for such a reward. Mr. Eddington could easily be discovered. He must leave soon.

She pulled her skirt again but the thorns would not let go.

Finch stepped closer and took her chin in his hand. He lowered his mouth, challenge in his eyes.

She swallowed, but did not look away.

His lips hovered near hers. His eyes taunted her, daring her to move, to fight back, to protest.

But she didn't. Finch would enjoy her struggle too much.

He turned her face and kissed her on the cheek. "Good chaste Katherine, 'twill not be long before you do what I say in all things."

As panic surged through her, she wrenched her skirt, ripping the fine wool off the thorny branch.

Finch's cold blue eyes raked over her.

"I am not yet your wife." Katherine took a step back. She turned away. Almost tripping over Montford, she scooped up the kitten and hurried from the garden. She must leave this night, before she could say the spousals that would legally bind her to Finch.

She would *never* be his wife.

Nicholas examined the cottage wall by the wavering light of a candle. With surprise, he saw his initials—all five of them—just as he'd carved them seventeen years ago in crude block letters. He had wanted to leave a part of himself behind before departing for Holland and had spent the better part of a week chipping them into the stone.

So long ago.

Had that sad young boy really been he? Or had it been a different Nicholas still reeling from the death of his mother, the child who believed his father's promise that they would be back soon. He hadn't known that in leaving Ashfield, his childhood was over.

He let out a long breath as he moved the candle lower. In the flickering light another set of initials appeared. Not carved as deeply as his, but with more style. K A W, no doubt for

Katherine Welles. But what did the A stand for?

Angel?

For that's what she'd been. Now that the fog and sweats had diminished, along with the terrible pounding in his head, he knew she had saved his life.

As far as he could tell, he'd been here a week, asleep for the most part. He needed to get back to the inn where he'd left Henry suffering from a toothache, telling the man he'd be gone a few short hours, and only to reconnoiter, not to strike. His old friend would be beside himself with worry.

That disastrous evening had placed him closer to achieving his goal of reclaiming Ashfield, the reason he had returned to England. With his ancestral estate nearby, and its heiress nursing him back to health, it seemed there ought to be a myriad of opportunities open to him. But he had not yet come up with one, except abduction. And that seemed so...well, old-fashioned.

"Mr. Eddington?"

Nicholas blew out the candle and turned to see Katherine come through the door. Winded and red-cheeked, her eyes sparkled, but her brow was furrowed.

"They've put a price on your head," she exclaimed. "Five gold sovereigns, I've just heard."

Maybe he could make her smile. "My...head?" He lifted his good hand to that part of his body. "'Tis not so much money. Surely 'tis worth more than that?"

She looked at him as if he'd suddenly gone daft.

He grinned. "At least it is worth much more to me."

She frowned. "'Tis not a jest. The money is enough to make your capture appealing to many."

"To you Mistress Welles?"

"Of course not."

"Have you informed anyone of my presence?"

"Of course not," she repeated, snapping the words out this time.

"Then there should be none who know where I am."

"They will look for you in earnest now. You can no longer stay here. 'Tisn't safe. Even those who are afraid of Witches'

31

Rock would come here for such a reward."

Nicholas nodded. She was right. He could tarry no longer. Walking to the doorway, he looked outside. The sky was a cloudless blue. The late fall sun shone weekly on the dry ground.

"You are right. 'Tis time for me to go."

"Indeed you must." She spoke with surprising vehemence. "But are you well enough?" She added almost timidly. "I think your arm must pain you sorely."

"My arm is much recovered." He raised it to show her, concealing a grimace behind a tight smile. "And my head— perhaps due to the increased value—works better as well." He shook it gently from side to side. "I must thank you for caring for me as you have, and for saving my life. No doubt at great risk to yourself."

"Nay there was scant risk, only that I might not succeed."

Had his confident angel thought she might fail? That was hard to imagine. Then again, she did not seem the type to take on adventure, or put herself at risk. Yet she had done so.

She stood quietly for a long moment as if coming to a decision. Then, in a jerky motion, she reached inside her cloak and pulled out a small bundle. "You must be hungry and I have brought your dinner."

"'Tis a fine day. I would much prefer to eat out-of-doors. Stay with me, mistress. Your good company will improve my appetite."

"It is not safe for you to be abroad in plain sight," Katherine protested.

Nicholas smiled. "If anyone should come upon us, we will say I am your...cousin, just arrived. They will have no reason to doubt you say the truth."

Katherine shook her head. "I do not tell tales well."

"Then, should we be discovered, you must let me do the talking."

Katherine frowned, but then nodded. He took her elbow with the hand of his good arm, and they left the cottage. She led him the short distance to a grassy area fringed by oak trees near a stream. It was a lovely spot he'd not seen for many years, reminding him, again, of how much he'd missed his home.

She opened out the bundle onto the ground then unwrapped a plain meal of brown bread and cheese. "My apologies for the simplicity of the fare."

"I thank you for it."

She nodded, but he could see she paid him little mind.

They sat across from each other, the cloth in-between. Nicholas sprawled his long legs out to the side, while she curled up more like a cat.

He bit heartily into the cheese. "Will you join me?" He ripped the bread in half and held out a piece to her.

She pulled off a chunk and put the rest on the cloth.

Nicholas watched her fidget while he ate. She chewed as if unaware she was eating. Before long, she was tearing off bits of the bread and tossing them toward the trees, where some lucky squirrel would come along and find them. He wondered what was on her mind, but let her bide as he ate, eyeing her openly as he chewed.

In the light of day he could see that the hair peeping out of her white cap was the color of honey, and not dark as he had thought. What would she look like with it flowing free?

As always, she wore black. In the bright sunlight, he could see how little it became her. Her creamy skin should be set against peach, deep blue or dark green. Black made her look stern. Simply cut and unadorned, the dress ought to have been worn by a widowed grandmother, not a young woman.

How old was she? He'd made inquiries about her family when he was in London, but had found little information about her. She was unmarried and heiress to the estate since the death of her brother, Edward, in an accident of some sort. Her mother had died recently. Perhaps that was the reason for the unrelieved black. That, and because she was a Puritan.

Of Gerald Welles, he'd learned more. An ambitious man, he had benefited under Cromwell's protectorate. His financial support had been rewarded with Ashfield, but his dreams of nobility had not been fulfilled. Since the return of the monarchy, he had kept mainly to the country. Perhaps, like others of his ilk, he waited for his Puritan-cropped hair to grow to a fashionable length.

Nicholas scowled and bit hard on the bread.

Katherine looked up and caught his eyes on her. "I was wondering where you will go," she said.

"I had not thought much on it," he lied.

Her eyes looked the most changed in daylight. The sun revealed flecks of gold, yellow, and green. The colors of autumn.

"Oh." She chewed another bite of the bread then looked straight at him. "I was hoping…"

"Yes?" he prodded when she did not continue. Clearly, his angel had something on her mind.

"It seemed to me, when I thought on it, you might not be returning to your life of crime straight away, until you are completely recovered that is. But…if you will be going toward London to meet up with your gang…well then I would be most obliged if you would take me with you." The last part came out all in a rush.

Nicholas almost choked on the bread as he swallowed it. Would it be so easy then? He need not lift a finger or even make a plan? He carefully drew his face into a look of thoughtfulness, trying valiantly to suppress the grin that threatened to appear.

"You have made an interesting request," he said, his expression under rigid control. "And why would you be going to London?"

A flash of apprehension lit her eyes, and he guessed she was deciding what to tell him.

"My father has resolved I am to marry."

"You are not over young for it."

"Yes." Katherine reacted to his bluntness with no vanity. "I have been in mourning this past fifteen-month. First my brother Edward, and then my dear mother. Now my father says 'tis time, he is willing to wait no longer, and he has made a match with our neighbor, Richard Finch, the man who shot you." She let out a deep sigh.

Nicholas turned away before she could see the pity he knew to be in his eyes. It would be a grave misfortune for his serious caretaker to marry that cold-hearted bastard. He wouldn't teach her how to laugh. More likely, his petty cruelties would make her more serious, even dour.

She must have taken his lack of response to mean he did not approve her request, because he turned back to see her frowning.

"I shall not marry him. I will get to London, somehow." She looked away. "I had just thought you might do me this favor."

"But of course I will, mistress," he smiled—a gentle curve of the lips instead of the grin that still threatened. "It seems I owe this neighbor of yours a favor as well." He rubbed his bandaged arm. "Since the Raven is mightier than the Finch, I shall aid you on your flight." He popped the last bit of cheese into his mouth. "What are your intentions once in London?"

"I shall stay with my cousin, Alicia Pemberton. She has over many children to manage on her own, and I will be glad to help her."

Nicholas brushed crumbs from the front of his shirt. "When shall we leave?"

She caught his eye, a tentative quick look for reassurance, and he nodded.

"Tonight?" she said, visibly relaxing. "'Twould be best for me to be gone before the morrow. And, ready or not, 'twould be best for you to be gone even now. I vow I will not be any trouble. I will continue to care for your injuries and help in other ways as I can."

Nicholas repressed a smile. If anyone needed help getting to London, it would be she, not he. Yet, if it made her more willing to travel with him, so much the better. "I am feeling quite recovered from this fine sunshine. With your good company, I shall not worry my health will suddenly fail. What say you, shall we leave at midnight?"

Katherine actually smiled. Not a big smile—nothing close to a grin—but the corners of her mouth turned up and the smallest twinkle flashed in her eyes. "If you truly think you are well enough?"

Nicholas nodded.

"Know you where Ashfield is?" She gathered the cloth into a

bundle and stood up brushing small bits of debris from her skirt.

He nodded again, rising to his feet.

"Meet me at the stove-house. 'Tis in the back garden, not far from the stables. I shall be ready."

"I do hope, mistress, you will be discreet. It is best that no one know of our plans unless you wish us discovered."

"I assure you, no one could wish to be discovered less than I." She looked at him seriously, and then cast her eyes downward. "There is just one concern I must discuss with you."

"Yes?"

"'Tis just that... I mean... You would not...?"

He could see her discomfort as she forced the words out.

"That is, while we are on the road...could you not...?" She toyed with the collar of her dress. "I mean I would like to get to London straight away, and if we have to stop while you hold up coaches...well..."

Comprehension finally dawned on Nicholas. "Do not fear, mistress," he raised her chin with a forefinger until she looked straight into his eyes. "For now, at least, my outlaw days are behind me. And I have business to attend in London that I have avoided overlong."

He could see it was not her collar she fingered, but a piece of green ribbon, its color incongruously bright against her black dress. It was just such a ribbon as women used to hold a keepsake from a lover. He should know; he'd given several away himself.

Could he have misjudged her completely? Might this drab Puritan miss be traveling to London to meet a lover and not a cousin?

"What is this?" he teased. "A bit of bright underplummage? Is this sparrow really a canary in disguise?"

He let his hand trail down her neck, and gave the ribbon a tug. She gasped as he pulled it out of her bodice.

Just as he suspected, there was something attached, but it was not what he had expected. Nicholas stared at the familiar old Chinese coin, warm in his hand.

My lucky piece.

Katherine deftly took it from his grasp and tucked it back into her dress. Fingers hovering protectively at the base of her throat, she eyed him warily as she moved away from him.

Nicholas cursed himself for treating her like one of the court ladies instead of a Puritan miss, and tried to make up for it with his fullest and most charming smile. "I was not going to steal it."

"'Tisn't proper for you to be so free with my person."

"And a charming person it is too," he made a courtly bow and straightened. "How did you come by such an item?"

"I found it in the cottage with other bits and pieces. Why do you ask?"

"It is from China. I am surprised to see it here. 'Tis an odd trinket for a Puritan lass."

"Puritan?" Her mouth took a firm line. "You say I am a Puritan because I look like one. What you truly see is an obedient daughter. But I will not be one for much longer." She sighed and looked towards the stream. A bird had discovered the bits of bread.

"Just who may *you* be, Mr. Eddington?"

"Naught but a simple outlaw."

"I think there is nothing simple about you. Are you a thief? No, I do not think so. You are an odd highwayman to be sure, for, by all accounts, you leave items of true value with their owners. Are you a noble, or a commoner? Perhaps one of the gentry? Are you English-born? There is something decidedly foreign about you. Be you Catholic or Protestant?"

Nicholas gave a wry smile. "If you must know, I was raised on the Book of Common Prayer, but I do not consider myself a religious man."

"And what of your gang? Why did they leave you to die and not return for you, or bring aid?"

"There is a simple answer to that. I have no gang."

Katherine blinked. "But I had heard—"

"One should not always believe what one is told."

Later, several hours after Katherine had left, Nicholas stood in the doorway of the cottage and watched the stars twinkle in the night sky. He named for himself the various constellations and reflected on what had happened.

When he'd come back to England, he'd been uncertain of what he really wanted. Of course, he had promised his father he would get Ashfield back—a promise he meant to keep. But as to whether *he* really wanted it, that was a question to which he had no answer.

Since arriving on England's shores, his goal had become quite clear. Nicholas tightened his fingers on the doorframe sending a shock of pain to his wounded arm.

He craved *revenge*.

Revenge for his father's impoverished and ignominious death in Holland. Revenge for the loneliness of growing up on his own in foreign lands. Revenge against those who had changed their clothing, religion, and loyalty with the tides of politics, and had therefore lost nothing.

He rubbed the muscles on his arm below the bandage. In exacting his revenge, he'd taken the coats from those turncoats, and the rest of their clothing as well. He'd taken their dignity and gifted them with a fine humiliation, at least for the nonce. And he'd had a good laugh.

But that wasn't enough. His blood still ran hot with the need for vengeance. He needed a better target. Bigger and more appropriate. More satisfying. With Cromwell dead and declared a traitor, he'd have to find a man who'd thought he could get away with such treachery.

Someone like Gerald Welles. After all, Welles was in possession of Ashfield.

But not for long. Nicholas scowled.

Tonight he'd be on his way to London, traveling with the man's daughter. Nicholas would have in his grasp the means to reclaim his patrimony. Plus, he'd be snatching Katherine and the estate from the clutches of his childhood enemy, Finch. A fine revenge, indeed. And a highly satisfying turn of events.

Better yet, he hadn't had to lift a finger to set this in motion.

Nicholas's lips pulled into a tight smile. Fate. Kismet. He'd been introduced to the concept during his time in the East. Yes, fate must be providing him with the means to achieve his goal. Just as it had to be a sign that Katherine A. Welles, ministering angel and the instrument of his retribution, wore his old lucky piece around her neck.

There was no question his luck had changed the moment he met her.

CHAPTER FOUR

"Katherine?" Nicholas's hushed voice echoed loudly in the night. He'd come early so he could take a good look at his old home. In the scant illumination of the crescent moon, he could see little had changed, though it seemed so much smaller and less grand than the Ashfield of his memory.

Then he saw her. In her dark hooded cloak, she'd blended in with the blackness. As she emerged from the shadows and walked toward him, the moon glinted off her forehead. She carried two bundles and cradled something in her arms.

"You are on time," she whispered, dropping her satchels.

He could see, now, she carried a very small cat.

He nodded, watching the moonlight play on her upturned face.

"I cannot help thinking," she scratched the feline behind the ears, "'tis too soon for you to be afoot."

He smiled. "I am quite ready, I assure you. I have no interest in spending any more time confined to that cottage. No, 'tis best we saddle up and be on the road quickly."

Katherine frowned. "But you do not have a horse."

"You are right," Nicholas said. "So 'tis a good thing we are here at your stables."

Katherine nodded. "We are to walk."

"Walk?" he raised an eyebrow. "No, we will not walk. Our progress would be so slow they would come upon us before the morrow. And yes, you are right, I am not recovered well enough to walk for several long days, but I am quite well enough to ride a horse."

"Oh." She was still frowning.

That did not bode well.

"So we will quietly go inside the stables, and you will help me pick a horse."

"But that would be stealing."

"Do you not live here?"

"Of course I do."

"Are these not your horses?"

"I suppose in a way they are."

"So you will accompany me into the stables, and we will select two suitable mounts and see they are returned at some point in the future."

She looked away from him. "No. I will not."

He tried to keep the annoyance out of his voice. "Katherine, you must be reasonable. Do you know how far it is to London?"

"'Tis a good distance, and will take several days on foot I have no doubt. But, you see, I do not ride."

A country lass who did not ride? And they were to travel to London? This was too absurd to contemplate. Nicholas ran impatient fingers through his hair. "What do you mean you do not ride?" He knew his voice was getting louder, but his frustration was rising as well.

"That is it. I do not ride," she repeated staunchly.

"Do you mean you 'do not' ride—or you 'will not' ride?"

She squared her shoulders, but did not look him in the eye. "It matters not. The result is the same."

"It matters much. Nevertheless, whether you *will not* ride or *do not* ride, we *will not go* unless you get up on a horse." He picked up a lumpy bundle and waved it at her.

With obvious reluctance, she raised her gaze to his. Along with the determination he expected to see, her eyes carried a mixture of sadness and desperation. He waited for her to speak, but she did not. In the silence, his exasperation grew. Would the wench continue to look at him like a wounded doe, unmovable and soundless as a statue?

At least she did not simper and bat her eyelashes at him. He was rarely able to resist such acts of deliberate coquetry. Nicholas's shoulder throbbed from the tension. He tried to relax and sound practical as he spoke. "Do you know how heavy this will be after walking for a mere hour? And then two? Three?" He dropped the bundle to the ground. It landed with a thud.

She looked away.

"But 'twill not tax us to load it on a horse." Cupping her chin, he pulled her gaze to his. "And no cat."

"You are mistaken."

Even though she did not say what he wanted to hear, Nicholas felt his approval grow. He disliked those who would not stand up for themselves.

But on this matter he would not budge. He would not complicate their travels with the addition of a cat, no matter how small. Nicholas scowled.

In answer, Katherine clutched the little beast protectively. Her eyes lost their sadness and flashed with new resolve. In the thin moonlight, she glowed with the ferocity of a lioness. "I will leave the bundles if I must, but Montford will come."

"Montford?" He hoped his voice sounded more curious than surprised. "'Tis an interesting name for a cat. How came you by it?"

"'Twas the family who lived here before the war. I have seen it in books and other places."

Nicholas felt oddly touched by this memorial to his family and knew not what to say. In the short silence that followed, he heard soft footfalls from behind. Letting go of Katherine's chin, he thrust her behind him as he spun around to face a tousled, sleepy-eyed young man wielding a pitchfork in his direction.

"Jeremy?" Katherine hissed loudly, stepping out from behind Nicholas. "I had hoped not to wake you."

Nicholas pushed her back behind him.

"It is quite all right," she whispered to Nicholas, shrugging off his hand and stepping out from behind him again.

The boy looked at her uncertainly then thrust the pitchfork at Nicholas. "Who is he?"

"'Tis of no importance," she answered.

"Seems mighty important to me, you being out here with him in the middle of the night." He glared at Nicholas and took a step forward, the sharp tines of the fork edging closer. "I would know why he is here."

Dressed roughly, the boy appeared to be a servant, probably a groom. What right had he to question Katherine? Or anyone else for that matter? Yet, by the way he held the pitchfork, it did not appear the lad would give up easily. Nicholas clenched his jaw. If the boy wanted a fight, why, then he would be pleased to give him one.

In one fluid move, Nicholas leapt to the side, positioning himself between the groom and Katherine, while whipping out his pistol.

The boy lunged toward him.

Nicholas jumped back, still holding Katherine. She bumped into his injured shoulder. He groaned, but kept his pistol aimed at the groom.

The gun glinted, cold and lethal in the weak moonlight.

"Both of you must stop this," Katherine said, her voice quiet but firm. "'Tis not your right to question me," she said to Jeremy. Then softer, to Nicholas, "Please, put away that weapon."

Nicholas kept his eyes fixed on Jeremy. "Your mistress is right." He lowered his arm, but kept it ready should the boy suddenly move again. "Let us talk inside. Is there anyone else in the stables?"

The boy shook his head.

Nicholas nodded at the pitchfork. "You can put that down before we go in."

Jeremy inclined his head stiffly and tossed the tool onto the ground. It hit a rock with a loud clang.

Nicholas sucked in a breath. He took Katherine's arm and waved at the boy with his gun. They followed him into the dark building.

Flint sparked onto tinder, illuminating the boy's face while he lit a lantern. The wavering light revealed neat, austere surroundings. Clean, oiled saddles hung tidily on pegs alongside harnesses and bridles, yet there was a feeling of disuse. Most of the stalls were empty. Nicholas lowered the firearm to his side.

Jeremy spoke to Katherine. "Is he that highwayman?"

"Who I am is of no concern to you," said Nicholas.

"'Tis of great concern," the young man affirmed.

Katherine shook off Nicholas's hand, and pulled back her hood. "Jeremy, this is Mr. Ed—"

"I am Katherine's cousin." Nicholas spoke over her.

Katherine blinked. "Ah, yes. Mr. Eddington will be accompanying me to London, to see my other cousin."

Jeremy eyed Nicholas. "He does not look like safe company, and 'tis a strange hour you have picked to begin your journey."

"'Twill be aright, Jeremy." Katherine sighed. "Let us be off with no trouble. I must go because Father has planned I will say my spousals tomorrow with Richard Finch."

Jeremy looked at Katherine. "I would have agreed to take you."

"I thank you for that, Jeremy. But, you see, my cousin is bound in that direction."

The lad frowned, caught in obvious indecision. Then he smiled at her, and Nicholas could see she had won him over.

Nicholas stepped forward. "We shall need two horses."

Jeremy shook his head. "She don't ride."

"All right," said Nicholas, almost shouting his frustration. "The only way to get to London I can think of if 'she don't ride' is for her to ride with me. Together. In which case, we shall only need one horse."

Katherine pursed her lips.

The little cat yawned and began to purr.

Nicholas took Katherine's lack of argument for agreement.

"I think 'twould be better," Jeremy said, addressing himself to Katherine, "if I get two horses." He put out a hand to still her protest. "I will accompany you. It will take me just a moment to make ready."

"No, Jeremy. I cannot ask that of you," Katherine said.

"You are not asking," he corrected her. "I will feel much better if I can see you are safe."

"Fine," agreed Nicholas looking heavenward. "While we talk, the night wanes. If we do not leave soon 'twill be morning." He turned to Jeremy. "You get two horses, and whatever else you require. And be quick."

He took Katherine by the arm and guided her through the door, then helped her collect her satchels. One was very heavy and held several book-shaped objects. Could they really *be* books? And she had thought she would walk to London carrying them?

Keen disappointment ran through Nicholas when he saw the mounts Jeremy led from the stables. Personal inspection of the stalls confirmed the lad's declaration that the two mares were the best Ashfield had to offer. And to think that these stables had once been renowned for their horseflesh.

He could feel Katherine tremble as he took her by the waist and lifted her onto their horse. Her complexion appeared waxen in the moonlight. In her eyes was the same dull resignation he'd seen on the faces of Christians sold in the slave markets of Algiers. He made an effort to be gentle while he settled her on the animal and mounted behind her, offering no further objections to the furry bundle of his namesake she had tucked in a fold of her cloak.

Katherine perched uneasily, not astride, but not sidesaddle either. Her heart pounded, and alarm ran through her veins. She adjusted her skirt.

Nicholas took the reins, tightening his arms around her, and pulled her into his warmth. But she could not relax. Dread clutched her heart with each slight movement of the mare.

"I have not been on a mount since...since Edward." The words stumbled out breathless and hesitant. Her heart pounded as the scene flashed through her mind. Her body felt, anew, the dawning horror as horse and rider missed the jump and fell, crashing down together. A gasp caught in her throat.

She felt a gentle squeeze. "'Tis sorry I am." Nicholas's

resonant voice brought with it a measure of calm, and his arms gave comfort. "This ride 'twill be aright. I will keep you safe." The prickly stubble of his beard grazed her cheek.

She heaved a shuddering breath and pushed the memory away.

He tightened his arms around her as he slapped the reins.

They started down the drive, through the long border of stately oak trees. Katherine's stomach pitched and tossed with each movement of the horse, even though they traveled slowly. They passed by the dark gatehouse, pausing while Jeremy unlatched and opened the gate. The loud and unavoidable creaking did not wake the old, deaf gatekeeper.

Katherine craned her neck to get a last glimpse of Ashfield. Even atop a horse, she was glad to be leaving—glad of every step that put distance between her and a terrible future. Glad, as well, to have a strong escort in Nicholas and a loyal one in Jeremy. Taking a deep breath, she turned her head frontward. She wished to never see Ashfield again.

As Nicholas urged the mount forward, her stomach lurched. She stifled a cry, grabbing at his hands. He tightened his arms around her. She felt pinpricks on her arm from Montford's claws as the cat readjusted inside her cloak.

"I'll keep you safe, lass," Nicholas said, his low voice rumbling in her ear.

A rush of warmth ran through her and she shivered.

When had he stopped calling her Katherine and started calling her lass? And when had she stopped thinking of him as Mr. Eddington, or the Raven, and started thinking of him as Nicholas?

Katherine dragged in a breath. Tree branches rustled in the light wind. The rhythmic clop-clop-clop of the horses' hooves echoed into the darkness, soothing her fears, lulling her. She sagged against him, easing her head into the curve of his neck, breathing in his exotic scent.

Katherine blinked hard and straightened up. What had come over her? Just because the man gave her comfort and promised her safety, did not mean she should not keep her wits about her.

What would she do if thieves set upon them? Or highwaymen? Would highwaymen give other highwayman trouble? Was there some sort of Brotherhood of Outlaws? Did they have a code of conduct? Katherine bit her lip. It seemed quite unlikely.

As important, would Nicholas be the gentleman she hoped he was? So far, his actions had been unpredictable: either alarming or protective. Letting out a slow sigh, she acknowledged it was too late to have doubts. He was her best chance for freedom, and she had already gone too far to turn back. He had said his outlaw days were behind him, at least for now. And even though she did not understand why, she felt safe in the shelter of his arms. She would have to be content with that.

Katherine took a couple easy breaths to settle her stomach. A heady courage began to replace the fear coursing through her veins. Even though Cousin Alicia didn't know she was coming, Katherine began to think for the first time in quite a long while that everything *could* turn out all right.

Katherine settled into Nicholas's arms. Before long, her regular breathing told him she'd fallen asleep. He'd carefully kept their pace slow and easy to allay her fright.

Assessing the moon's position, he surmised that even at this pace, they would reach the inn in three or four hours, arriving at dawn.

When he'd first returned to Dorsetshire, he'd deliberately chosen to stay some distance from Ashfield. Although he'd been gone seventeen years, and even though he bore scant resemblance to the angry eleven year-old boy who had left, memories could be long, and Nicholas had no desire to be recognized. He had given the innkeeper a false name, and so far, he was confident no one had noticed that the Earl of Ashton had returned.

But there was no question about it. He was back.

Nicholas looked down at his prize, watched her head bob with each plodding step of the horse. A wisp of hair had come loose from the prison of her cap and dangled across her tender nape. A sudden overwhelming need to nestle his face into that delicate curve possessed him. Instead, he readjusted her sleeping form. As her head repositioned into the crook of his neck, the scent of lavender wafted up to him. Nicholas closed his eyes and shuddered at the sudden rush of desire that ran through him.

The sound of horse hooves coming closer seeped into his awareness. He opened his eyes to see Jeremy had ridden up beside him.

He'd forgotten about the boy.

In the dim moonlight, he could see the lad wore an unmistakable scowl.

Nicholas scowled back.

Katherine cracked open an eye. They had stopped moving.

Dawn painted rosy streaks across the sky. A sign announced, by both picture and word, that they had arrived at the *Ram's Head Inn*. Warm inside the curve of Nicholas's arms, she yawned and looked around the well-tended courtyard. Two benches made from logs cut in half sat outside a sturdy wooden door. The windows were still shuttered against the night, but smoke poured out of a chimney at the back of the unassuming building, attesting to the beginning of a new day.

Nicholas dismounted, caught her by the waist and swung her down. Her legs buckled when her feet touched the ground, and she sagged against him, clutching Montford to her chest. Nicholas did not let go of her, but held her close—too close for the cat, wedged between them.

Montford mewed in protest.

Nicholas's eyes met hers. A jolt of physical awareness tingled through her, and all sleepiness vanished. Katherine gasped at her reaction. He held her steady for a long moment before putting her from him. This time, after a slight sway, she held her own weight. As soon as she was stable, he walked off.

Shaken and bereft of Nicholas's strong presence and warmth, Katherine began to shiver. She tightened her cloak against the morning chill and watched him give instructions to a stable boy.

Jeremy looked her way and their gazes met across the

courtyard.

She blushed, still overcome by her intense response to Nicholas.

The front door burst open. The innkeeper, a short stout man, flew out to greet them.

"Master Abernathy," he cried. "'Tis pleased I am at your safe return."

Abernathy? Katherine's head spun to Nicholas.

"Afraid I would not be back to pay my bill, you mean." Nicholas chuckled.

The innkeeper stopped in his tracks and acted as if he'd been stabbed in the heart. "You cut me to the quick," he exclaimed. "In your absence, Molly has been sulking and Henry off to his room. I am hoping your return will put all back as it should be."

"Then let us begin with my belly." Nicholas rubbed his stomach. "I have a powerful hunger this morn."

"Aye." The stout man nodded and cast a curious glance at Katherine as he led them inside.

Jeremy stayed behind with the stable boy and the horses.

The common room was crude but clean. Loud banging in the kitchen, accompanied by the smell of bread baking, set Katherine's stomach growling. The innkeeper settled them at a table. A few minutes later a sleepy-eyed serving girl set a loaf of warm bread, and an assortment of cold meats, cheese, and pickled herring before them.

Katherine washed down a bite of the cheese with small ale. Not so good as that made at Ashfield under her guidance, yet still marvelously thirst quenching, and perhaps better because she was *not* at Ashfield. A feeling of elation ran through her, and she smiled.

Nicholas stared at the rare sight of Katherine smiling. All severity gone, a glow radiated from within her. She almost looked pretty. Her lips, usually pulled into a thin line, looked soft. Kissable. It had been too many days since he'd been with a woman.

He was beginning to count how many, when his thoughts were disturbed by footsteps hastening down the hall. A man's voice burst into the peacefulness of the room.

"Nicky! Where ha' ye been?"

Nicholas's head whipped around as Henry advanced toward their table. The man's usually neat appearance was gone. His shirt was dirty, his eyes bloodshot, and a white cloth wrapped from the top of his head to his jaw made him look quite mad.

"Where have ye been?" Henry repeated. "It's worried to death, I've been, waiting for ye here. Back before morning, ye said." He swallowed, his large Adam's apple bobbing. "And when the horse came back without ye.... I'd heard ye were shot...thought ye were dead..." His voice trailed off as he looked at Katherine. "Who—?"

"Henry," Nicholas cut him off, alarmed the man might give it all away before he had a chance to warn him. "I did not wish to wake you, and my sister here—" he made a meaningful glance and nodded at Katherine.

He ignored the looks of astonishment on both Henry's and Katherine's faces and continued. "My sister and I needed to break our fast after our long journey, so I decided we should eat now and announce our presence to you after."

A commotion on the table diverted their attention. Montford clenched a piece of herring in her teeth. Growling, the kitten slowly backed to the table edge, hair straight up on an arched back.

Nicholas chuckled.

Katherine smiled. "Aright puss." She picked up the feline, avoiding four sets of sharp claws, and placed Montford at her feet on the wooden floor.

"Would you like to join us for a bite too?" Nicholas invited Henry.

"I thank ye, no." He rubbed one side of his bound jaw gently. "'Tis me tooth again. I cannot chew. 'Tis also making me a bit peevish."

"I had not noticed," Nicholas said drolly, picking up a bit of cheese with the tip of his knife and popping it into his mouth.

Katherine spoke to Henry. "Have you tried clove for your tooth?"

Henry shook his head and grimaced. "It's brandy I've been trying mostly, and a very strange decoction the landlord's daughter gave me." His mouth formed a crooked smile. "It made me tongue blister, it did, but it didn't help me tooth, except that me tongue hurt so bad I forgot about the tooth awhile."

Nicholas pulled a hunk of bread from the loaf. "You are well enough to travel?"

Henry pulled the ragged cloth from his head. "Aye," he nodded. "Where to now?"

"We are to London," Katherine told him.

Nicholas gave her a censuring frown. "Do not say it so loud, lass. Do you want the whole of Dorsetshire to know where we're headed?"

Katherine looked down at her lap.

At once Nicholas felt contrite. "In truth," he said more gently. "We need to be gone quick. We'll eat, I shall settle my account with the landlord, and we'll be back on the road." He turned to Henry. "We've brought a groom with us—a boy, and some sorry horse-flesh. The boy can help you in the stables." He sent the man a glance that said *I'll explain all later.*

Henry nodded and left the room.

"More riding so soon?" Katherine sighed, disappointment written across her face.

"We cannot stop here, lass. They would find us before supper. We need to stay well ahead of them."

"Do you think they come after us," she swallowed, "even now?"

"No." He smiled. "My guess is they are just discovering your absence, and within the next few hours will be on the road in pursuit. Still, 'tis best we get on our way soon."

She nodded; her mouth drew into a tight line.

"Cheer up, lass. I will not let them get you." Nicholas took a bite of the crusty bread. "Now it is time to eat. 'Twill be a long day on the road, and we won't stop again before nightfall."

At the thought of getting back on a horse, Katherine's muscles groaned. Nicholas's arms had been comfortable, but she had not slept well. Still, they had made much better progress than had they been on foot.

As the room filled with villagers stopping in for their morning draught before moving on, Katherine made an effort to eat. Each time someone walked in, she sank as far into the solid oak bench as possible, but no one looked at her.

Nicholas, on the other hand, drew the eye. Though not exactly handsome, his presence was commanding. The streak of white running through his otherwise ebony hair was a striking bit of audacity. Thank goodness, they would be looking for her and not him. As if to prove this, a loud voice cut through the general buzz of conversation.

"Nicky!" A robust serving-maid headed in their direction with two large tankards grasped in one hand, her face all smiles. "'Tis glad I am t'see ye returned in one piece," she exclaimed. "When yer horse came back w'out ye, 'twas thought ye'd come to some harm."

"Molly," Nicholas brought his hand about her waist and pulled her to him, planting a kiss on an ample breast that threatened to burst from her tight bodice. "Surely I missed you, my girl."

"Away w' ye, now," said Molly, batting at his hand.

Katherine pursed her lips. Heat rushed to her cheeks. She glanced around the room, but no one seemed to notice. Yet, in such proximity, she could not avoid it. Keeping her eyes averted from Nicholas and the maid, she swallowed, and pushed her mug away.

"Pray excuse me," she mumbled and rose.

Nicholas put a staying hand upon her arm. He shook his head, his eyes urging her back into her seat. Katherine shrugged him off, but sat down anyway.

"Not now, Molly, you can see my sister does not approve."

Molly eyed Katherine and clucked her tongue. "Is she a Puritan, or one of them Quakers?"

He shook his head. "Nay, she is a widow."

Molly extricated herself from Nicholas's embrace and smoothed her skirt with her hands. Then she reached over and gave Katherine's shoulder a pat. "Sorry I am to hear of it. I miss me Harry, I do. It's been almost two years and I still grieve for the scamp." She sighed, and then her smile returned as she turned to yell at a couple of farmers who had been calling her, "Comin', comin', cannot ye see I'm busy?" She guffawed before bouncing off to serve them.

Katherine looked at the table, avoiding Nicholas's gaze.

"You disapprove?" he asked.

"'Tis of no matter whether I approve or not," she answered. "But 'tis not seemly, nor prudent to draw attention in a public place."

"Such behavior is common in a place like this."

Katherine sniffed. "That may be so. I would not know."

Nicholas reached across the table and took her hand, cradling it between his two larger ones. He drew slow circles on her palm with a finger, sending strange feelings through her. She tried to pull her hand away but he did not release it. Finally, she looked at him.

"I am a man," he said simply.

Katherine let out a shuddering sigh and nodded.

He loosened his hold.

She snatched her hand back into her lap just as Henry approached the table, carrying a steaming mug. Clothing straightened, he looked almost presentable.

Nicholas took the cup and brought it not to his mouth, but to his nose, and inhaled deeply.

The delicious scent wrapped around Katherine, exotic and earthy. "It smells wondrous. What is it?" She sniffed the air. "Is that what you do with it?"

Nicholas laughed. "Nay. I drink it," and he proved this by taking a big gulp. He held the mug out to her. "Coffee."

She brought it to her lips and sipped. He watched as her eyes widened, then her mouth pulled into a grimace. "Why, 'tis bitter." She looked at him reproachfully and put the cup on the table.

Nicholas smiled, taking the mug back up. "Only at first." He took another big drink. "Later 'tis pleasing. Very pleasing." Just like lovemaking, he thought, and then shook his head.

Why did his mind stray to carnal pleasures when he was with

her, this drab Puritan? Too bad there was no time to slake his lust with Molly. He drained the last of the stimulating brew and turned to Henry, who had fallen into conversation at one of the tables nearby. "Are we ready then?"

CHAPTER FIVE

"Who are your new friends, Nicky?" Henry kept his voice down and inclined his head toward other end of the yard where Jeremy readied three fresh mounts. Katherine stood to the side, holding her cat.

"She isn't my sister, that's for certain." Nicholas chuckled.

"I know that. Your sister is in France."

"Listen," Nicholas's voice took on a conspiratorial tone. "She is heiress to Ashfield."

Henry's eyes grew large.

"And, she is to marry Dickon Finch."

"No!"

Nicholas nodded.

Henry rubbed his jaw. "Then what is she doing with *you*?"

"She doesn't know who I am, or that I have a connection to Ashfield. Thinks I'm a Nicholas Eddington, got that idea while I was ill,"—and then at Henry's expression—"nothing to worry about, just a bullet to the arm. I'm quite recovered, I assure you." To prove this he raised his arm, waved it back and forth, up and down. "See?" he said smiling, even though showing it didn't hurt at all made it hurt quite a bit.

"She does not want to marry Dickon. Who would blame her? She thinks I'm helping her run off to London—which I am, in a way." He winked. "She knows I'm the Raven."

"Are you sure you're alright Nicky? Maybe that bullet addled yer brains?" Henry shook his head. "What can you possibly be doing with her? And who is the boy?"

"He came long to make sure I do her no harm."

"Mayhap a good thing." Henry frowned. "I know this is asking a lot of ye, but have ye made any sort of a plan?"

Nicholas looked across the yard at Katherine and Jeremy, in quiet conversation. She smiled up at Jeremy in a way he found most annoying. What were his plans for the lass?

It had seemed so simple back at the cottage: through her, he would wreak his revenge. But how, exactly? Would it be possible to hurt her father and Finch without hurting her, and still fulfill the promise he made to his father? He kicked at a rock with the toe of his boot.

"Not exactly," he admitted. "But by keeping her with me, I at least foil the plans of Finch and her father to unite their properties."

"That old friend of yours was here t'other day, the day after you disappeared, looking for the Raven. I fear he might have recognized me. It has been many years, of course—"

"And you haven't changed a bit, have you my friend." Nicholas teased, remembering a younger and wider Henry, as he had been when they left Ashfield. The man's hair, then brown, had long since turned gray.

"We must travel where we are not known. Until I am certain what game I play, I don't wish Katherine to discover who I am. Mayhap we should take the Salisbury road. What do you think?"

Henry furled his brow. "I do not recall the country lanes at all well, Nicky. But since we had best get going, any road should do as long as we aim in the right direction."

Gerald Welles watched through the tall mullioned window as the elegant Finch coach wound its way up the drive. His empty belly clenched. This would not go well; he knew it.

Nothing had gone as it should since he'd awakened this morning to discover his household at a standstill. There had been no satisfactory explanation, except that Katherine was not there to make it go.

He'd not been alarmed, at least not at first. After all, she was generally a sensible girl who did not disobey or turn up missing. Still, it was too easy to remember how she'd resisted him about Finch. Wilfred had often warned him about sparing the rod, and Gerald was beginning to think his father might have been right. Perhaps what the girl needed was a good beating.

Something he would attend to as soon as she came back.

While he'd waited for his breakfast, he'd set the servants to look for her. Instead of Katherine, they'd found a note: a list of tasks underway and what still needed doing. Gerald wondered if that might be her way of saying good-bye. This became more likely when Lucy discovered Katherine's little cat was gone. Then news came from the stables that Jeremy and two mounts were absent as well.

That was bad.

Very bad.

So bad, Gerald lost his appetite and left his breakfast uneaten. The anxiety of what to tell his father set his knees knocking. And now, drat it all, Finch was arriving early.

Outside the window, the coach came to a stop. The coachman hopped down from his perch and helped Finch out of the cab. Gerald hurried to the antechamber, preferring to meet Finch in the smaller room.

At the sound of Finch's imperious steps clicking across the stone floor, Gerald's stomach twisted into a hard knot and his mind went blank. He tried to compose himself before the other man barreled into the small room, the Ashfield butler in tow.

"Is my bride ready for our espousals?" asked Finch, without even the courtesy of a greeting. He dismissed the servant as if this were his house already.

"She's gone," Gerald blurted out, not meaning to say that at all.

"Gone?" Finch squeaked. He cleared his throat. "What do

you mean she is gone? Where did she go?"

"Not far, not far. I-I am sure she will return soon. A touch of the megrims is all, I think. The gentle sex..." Gerald tried to smile but failed. He had to protect Katherine, not that she would appreciate it. The chit didn't know what was best for her; women rarely did. He'd secured a very advantageous match for her, and she was ruining it all.

"She knew we were to say our espousals today." Finch's eyes narrowed. "Has she gone off to the woods again? I do not approve. 'Tis dangerous." He cracked his knuckles.

Gerald flinched with each pop. "I shall send word when she is back," he said, trying to gain control of the exchange. "I will lock her up. You have my word on it."

"You should have locked her up before. She is a disobedient daughter, which is not to your credit." Finch waved a finger at him. "I will not have a disobedient wife to discredit me." He grasped the hilt of his dress sword, pulled the blade out halfway, and then shoved it back inside its scabbard. "She will not be disobedient long." He turned and left without so much as a good-bye.

Gerald sank onto the stone seat. With the two best horses gone, he'd have to send Horace and Stephen on the remaining mounts. They'd find them.

They had to.

Once clear of the village, the four riders passed hills dotted with small farmhouses and sheep, picturesque under a crystal-blue sky. A bucolic and peaceful scene that did not match Nicholas's irritated mood.

Feeling thus as a younger man, he'd have picked a fight, calling out the biggest, brawniest opponent he could find and emerging a bloody, yet usually triumphant, mess. At twenty-eight he was too old for that. And who would he fight anyway? Jeremy? He let out a derisive snort.

Katherine made a disapproving shrug.

It all came from lack of sexual activity. He could think of no other reason that she should fill his thoughts. Instead of watching the landscape as they traveled past, or thinking of what to do next, Katherine appeared in his mind's eye. Not as she sat, stiff before him on the horse, but a different Katherine, a winsome, responsive, full-blooded woman.

This other Katherine did not wear her hair bound under an ugly white cap, but wore it flowing free. Long and silken, he could imagine it spilling across his pillow. Her mouth, instead of drawn in a tight line, was soft, yielding, and full of erotic promise. Her eyes, instead of sad and wary, were beckoning, warm, and hungry. For him.

A dream Katherine to be sure. He cursed silently and shifted in the saddle to ease the tightness in his breeches.

Katherine's Puritan upbringing did not bode well for bed sport. He'd heard that Puritans regarded bedding with the same dry religious conviction as they did everything else. Likely for Katherine, fornication would be a cold perfunctory joining purely for the begetting of children. No doubt she would be as wooden in bed as she sat before him now.

And a virgin, too. Although some men preferred them innocent, that chaste state was not at all to his taste. He preferred a seasoned woman, one who could match his level of passion and delight in sex play.

Nicholas grimaced and shifted in the saddle again. Taking a deep breath, he acknowledged that traveling with Katherine presented complications he had not foreseen.

He raised his arm in a signal to stop. "We can rest now," he said, and at Katherine's pleased smile, he added, "but only for a moment." Although he'd been aching for her to smile, perversely, he now wished to crush it.

He dismounted, and then helped her down, putting her away from him with haste.

Montford sprang from her arms and darted off into a thicket.

"I will not wait for you to find your cat," Nicholas warned.

"My kitten will come when I call," she said, her voice a trifle haughty.

It had better, he thought, turning away.

After Nicholas and the other men went off, Katherine found a group of bushes to seek her ease.

"Montford," she whispered when she was done. Then louder, "Where'd you go, puss? Will you make me a liar?" A rustling in the far undergrowth caught her attention. In a flash of grey fur, Montford dashed across the clearing and scampered up a stately old oak. Shading her eyes against the late afternoon sun, Katherine spied her kitten several branches up and well out of reach.

"Montford," she pleaded. "Nicholas said he would not wait, and I think he's a man of his word. At least I've been hoping so."

That didn't budge the cat, except, perhaps, to send Montford higher up into the branches. The kitten's movement dislodged several leaves and an acorn, which hit Katherine squarely on the forehead. She let out a yelp and jumped back at the sudden pain.

Rubbing her brow, she vowed she would not leave without her kitten, no matter what Nicholas said. If he wanted to go on, then he would have to leave without both of them.

She looked around the clearing. Night would soon obscure the shadows and plunge the woods in darkness. She would be prey to any wild animal or thief that happened by. Katherine shuddered and clenched her hands into fists. She could not let it come to that. "Montford!"

Nicholas, returning at that moment, winced at hearing his name, and hoped Jeremy did not see the astonished look on Henry's face.

"'Tis her cat," he hissed to his friend. "She gave it the family surname, I forgot to tell you."

In an instant, Nicholas could see what had happened. Speaking in his normal tone, he addressed the two men. "Leave this to me."

Unable to resist toying with Katherine, he sauntered over to her. "Lost your cat up a tree, have you?" He smirked.

She looked away.

He took hold of her up-thrust chin, slowly turned her face to his, and looked straight in her eyes. "And you want me to get it back for you?"

She swallowed deeply and nodded. A plaintive meow from up in the branches echoed her assent.

He looked into the tawny depths of her eyes. She looked back warily. At this range, he could kiss her.

That was it. He could solve both their problems. She would get her cat back, and he could put the fantasy Katherine out of his mind with one harmless act.

Nicholas smiled. "I will demand payment."

Her delicate brows drew together.

"Don't worry lass, 'tis a payment you can afford." He caught a whiff of lavender. "All I ask is one kiss."

Her eyes widened. He saw a flash of alarm just before it was replaced by a look of reluctant curiosity. Then she turned her head away and he could no longer read her eyes. Montford's pleas grew louder.

"Please," she said, arms crossed over her chest.

He bent his head and spoke into her ear. "Ah, lass. A kiss is naught to be feared. 'Tis one of the wondrous things a woman can share with a man."

"'Twill be payment for your service, and naught else."

"As you wish," he grinned, certain she was right. "But I will collect."

With that, he walked over to the tree, grabbed hold of the two lowest branches, thrust a leg into the "V" at the bottom and began his ascent.

As Jeremy and Henry joined her, Katherine's stomach knotted. They stood, a somber threesome, necks craned to watch his progress. The branches above swayed as Nicholas climbed. A loud crack sounded, and a small branch came plummeting down. Jeremy grabbed Katherine and pulled her to safety.

"You aright, Nick?" Henry called up.

"Quite," Nicholas's terse reply came down.

"And Montford?" Katherine now realized that for Nicholas to bring down the cat, he'd only be able to use one hand for climbing. That, and his recent arm wound, made it seem an impossible task.

How could she have asked it of him?

How could he dare it for a kiss?

If he did succeed, she would have to pay the forfeit, but for him not to succeed was unthinkable.

"Your puss is fine." Nicholas called down, sounding like he spoke through clenched teeth.

"Oh, do be careful," she cried.

"'Twill be just a moment longer," he called back.

They all watched as the branches dipped and swayed, signaling Nicholas's descent. Katherine was surprised to see him hop down from the last branches with both hands free.

Katherine heard a muffled meow. "But where is my kitten?"

Nicholas laughed and held his coat open on one side. Montford's head peeked out from the inside pocket.

"Here is your puss—safe." Nicholas's voice sounded husky in the cool afternoon air. He handed Montford off to Jeremy. "You take this mischief-maker and do not let go."

Katherine swallowed. Nicholas's part of the bargain was fulfilled. Would he kiss her now? Surely not with Jeremy and Henry present!

"If you will excuse us?" Nicholas nodded dismissal at the two men.

Jeremy scowled as Henry took his free arm and drew the boy toward the horses. Katherine saw him turn his head twice to send her an inquiring look. Both times, she shook her head slightly. She would not go back on her word.

Nicholas's sense of triumph faded as he wrapped an arm around Katherine's trembling shoulders and led her to a fallen tree branch behind a copse. For a moment, he was sorry that a small dalliance such as this could cause her so much consternation.

But he had to go through with it. It was the only way he could think of to rid himself of the fantasy Katherine.

He looked her over. She could not be more different from the Katherine of his vision. Alarm filled her eyes. Her lips were drawn into a hard line and her cheeks, instead of being rosy, were wan. Her breath came out in little puffs. He hoped she wouldn't swoon.

"Shall we?" he asked.

"Yes." Her voice was almost a whisper. "Can we get it over with?" Her words echoed his thoughts, yet the pleading he saw in her eyes just before she clamped them shut, did not.

"No, lass." He put a hand to each cheek. "Open your eyes. Look at me now."

Katherine cracked them open.

He searched their depths for that other Katherine, but saw naught reflected back. Her cheeks felt like fine porcelain under his hands. As his mouth hovered over hers, she let out a whimper.

Should he stop? But that would not vanquish the dream Katherine. No, he must prove to his errant body she did not exist. Then she would cease to haunt his waking hours, and allow him a peaceful rest this night. It was just a kiss after all. No great matter.

He gently rubbed his thumbs across her cheekbones until she relaxed, just a bit. Again, his mouth began the descent toward hers. This time she did not whimper. Nor did he stop.

Her lips were cold. Nicholas plied them gently, yet they did not yield sweetness.

The frustration of the ride today and the night before welled up in him like a rising tide. Nicholas redoubled his efforts. His hands slid behind her head to hold it against the onslaught of his mouth, but instead of the silken masses of hair he'd imagined, he felt only the fine fabric of her cap. He yanked the strings of her bonnet free where it fastened beneath her chin and cast it away, smothering her surprised gasp with his mouth. One by one, he plucked the pins from her hair and tossed them into the copse.

Her hair fell over his hands like a mantle. The scent of lavender wafted about him. And then he felt a tiny, almost imperceptible, spark of response.

With renewed vigor, he tugged her bottom lip, then the top one with his teeth. Running a hand through her luxuriant mass of hair, he suckled each lip in turn. He coaxed her mouth open and ran his tongue over the silken interior.

Katherine melted into his arms. She touched his face, running a finger along his cheek to his eyebrow and into his hair. Shivers coursed through him. Her velvety tongue probed his mouth in a tentative response that sent his blood pounding. Nicholas groaned.

Wrenching his lips from hers, he gazed deep into her eyes...

The eyes of that *other* Katherine.

CHAPTER SIX

Just past nightfall, the four travelers dragged into the stable yard of the *Crown and Crowe* in Salisbury. A hostler came forward to claim their mounts.

Katherine slid wearily off the horse into Nicholas's waiting arms. He held her for a long moment in the soft moonlight, his expression unreadable, then put her from him. Neither broke the awkward silence that had stayed between them since the kiss.

More than anything, Katherine wanted to be alone, without Nicholas's compelling presence, without his arms around her, his scent enveloping her. A bath to ease the stiffness in her muscles would be nice, she thought, hobbling toward the welcoming shafts of light that beamed through the windows.

As she stepped into the common room, the warmth from a large fireplace rushed up to greet her. The crowd seemed congenial, not too boisterous. The luscious aroma of cooking food beckoned her hungry stomach.

"Welcome, welcome," the innkeeper cried as he hastened to them.

"A private room for the night," said Nicholas without ado. "My wife tires," he squeezed Katherine's forearm. Though smiling, his eyes forbade contradiction. "We require a meal sent up, and I would pay well for the speedy delivery of a hot bath."

"Of course," the innkeeper responded. "Cassie!" A round, merry-looking woman bustled up.

Wife? Katherine did not wish to spend this night with him. As much as she wanted a bath, she would not bathe in his presence, or suffer his bathing in hers. It was not right. As soon as the woman left, she'd tell him so.

Cassie led them up a flight of stairs, down a short hallway to a small, but comfortable room. She tilted her candle flame to the wick of a lamp. The growing light cheered the room, as did the fire the woman kindled in the hearth. Montford jumped out of Katherine's arms and bounced off to search the corners and under the quilted bed.

"The bath will be up soon. Ye look tired," she looked kindly at Katherine. "I'll send a sack-posset up w'yer meal. 'Twill help ye sleep well this night." Then she left, closing the door behind her. Katherine was alone with Nicholas.

"Wife?" she said sharply.

He pulled off his hat and walked toward her, managing to look apologetic and predatory at the same time. "It was the only way."

Katherine took a step back. "I thought I was your sister, or your cousin." She was unable to control the trembling in her voice. "I'll not stay here with you. 'Tis not right."

"We have no choice, lass. You cannot stay in a room by yourself. 'Tis too dangerous. You haven't a maidservant to attend you. If 'tis thought we are married you will come to no harm."

"I have entrusted my safety to you, Nicholas. Not my reason." She raised a finger to her lips. She did not trust him—or his kisses. Katherine frowned as a new thought came to her. "Do you have a wife?"

He looked at her as if puzzled by the question. "No."

"Good." Katherine nodded. She knew so little about him. This lack of knowledge hadn't prevented her from asking his help. But now, it bothered her.

"If you had a wife how would you treat her? Would you demand her obedience?"

"I would expect her to comply with my wishes," Nicholas

frowned. He shook his head. "I do not see—"

"Would you beat her if she did not do as you say?"

"Katherine, I have not thought to have a wife. I have no use for one. I have no wish for one."

Katherine sighed. "I have always thought to have a husband, whether I wished one or no." She looked directly at him. "And it seems this is no different. But you are not my husband, Nicholas. You will spend this night on the floor."

"I look forward to it," Nicholas answered dryly.

"And you will leave while I bathe."

"'Twas always my intention." He nodded and put on his hat. "I ordered the bath for you. I shall wash with Henry."

"Oh," she said feeling foolish for having thought otherwise.

Turning to the fire, he added a bit more kindling, and prodded it with the poker. Finally, a rap on the door announced the arrival of the bath. Ushering the servants in, he supervised the placement of the tub, and followed them out.

Katherine experienced a wave of relief as she shut the door and latched it behind him. She took off her dusty cloak, shoes, and stockings. Letting out a long sigh, she wriggled her bare toes on the cold wood floor.

Montford jumped out from under the bed and attacked. Rolling onto her back, the kitten bit and kicked Katherine's foot while she jiggled it.

"Ouch!" She pulled her foot away when a sharp tooth bit into her ankle. "That's enough, puss."

Divesting herself of her clothing, even the Chinese coin on its green ribbon, Katherine walked naked to the tub and eased herself into the hot steamy water. The innkeeper's wife had provided a new bar of Castile soap. Wistfully, Katherine thought of the lavender soap back at Ashfield, made just this autumn, each bar wrapped and stored away.

She splashed her face with hot water. There was no going back, so there would be no looking back.

Submerging to her chin, Katherine closed her eyes. The hot water soothed her aching muscles and lulled the tension from her mind. She drifted on the visions she'd seen earlier that day of the countryside: farmers working in the fields, sheep grazing, the small thatched cottages they had passed. But then the image of Nicholas's face appeared before her, his eyes searching hers and his lips moving closer, closer...

Katherine opened her eyes and sat up sending a wave of water sloshing onto the floor. She took a guilty look around the room, but there was no one to see her discomfiture, no one to be aware of her thoughts. She was still alone but for Montford, who now slept on the center of the bed.

Resolving to set her mind on other things, she picked up the bar of soap, dunked it in the water, and worked up a lather with her hands. But soon, massaging the soap through her hair made her think of *his* hands running through her hair, soaping her arms brought to mind *his* hand on her arm as he'd steered her up the stairs. Everywhere she washed, she could feel his hands upon her, a strange, unsettling, yet pleasant sensation. She watched her nipples grow into firm pebbles, saw the soap trail down the valley between her breasts—breasts that had become sensitive when he'd kissed her.

A surge of heat ran through her. Never had she imagined a kiss to be that way. She'd melted like winter snow in the spring sun. If he hadn't stopped, she was sure she'd have become a puddle at his feet.

Disconcerted, Katherine dunked under the water, rinsing the lather from her arms and breasts with brusque, almost harsh, motions.

Leaning back against the side of the tub, she sighed. This bath was not bringing the calm she needed. She lifted a leg out of the water, ran the soap from her toes to the top of her thigh, and then repeated on the other side. That left the place where her legs joined. Her woman's place. Another rush of warmth coursed through her. That place had felt his kiss as well. He had made her ache, as if she were coming down with the ague.

That must be it, she thought, lowering herself back into the water. Nicholas gave her a fever. Maybe she needed a dose of comfrey and willow bark tea.

Or to kiss him again.

Katherine immersed her face in the water and scrubbed her skin, getting just enough soap into her eyes to burn, as if to punish herself for such wayward thoughts.

She rinsed her hair and shivered. The water had cooled. She must be well done with her bath and dressed when Nicholas returned, and have her thoughts under control as well.

Katherine rose from the tub and dried herself, not minding at all when the coarse towel abraded her tender skin. Taking a wrinkled but clean gown from a satchel, she dressed without her stays and petticoats, knowing she would sleep in what she wore.

After a brief search through her other bag, Katherine found her comb. Pulling a stool before the fire, determined to cast her mind from Nicholas, she tried to remember her Latin verbs and combed her hair until all the knots were gone.

Downstairs in the common room, Nicholas sat across from Jeremy at a rough wooden table not far from the fire. The atmosphere between them bristled with tension. Impatient to be done with a necessary ploy, Nicholas spoke overloud. "Now, lad, which road d'ye think will be the best to take us to Portsmouth?" He gave the boy a broad wink.

"Portsmouth?" Jeremy looked up, startled. "But I tho—ow!!" He shot an angry look at Nicholas and reached down to rub his shin. "Ye did not have to kick me!"

"Shhh," Nicholas hissed. "We want them to think 'tis where we're going in case we're asked about."

"Oh," Jeremy looked down, a hot red tinge flushing his ears. "I shoulda thought o' that."

Nicholas said louder, "It seems we should go by Alderbury. Or d'ye think the Bodenham road would be better?"

Jeremy cleared his throat and spoke, eyes looking daggers at Nicholas. "I reckon 'twould be best to take the Bodenham road."

"No 'twon't," a gruff voice from the next table cut in. "The Bodenham road runs a mite longer, by tak'n ye through Downton and Bramshaw." The man took a long draught on his ale, letting a dribble run down his chin. "Take the Alderbury road, 'twill get ye there sooner."

"True enough, Tom, unless it rains tonight," said another voice from the same table. "Me bunions are telling me 'twill rain something fierce. When that happens the Alderbury road washes out and ye canna take it. Then ye'd have to go by Bodenham instead."

Nicholas looked over the rough-clad workers and nodded. "My thanks for the information."

Turning back to his table, he flashed Jeremy an apologetic glance. He hoped he'd not done serious damage to the young man's leg. He should have given him an idea of what he was doing, but he'd not been thinking properly since kissing Katherine. It was the curse of a woman to muddle a man's mind, but who would have ever thought this plain Puritan would ignite such a passion in his loins? Nicholas scowled, adjusting himself on the bench. It was becoming very clear that he would need to be rid of her soon. He should be ransoming her back to her father instead of kissing her in the woods.

Had he been thinking at all since returning to England?

On the face of it, it seemed extremely doubtful her father would just hand over Ashfield, even for the return of his daughter. Clearly, Nicholas would have to come up with some sort of a trade that would give both of them what they wanted. He frowned, and then smiled as a thought began to form in his mind.

Henry returned from the kitchen bearing a steaming cup of coffee. Jeremy sniffed, wrinkling his nose in suspicion. "What is that?"

"'Tis a drink from Turkey," Nicholas said, taking a big gulp and feeling the hot brew trail all the way to his stomach.

Lord, he was weary. He'd not really slept since the day before yesterday. His arm ached like the devil, a reminder of his last bit of foolishness. What he really needed was sleep, but sharing a room with Katherine—on the floor at that—would not make it easy. Besides, he had one last task to perform this day, and it had to wait until the lass slept.

A small maid bearing two heavy mugs of ale arrived at the table. With a timid smile, she placed one before Jeremy. As she served Henry, the man from the next table, who'd first spoken to Nicholas, reached over and gave her bottom a pinch. She jumped, spilling ale down Henry's linen shirt.

Her face paled. "I-I'm sorry, I am." She looked at Henry unhappily. "I-I'll refill it and g-get a cloth to mop ye up."

As she moved to leave, Henry grasped her arm. "'Tis no mind, truly. 'Twas an accident of no account."

"Our Grace is a clumsy one," asserted the man who'd pinched her, "but she has a nice backside which makes up for it." He guffawed at his own cleverness and took another draught of ale.

Nicholas scowled, his temper rising. As a lad, he'd seen too much of that kind of intimidation on the seamy streets of Amsterdam. Turning to face the oaf, he clenched his teeth to hold back the full force of his anger. "Leave her be," he commanded, and watched the range of expressions from belligerence to deference run over the man's face.

Finally the man spoke. "I didn't mean nothing by it." He took a big swig of ale then, banged the empty mug on the table, and barked at the wench. "Get me another, and quick."

With butterfly movements, the maid picked up the empty tankard and retreated to the kitchen. Nicholas gulped down the rest of his coffee and stood up.

"Where you goin'?" Jeremy eyed him narrowly.

Nicholas took a deep breath. It was getting harder and harder to avoid loosing his temper tonight. "'Tis naught to you where I go or what I do, lad."

"You go to my mistress?"

Nicholas sighed and sat down again. "She cannot stay in an inn like this by herself. She needs protection."

"I'm all the protection she needs." Jeremy glared at him.

"You are nothing close to the protection she needs," Nicholas snapped. "You are just a country lad, whereas I—" Nicholas stopped. He took a deep breath and let it out before continuing. "I am considerably more experienced in the ways of the world."

"'Tis what worries me." Jeremy looked grim.

Nicholas cocked a dark eyebrow at the lad. "Just what is she to you?"

Jeremy spent a long moment looking around the room before he turned his light blue eyes on Nicholas. "She's my mistress, she is. Good and kind." His eyes turned challenging. "I won't see you harm her, else you might come to some harm yerself."

"Do you threaten me?"

"Take it as ye will." Jeremy took a deep draught of his ale.

How was it, Nicholas thought again, that such a missish Puritan could stir such a fever in the blood? He and Jeremy seemed due for a fight. He shook his head wearily. Not tonight.

He took a deep breath and expelled it. "I bid you goodnight," he said as the maid returned.

She smiled shyly and put down a heavy tray, laden with supper. Then, pulling a clean rag out from under one arm, she began to dab at Henry's shirt.

Henry sputtered and took the cloth from her. "I-I can do it meself, thank ye."

She nodded and smiled at him.

Then, she took the tankard to the next table. Glaring at the offensive man, she plunked it down hard in front of him, sloshing liquid down the sides. She turned and walked, head high, back to the kitchen.

༄

A sharp knock set Katherine's pulse racing. Rising from the stool, she walked to the door. "Who is it?" she called just to be sure.

"'Tis me with supper," Nicholas barked from the other side.

"Then I shall have to let you in," she said, drawing the latch.

He stood to one side while the innkeeper and his helper brought in a tray of food and placed it on a table. They bowed, and at Nicholas's motion, picked up the heavy tub, struggling with it until they were out of the room. Nicholas closed and latched the door behind them.

"Let us eat," he said, his voice almost a growl. He pulled two stools to the table.

Katherine nodded and sat down. As she served the hot mutton stew and root vegetables, Montford jumped into her lap and sniffed at the table.

Nicholas scowled. "I will not eat my supper with a cat."

Dropping the kitten to the floor, Katherine bowed her head to avoid Nicholas's ill temper. She picked at her food and sipped the sweet sack-posset the landlord's wife had sent. In the oppressive, awkward silence, she couldn't help thinking that Montford would have been much better company. Why had Nicholas become so grumpy?

She observed him out of the corner of her eye. He ate with the same lack of enthusiasm she did. Was it for the same reason? Had he also found the kiss alarming? Did he find her nearness as disturbing as she did his? Katherine knew so little about him. As her drink's rich warmth eased her nerves, she found the courage to find out more about him. "Nicholas?"

"Umh?" He raised an eyebrow and took a bite of the stew.

"Have you always been a highwayman?"

"No."

Not much of an answer, but it was something, so Katherine continued. "Why do you...do it?" She toyed with her food. "Your earnings could not be much from stealing clothes."

"I do it to expose the hypocrites among us."

"I don't understand."

He fixed his eyes on her. "I do not like Puritans. I especially do not care for those who forgot they are Puritans now the King has returned. I do not like turncoats," he glared.

"I'm not a turncoat." Katherine's voice was almost a squeak.

Starting at her waist, his eyes slowly traveled up her body, searing her with heat until he connected with her eyes. "No."

Katherine's heart pounded. She crossed her arms over her chest. "England is not at war anymore," she said, her voice almost a whisper.

"No, it is not." He frowned. "I guess 'twas sort of a joke, perhaps for my benefit. No one else seems to understand."

"'Twas a dangerous joke." Katherine found herself wanting to scold him. At the same time, a smile tugged at the corners of her mouth.

"Ah," he said, his voice low, resonant. Making a fork of his first two fingers, he brought them to her lips, pushing the corners up gently. "That is something you should do more often." He nodded. The twinkle had returned to his eyes. "It makes you very pretty, indeed."

"Fie." She looked down at her food.

"Now 'tis my turn to ask you a question," he said, pulling a hunk of bread off the loaf. "If you are not a Puritan, what are you?"

Katherine rearranged the food on her plate while she thought. "I seem to know what I am not, but not what I am." She sighed. "I was raised a Puritan, but I am not one. I have always been a good daughter, but I am not one anymore. I was to have been John Perkins wife, yet that is not to be so. Then, I was to be married to Richard Finch, but I pray I will not be."

"You leave behind two suitors?" Nicholas smiled a devastating and flirtatious smile. "I did not know I travel with a heartbreaker. I had best use care lest you break mine."

Katherine knew he teased her. Even so, she blushed. "I do not break hearts. Richard Finch does not have one, and John? Our marriage had been arranged years ago. Now his family will move to the New World. His father offered to break our betrothal so my father would not have to see me go. Had they asked me, I should have told them I'd be happy to emigrate to America. In truth, I barely knew John, though he did seem very pleasant."

"Pleasant?" Nicholas scoffed and put down his fork. "I would seek passion should I ever decide to find my match. Yet, 'tis not a likely thing for me to do for some time. I fear I have little to recommend myself to a wife. I snore when I sleep, make bad jokes, and find myself in trouble all too often. Should I find the woman of my heart, I would like her too much to impose myself upon her good nature."

A loud clap of thunder broke outside, shaking the room.

Katherine watched the brilliant blaze of lightning out the window. Raindrops pattered on the roof. The weather reminded her of the night she met Nicholas. Yet so much was different—he was no longer helpless; she was no longer the one in control.

Katherine shivered. Although she had asked for his protection, since the kiss she was no longer safe with him. There was danger in his presence; a danger she did not understand, exciting and distressing all at once. Firelight played across one side of his face, while the other side remained dark, shadowed and mysterious.

He broke the silence. "Tell me of your life, of your family."

Katherine picked a small piece of mutton off her plate and put it on the floor for Montford. "My mother died a few months ago. My brother a year before. I think it broke her heart when Edward died. So sudden." Her voice caught as emotion flooded her.

Nicholas gave her hand a quick squeeze. A flash of heat ran from his hand to hers, warming her, easing her heart. Perhaps because of the kindness in his eyes, or maybe the wine in the sack-posset, Katherine found her tongue loosening.

"I miss them both so much. Especially Edward, who was also my dear friend. I always depended on his good counsel." She took another sip of her drink. "Some might say 'tis my good fortune to be heiress to Ashfield. Yet, I never wished it. I do not want to be bought or sold with the property. I do not think my mother would have allowed it. But she is gone and cannot help me."

They were quiet for a moment while the fire sparked and rain beat upon the window.

"I, too, miss my mother," Nicholas said. "I do not remember her well; she died a long time ago—so long that I am no longer the same Nicholas she knew. That boy is gone."

Katherine remembered how tender he had looked, calling to his mother in delirium. Maybe the boy was not completely gone, but perhaps it was best Nicholas not know this.

"Where did that boy go?"

Nicholas leaned back on his stool. "First he went to

Amsterdam. Then, several years later, when his father died, he went to France. He did not stay there long, but traveled for many years, seeking his fortune in strange and exotic places." Nicholas put down his fork and smiled. "He got into more than one scrape of his own making. And finally, here he sits before you now—in the land of his birth, a land he should call home—not certain of his welcome or of his own feelings about the place."

She was not surprised to hear he was just returning from exile. The wars had sent many English families abroad.

"Do you have no relations here? No brothers or sisters?"

"I have a sister. I lived with her in France. She is much older and not over fond of me. I found her company," he paused, and ran a hand through his hair. "I found it confining. I had wanderlust in my eyes, and was not accustomed to being told what to do. We argued. I did not stay with her long."

Katherine nodded, repressing a yawn.

"I see 'tis time for you to be abed. We have much traveling to do on the morrow. We will aim for Winchester, staying on the back roads as we did today. We shall journey through small market towns and villages so 'twill be harder for Finch and your father to find us." He tapped a fingertip on the table. "I do not like to plan too much. When outrunning the fox, I have found 'tis best to keep my eyes ahead. That is what we will do."

He rose and went to the fire. "Should they chance to come upon this place, I have let it be known to the locals downstairs that we are on our way to Portsmouth—which is not on the way to London, but a likely destination nonetheless. We should be safe for now."

Katherine did not feel entirely heartened by this. She always had a plan and was prepared to change it when need be.

Nicholas poked at the flames. "I shall settle here on the floor."

Their eyes met across the short distance. Katherine found it hard to breathe. Like a warm caress, he gazed upon her, reminding her of his strong arms when they held her on the horse, of the feel of them around her when they kissed.

"Goodnight, Katherine."

Dragging in a breath, she turned away and quickly got into bed. She heard him settle before the fire. She could not think he would be comfortable there, even though it would be no worse than the dirt floor he'd slept on in the cottage. It was unlikely she would be comfortable on the lumpy mattress either, even with Montford purring beside her.

Trying to sleep in the same room as Nicholas unsettled her nerves in the most annoying way. Every breath, every rustle of clothing as he made minor shifts in position, came to her. His very nearness set her heart pounding and her senses on alert.

Katherine pulled the bed covers over her head and wondered if she'd ever be able to sleep.

He must have fallen asleep. The next thing Nicholas knew, the rain had died down, and the fire was reduced to embers. He heard Katherine's rhythmic breathing, signaling that she slept.

Tonight when she'd opened the door, a Katherine unlike any Katherine he'd seen thus far had greeted him. Except for the black dress, this Katherine more resembled a sprite or naiad, with her damp hair trailing down to her waist in gentle waves, and her bare feet peeking out from the bottom of her dress—a dress that fell with her natural silhouette. He could see she'd left off her petticoats and stays. It made her look young and very appealing.

He'd wanted her for dinner instead of stewed mutton.

Nicholas rose and lit the lamp. He retrieved the paper, pen, and ink he had procured earlier, and sat at the table. Carefully trimming the end of the quill, he let his fingers run up and down the feather. As he smoothed the strands back together, he thought about his conversation with Katherine.

Wife.

He had no use for a wife, nor did he wish one. Were he to pick a wife, it would be someone with fire and wit, not a somber lass like Katherine.

Yet, it was such a simple and obvious solution. If he married Katherine and got her with a son, the only thing to prevent him from getting back Ashfield would be if Gerald Welles remarried and got himself a son.

Would the man do that?

If he did, Nicholas could still pursue his petition with the King. Even though Charles avoided making any decision he could put off, he had restored some estates to their rightful owners.

Nicholas dipped the pen into the ink. There would be no hurrying the King, but he could threaten Gerald Welles with the petition. Though the man held little love for his daughter, he had great respect for his purse, and would not like the possibility of losing both.

A slight stirring came from the bed. Nicholas froze. Casting a look over his shoulder, he could not see Katherine in the shadows, but a light snore indicated she had settled back to sleep.

He let out a breath.

Katherine did not want to be heiress to Ashfield, so he would fix that for her. Perhaps it would be a bit like buying and selling her, but was it his fault women were bought and sold? No more than it had been his fault when he had been bought and sold in the slave markets.

He would simply do what opportunity offered.

He had to.

Keeping his back to Katherine, he began to write.

CHAPTER SEVEN

"Come in."

The massive door inched open, and a short stocky man sidled into the room. He inched across the long carpet to stand patiently before a large table, feet planted wide. With strong stubby fingers, he pulled off his hat.

Richard Finch looked up from his work, but did not smile.

"What news have you, Jakes?" Knowing Welles was not to be trusted, he'd not waited for word. The man was an idiot and a liar who had what Finch wanted, which was not the man's daughter. Finch wanted Ashfield, and she was the key.

"Well, yer Lordship, I sent word to the informers just like ye said."

"And?" Richard prodded, regretting that conversations with Jakes always ran like this—a series of questions necessitated by incomplete answers. Yet the man did make up for his stupidity by his tenacious loyalty, unsurpassed dependability, and a complete lack of scruples.

"She's been seen, she has. On the Salisbury road."

"Good work. Bring her back." Richard waved him off, but Jakes made no motion to leave. Instead, he frowned at the ground, twisting his hat.

"Out with it, man. What else have you to say?"

Jakes cleared his throat and blinked his bulbous eyes. "She were with three men."

"Three men!" The words hit the back wall like a gunshot. Finch rose from his chair. "You are sure of this?"

Jakes nodded, although his face remained impassive. His hands calmed.

"And?" Richard picked up a letter knife and balanced the flat side on the tip of his forefinger. "Who were they?"

Jakes frowned, making deep furrows in his forehead. "A lad of mayhap eighteen. My man thought it might be Jeremy Haywood. But he did not know t'other two."

Jeremy Haywood? Was this a romantic assignation? But that did not explain the other two men. "Did he tell you what they looked like?"

"The man she rode with was big with black hair, and white in it. Like this," with one hand he drew a line from the top of his head down over his left ear. "T'other man, his hair be gray, and him older." He cleared his throat again. "My man, he thought, well, the first man was quality, an' the second man his servant."

Richard leaned back in his chair and began to clean and pare his nails with the letter knife.

Three men. That changed the situation significantly. Marrying Katherine was fast becoming much more of a challenge than he expected. He had not known she had this kind of pluck. Catching her was becoming more appealing. Once he had her, he'd have to punish her, of course. How long it would take her to plead for him to stop? He grew hard just from the thought of it.

"Well, Jakes," Finch held the knife by both ends, running his thumbs over the sharp edge, "I think 'twould be best if I accompany you to Salisbury."

Jakes nodded and twisted his hat.

Sunlight streamed through the small window, landing in a warm pool on Katherine's face. She yawned and stretched all the way from her toes to the top of her head. Opening her eyes, she gasped at the unfamiliar surroundings, and then memory came back in a rush. Sitting up, she clasped the blanket to her bosom. Her heart hammered as she looked around the room.

Where could Nicholas be? Had he gone? Left her?

And where was Montford?

"Kitty, kitty, kitty?" But there was no response, no thump from a cat jumping up on the bed.

Katherine looked at her hands, clutching the counterpane to her fully clothed body. Shaking her head at this silly show of modesty, she threw off the covers and got out of bed. She looked everywhere, but found no trace of the cat. As she searched, the conviction grew that wherever she found Nicholas, she would find Montford as well.

She quickly donned her stays and petticoats, noting with exasperation that the black dress she'd slept in had become a wrinkled mess, another reason to hate the ugly gown. No doubt she looked like a scullery maid. Regretting the loss of her hairpins, she twisted her unruly hair into a coil and jammed on her cap, then shoved on her stockings and shoes. One last survey of the room showed Montford had not materialized.

Flinging open the door, she stopped short. Nicholas stood—hand poised to knock—blocking her exit.

Katherine stepped back in surprise.

Clean-shaven, dressed in a turquoise brocaded waistcoat and full-cut fawn breeches that tied below each knee with a red sash, Nicholas looked quite magnificent. The sleeves of his white shirt ended in flounces that danced with his hands as he bowed. A lace-trimmed cravat graced his neck. Black leather shoes with red heels and ribbon ties had replaced his boots. His hair, no longer pulled back tightly, hung in loose curls, giving him a less severe, more carefree look. He carried a bundle in one hand and a basket in the other.

"What have you done with Montford?" she demanded.

In answer, a loud "meow" came from inside the basket.

"As you hear, your cat is safe. And our journey will be much easier with him secure in this basket." Nicholas strode into the room, kicking the door shut. No sooner had he placed the basket on the table, than Montford hopped out. Nicholas chuckled. "Of course, we'll have to tie the latch to keep him inside."

"'Tis a prison," she sniffed. "And Montford is a girl."

"Really?" He registered surprise. But, just because Montford was his name—and the name of every male heir in the family for the past three centuries—why should the cat be a boy? Nicholas swallowed a laugh after catching Katherine's stern expression. She fingered the basket while chewing on her lip, and he remembered her other concern. "'Tis not a prison; the basket will keep your cat safe." Then he pushed forward the bundle. "And this, lass, is for you." He unfolded the package and revealed a peach silk and lace bodice, with matching skirt and petticoat.

During the long ride, Nicholas had imagined what Katherine would look like in fashionable clothing instead of the dour dress she wore. He'd envisioned golden satin to highlight her tawny eyes, a low cut bodice to show her bust to advantage. He had not been able to find that combination—in truth he had not looked—but a dealer in used goods had displayed these garments. They had caught Nicholas's eye, and the bargaining had been pleasant.

Katherine reached out a hand and then snatched it back without touching the fabric. She shook her head. "No."

"I beg your pardon?"

"I cannot accept this."

Didn't women like gifts of pretty things? But, Katherine was not like the women of his acquaintance. "You must," he said reasonably.

"I cannot." Her eyes lingered on the rich garments.

"Katherine, lass," his voice softened. He sounded like someone speaking to a young child. "They will be looking for a Puritan, in plain garb. So you must look like a Cavalier lady. And truly, 'tis not so fancy. See it not as clothing," he coaxed, "but as a disguise."

Her lips pursed as she scrutinized the garments, from the décolleté bodice to the water-stained skirt. He could see that in spite of herself, she wanted them.

"I'm sorry 'tis not new," he fingered the hem. "We haven't

time to wait for them to be made."

"I've never dressed like...like..."

"Like a Lady?"

A smile appeared on Katherine's face, as if rays of sunshine peaked out from behind clouds. "Like a bird."

He smiled at her attempt at humor. "Afraid the cat will catch you?"

She shook her head, serious again and eyed the clothing longingly. "Maybe they will not fit."

"Oh, I think they will. Perhaps the skirt is a bit long. You must put it on, and we shall see." He pushed the garments toward her. "There is much to prepare for our departure. I shall return shortly with our morning repast."

She ran a fingertip over the shiny fabric. "I had thought we'd be on the road well before now."

"And we would be, had it not been for last night's rain. The roads have turned to mud. 'Twas either wait for the sun to dry them, or get bogged down in the muck. Besides," he grinned, "you looked so charming in sleep, I had not the heart to wake you."

Katherine turned away. A hot flush ran up her neck. She did not like to think of him watching her while she slept. "Time is passing," she said, an edge to her voice.

"Then I leave you, lass. But do not tarry, we must be on the road to Winchester soon, if we are to arrive before nightfall."

As soon as she heard the door close, Katherine picked up the skirt. Fingering the folds of lustrous fabric, she watched the color change in the light.

She had never worn anything so fine, so pretty. So...revealing.

Nicholas had mistaken her hesitance to wear the dress for aversion. But nothing could be further from the truth. She had only hoped to wear a garment of such beautiful color with such lovely bits of lace at the bodice, never believing it to be possible.

Katherine eagerly worked the fastenings of her black dress and stepped out of the ugly garment. Despite her haste, she folded it carefully and put it aside. Raising the new petticoat over her head, she marveled at the feel of the cool silky fabric sliding down her body. Nicholas had been right about the length. The hem ended in a puddle at her feet. She rolled it up at the middle before tying it tight and then put on the skirt. The bodice fit properly and fell into a "V" below her waist. She peered at her bosom. The neckline seemed impossibly low. Indecently low. She pulled at the top of her smock, but it made no difference.

And no matter how she tried, she could not fasten the bodice in the back. Without a maid to help, she'd barely managed her stays that morning, which added to the problem.

Katherine chewed on her lower lip. She had not brought a shawl or any kind of cover-up. Instead, she'd brought her herb journals. At the time, it had seemed the right thing to do. But, she could not wear the books. She let out an exasperated sigh just as she heard a sharp rap on the door.

In the hallway, Nicholas balanced a food-laden tray on one hand, while he knocked on the door with the other. What took her so long? Mayhap she had not finished dressing. Women could take a very long time to accomplish such a simple task. But then he heard footsteps approach, and the door flew open. Katherine stood to one side. She looked at him warily. From what he could see, the garments fit her well, and the color looked pleasing on her fair skin. Of course, it would look nicer without the ugly cap that hid her silky hair.

And the cat she wore as a modesty piece across her breast.

"I like it very much," he said, trying hard not to laugh as he put the tray down on the table.

She backed toward the fireplace. "I could not manage without my maid. Could you please send a serving-woman to attend me?"

"I shall assist you."

"Oh no," she squeaked. A becoming flush colored her cheeks.

"'Twill take just a moment. Then we can eat and be gone the sooner."

She looked away then turned her back to him.

Nicholas smiled. Though he preferred to undress a woman, he also liked dressing one, when her smooth skin and tender flesh settled into the confines of whalebone and lace. He tugged the strings, tightening them with ease, savoring the smell of lavender and woman that was Katherine. Smoothing the fabric, he let her go.

They sat down at the table and ate in haste. Katherine juggled the cat in one hand and her food in the other, barely managing to keep the cat and the food apart. Nicholas found their antics amusing and could not tell who got the bigger meal, Katherine or Montford.

Soon they were on their way downstairs to the stables, Montford, now latched into the basket, and the pretty vision of Katherine in her new dress covered by her drab cloak, ruining the disguise completely.

The rain had left the air crisp and—just as Nicholas had said—the ground a muddy mess. Katherine wished she had her pattens to keep her feet above the muck as she walked across the courtyard on tiptoe, her skirt carried high to keep the hem out of the mud.

Jeremy had the mounts ready. Nicholas tied her bundles onto the back of their horse, and they were off.

The going was slow. The roads, what could be seen of them, had turned to a deep quagmire, making the horses skittish. After leaving Salisbury, they'd not even seen a signpost, and Katherine realized how impossible traveling on foot would have been under these conditions.

After following a set of barely visible carriage tracks, they'd been dismayed to see them disappear into several inches of standing water. They'd coaxed their balking mounts through the sludge, yet had not discovered a trail at the other side.

To Katherine's great relief, Nicholas decided at that point to rest and water the nervous horses. Not far from there, they found a high grassy mound, with a stream running down the side.

Henry helped her dismount. Nicholas led their mount to the

stream, paying her no mind.

The day had warmed. Katherine would have found it pleasant, had she not been wearing the heavy cloak. She knew she should take it off, yet she felt unaccountably shy in such revealing and fancy attire. She put down the basket containing Montford. Knees shaky from disuse, she hiked up her skirt to keep from tripping, and walked over the rise. Upstream from the men and horses, around a bend, she found a place hidden by tall beech trees where she could have some privacy. The water looked brisk and inviting. She looked around before removing her cloak. The gentle breeze stroked her overheated skin. She breathed deeply and reached down into the cold stream.

"You look wondrous fine, mistress."

She whirled around to see Jeremy smiling at her in approval. "Fie, I want no compliments from you Jeremy Haywood," she said, pleased, none-the-less. She looked at her cloak where she'd left it carefully folded. In her new dress, she did not feel as exposed with Jeremy as she had with Nicholas.

Jeremy's smile faded to a look of discomfort. He cleared his throat. "Last night...this cousin of yours...he did not do anything..." His voice bumped up several notes, "improper, did he, mistress?"

"Nay, he did not," Katherine assured him. "He behaved as a gentleman."

"I cannot trust him," Jeremy avowed, screwing his forehead into wrinkled furrows. "There is something not right about him."

"You are correct, Jeremy. He is not as he seems." Katherine hoped to fend off his suspicions, and she disliked perpetuating a lie. "He is not my cousin."

"Oh." Jeremy looked at her strangely. "Then who is he and why does he help you? I cannot imagine it is out of the goodness of his heart. He does not seem to use that organ overmuch."

Katherine looked up into Jeremy's sky-blue eyes—eyes that reminded her inexplicably of Edward sometimes. She could not tell him about the wound, or of tending Nicholas in the cottage. "I did him a service, and so he helps me in return. He would be traveling to London in any case."

Jeremy frowned. "We're not so far from Ashfield. I would take you back there myself."

"Jeremy, I have not come this far to turn back now. I will never go back to Ashfield. I will not marry Finch. I'd as soon die. So, you see, I have no choice."

"'Tis brave you are, mistress."

Katherine scoffed. "Brave? I think not. 'Twould have been brave to stay. No, Jeremy. Do not think it. I have run away because I have not the courage to face the future father had made for me." She looked around at the trees and verdant scenery. "But I find I like to travel. There is much to see."

She started toward the stream, and he followed her.

"What of you?" she asked. "Are you sorry you have come? I greatly fear you cannot return either. Father would sooner turn you out than have you back. You must continue on this journey as well. What will you do when we get to London?"

A bright smile started at the corners of his mouth and traveled to his eyes, banishing the concern she'd seen there moments before. "There was not much for me at Ashfield, you ken? But, London?" He said it with reverence. "A man can make his fortune there."

As he spoke, his shoulders went back and his chin up, and Katherine saw him as the lad he might have been, had he not been born to the stables. With grand clothing, such as she now wore, he might look nice indeed. Who would know he was naught but a servant?

Nicholas leaned against the smooth gray bark of a beech tree, just out of sight of Katherine and Jeremy. A gentle breeze ran through the leaves, clean and shiny green from the night's rain. He could hear the babble of their voices, but could not make out their words. They looked companionable, even intimate. Watching them in discourse, Nicholas experienced a flash of irritation. He rubbed at his temples, and sighed.

The lass looked comely enough, now that she'd taken off the cloak. With a smile on her face, holding the hem of her dress above the mud, the dour Puritan was gone. Except for that damned cap.

It would have to go next.

Why did he even care? With his plan well along the road to fruition, should he not leave well enough alone? He'd posted the letter this morning. If all went well, she'd be off his hands as soon as they got to London.

Then, at long last, the vow he'd made to his father would be fulfilled. He could get on with his life.

Not bad for a fortnight's work, he thought with satisfaction.

Nicholas watched Katherine venture into the stream, tiptoeing along a series of flat rocks. Jeremy hovered on the bank nearby. She gathered her skirt in one hand and reached down into the water with the other. Suddenly she lost her balance and teetered backward, landing on her bottom with a small shriek.

Nicholas started forward, but stopped short as he realized she needed no help. Instead of the tears and indignation he would expect from a damsel in this type of distress, gay peals of laughter rang through the autumn air. Lazy sunshine filtered down through the leaves to dance upon her where she sat in the water, leaning back on both arms, bust forward. Her face tilted up like a joyous and pagan sun worshipper.

If a smile had lightened her dour looks, and a dress made her look less sallow, this exuberant laughter transformed her. She possessed a radiance and sensuality reminiscent of a painting he'd once seen by the artist and diplomat Rubens. He watched, still enchanted, as her lusty laugh gave way to girlish giggles. Jeremy, who had given into the infectious hilarity, held out a hand, and she accepted it. He pretended for a moment to throw her back in the water before pulling her out. They stood together on the stream bank, laughing with an open affection.

Nicholas stepped away from the tree into the clearing. Katherine saw him first, then Jeremy. Their laughter faded as they stood facing him like two naughty children. Her grin slowly turned into the mask she wore so much of the time. Nicholas watched the missish Puritan replace the delightful hoyden he'd admired but a moment before.

He turned away. The sooner he got the two of them off his hands the better.

Katherine stood in a spot of sunshine and fanned out her skirts. A distinct chill had come over her, not from the cold water, but from Nicholas. She watched him stride over to a fallen tree branch, bread and cheese in hand. Raising one foot up on the branch, he leaned forward, an elbow to one knee with his back to them, his displeasure evident by the tilt of his wide shoulders.

Katherine sighed. How ungrateful of her to ruin the dress. The minor water stain on the bottom had been nothing compared to the new one it would have when dry. And Nicholas would have to suffer a soggy traveling companion as well.

Henry brought her a chunk of cheese and a piece of bread. "We have only water to wash it down w'."

"I've water a'plenty," she said, wringing out the hem of her dress.

"That ye do, mistress." Henry made a half-smile and walked off.

She sighed and bit into the bread. It wasn't as if she'd tried to fall in the water. She'd simply been startled by her own reflection. Her likeness had looked so completely unfamiliar, like another woman altogether. For a moment, she'd wondered if perhaps fairies played a trick on her. What a ridiculous thought!

But she should not have been wearing her new finery and walking in a stream overfull from the night's rain. No wonder Nicholas was angry with her.

Back on the horse, Nicholas was grateful they'd placed a blanket between them. It not only kept him from getting wet, but also concealed his insistent erection. In spite of his irritation at Katherine, or perhaps because of it, he found himself wanting to drag her off to a secluded spot where he could make hard love to her until his good humor returned.

"I'm sorry I've ruined the dress," she said softly.

"The dress?" He shook his head. "No mind. We can always find another."

"'Twas a nice gift, and I've misused it."

"It matters not. 'Twas stained before and 'twill still work as a disguise."

She was quiet again, and so was he.

For several hours, they followed a road they'd discovered after fording the stream a ways. Blessedly, it had stayed a road.

Katherine's body relaxed into his, and he could tell she'd drifted off to sleep. Montford awoke, complained mournfully, and quieted again. Occasionally Henry and Jeremy could be heard talking together.

As the sun slowly made its fiery descent, they reached the outskirts of a town. Nicholas scanned the buildings. They came to a halt in the courtyard of friendly looking inn on the main thoroughfare that proclaimed to be the *Black Swan*.

Henry helped Katherine to dismount. Nicholas followed. Jeremy assisted the hostler with the horses.

"I thought Winchester had a Cathedral." Nicholas voiced his thoughts aloud.

Henry shook his head. "Me memory fails me, lad."

The hostler, who had overheard this conversation, stopped and raised his eyes to Nicholas. "Winchester ye say?"

Nicholas nodded impatiently.

The hostler lowered his gaze, and shook his head. "This nay be Winchester, milord. Ye be in Devizes."

CHAPTER EIGHT

Nicholas's belly laughs filled the courtyard, reverberating from wall to wall, compelling those who heard it to join in. Katherine's giggles mingled with Jeremy's chuckles and Henry's snorts. After a difficult moment of trying to keep a grave face, even the hostler began to chortle. Nicholas pounded the man on the back between guffaws, the thumps adding punctuation to the mirth as the two men laughed together like old friends reliving a bit of fun over a pint.

"Devizes?" Nicholas clutched at his middle.

"Y-yes, m'-m'-milor—" the hostler hooted, unable to finish.

"T-tell me, my good man," Nicholas wiped tears from his cheeks, "is Devizes closer or f-farther from London than Salisbury?"

The hostler quieted, cast his eyes down, and scratched the top of his head. "'At's a difficult question, milord."

Nicholas's expression turned serious. He reached into the pocket of his cloak, pulled out a coin, and flipped it to the servant. "Try."

The man bit the coin, and then tucked it into a pocket. He pursed his lips and furrowed his brow before speaking. "If you was a bird and was to fly there, I'd have to say we was a mite further. But since you hain't a bird you'll be takin' the roads. It'll probably take you the about the same as if you was startin' out from Salisbury." He rubbed his nose with a none-too-clean finger. One side of his mouth curled into a lopsided smile. "Although I can't say from personal experience, ye know, see'n as I hain't never been to Lunnon."

Nicholas sighed. "Hain't never been to London," he repeated then shook his head.

Katherine watched Nicholas's mood change, mirroring the darkening sky as the last rays of the sun disappeared into twilight. Now that the gaiety was over, a troubling thought came to take its place. She examined Nicholas soberly. From his plumed hat to the red ribbons on his black leather shoes, he cut a truly dashing figure. He spoke with innate assurance as he gave instructions to the other men.

But was he capable of getting them to London?

Katherine swallowed her frustration. He had told her he had not been back in England long. Still, if he was unsure of how to get to London, he should have asked for directions.

Richard Finch shrugged off the chill and stepped into the *Crowne and Crow* in Salisbury. Jakes already stood at the far end of the public room, blocking the back exit. Another man followed Finch in and covered the entrance once they were inside.

Conversations quieted, then broke off completely, as more and more eyes came to rest on him. He could feel their fear. It sizzled in the air and warmed his blood. He waited, drawing out the moment until he could almost hear the pounding of their hearts.

Finally, he spoke. "I seek information." He cracked his knuckles.

A shudder ran through the room.

"I look for someone." He enunciated each word slowly and clearly. "In fact, I look for a group. A young woman and three men. One of the men has dark hair with a streak of white. One of them is young, perhaps twenty, and the other is much older.

Can anyone give me information?"

Rustling and coughs greeted his request, but no one spoke. Cowards, the lot of them, and not yet frightened enough. But they would be. He would get what he needed one way or the other.

Finch clasped his hands behind his back. "Of course, I'd like this information to be voluntary." His voice trailed off as his eyes rested on a small figure clinging to the shadows in the very back. His gaze trailed down her slight body, then back up to her face, pinning her in place, a rabbit caught in his snare. He would start with her. An easy victim, she would not be much of a challenge.

Unlike Katherine.

He had not expected her to be so defiant. She would be sorry for it. Once he caught her—and he would catch her—he would delight in making her scream. She would beg for his mercy, but there would be none.

He turned his attention back to the motley group before him. "I have reason to believe they stayed here last night." One broken nose and two sprained wrists had provided the reliable information that they had not stayed in any of the other establishments. "I would be willing to pay."

"Aye, they did." One of the men in the front spoke. He swallowed. "Although I dunno about the woman. I did see three men and one had hair like you say." Although the man kept his eyes averted, he shrank under Finch's scrutiny. Then he grabbed his ale, drained the tankard and banged it on the table. "Grace," he bellowed.

There was a movement in the shadows at the back of the room.

"Come here," said Finch, his voice low, commanding.

The small figure stepped forward without much grace at all. She smoothed her apron with a shaking hand.

Finch crooked a finger. "Closer."

After several hesitant steps, she came to stand before him.

"Did you see the men I described?"

She nodded.

"And what of the woman?"

"I saw only the gentlemen." Her words came out faintly.

"Well, at least you are all in agreement." Finch looked at the man at the table. "Did you learn anything that would be of interest to me? Such as where they were headed?"

"'At I did, sir," said the man. "They was off ta Portsmouth this morn." The other two men at the table nodded their heads in corroboration.

The little maid twisted her hands in the end of her apron. Something was wrong. He hadn't threatened her yet.

"Portsmouth you say? And how did you come by this information?"

"I heard 'em talking about it, I did. We, that is me friends and meself." He nodded to include the other two men sitting with him at the table. Both looked very unhappy to have Finch's attention directed their way. "We talked about the roads with the rains and all. Miles here said they should go by the Bodenham Road, and I said they should go by the Alderbury Road but to Portsmouth they was bound, I vow."

"'Tis not true!"

All eyes turned to stare at the little maid.

"He's lyin'." Grace nodded rather fiercely at the man who'd done all the talking. "I heard it perfectly well. They said they was off to Marlborough."

"Marlborough?" Finch nodded. "I'd have expected Winchester or Andover. But the thought of them going off to Portsmouth is preposterous."

"B-b-but I overheard them," the man at the table sputtered.

Finch leveled the rough worker with his gaze. "And Grace says ye did not."

He turned to her. "I hope you're right gel, because if *you* are lying I will be very unhappy."

He grasped her by the chin. And stared hard into her eyes, but she held her ground. Her gaze did not waiver. "Do not make me unhappy."

With a swift move, he released her chin and slapped her cheek soundly.

Not a whimper. Not a cry. She did not look away. If the chit was lying, she was very good at it.

Finch nodded to Jakes. "Take them outside and find out if they are telling the truth."

Back in Devizes, a sober group sat at table in a private room of the *Black Swan*. Henry looked drawn and chewed his meal gingerly. Katherine guessed his tooth pained him again. Across from her sat Jeremy, a scowl darkening his countenance. Nicholas ate glumly beside her.

Katherine chewed each bite of the stewed mutton the innkeeper's wife had brought them, not really tasting it. Did every inn in Wiltshire serve the same thing? Not her favorite meal to begin with, she was quickly losing any appreciation she'd ever had for it.

The warmth from the fire joined with the moisture in her clothes, making Katherine wretched.

"I do not see why we cannot ask for directions," she said.

"We cannot ask directions else we will be more easily tracked. Whoever we ask will know where we go," Nicholas explained with exaggerated patience.

"Yes, but 'twill just be one person who would know, and Finch and my father cannot ask everyone." Katherine could not keep the exasperation from her voice. "It seems unlikely they would find the one person who you did ask. Nor is it likely that person would tell someone, who would tell someone, who would tell—"

"Enough!" Nicholas took a sip of coffee and put down his cup. "If we were to travel at night I would at least know our direction."

Katherine could not imagine a worse way of continuing the journey than traveling by night, and saw her doubts mirrored on Jeremy's face. Henry pushed away his plate and looked toward the door.

But Nicholas continued, apparently unperturbed by their lack of enthusiasm. "Traveling at night, we could use the stars to navigate, like a ship at sea." He stretched, and his long arm came to rest behind Katherine on the bench. She shifted in her seat, all too aware of his overwhelming presence. Not only was he too caught up in his own arrogant thinking, but he also took up more than his share of the bench.

"Of course," he continued, "to do it right would take the proper instruments. But an Arab taught me how to read the night sky."

Katherine scooted a bit further away from him. Henry took a draught of his ale. Jeremy cast an annoyed glance at Nicholas who moved his arm so he took the space Katherine had just given up.

Katherine squirmed.

Nicholas continued as if he had a rapt audience. "The Pole-star is the north star. It hangs at the top of the world, with the constellations all rotating around it. A very bright star, 'tis not difficult to find. Once we know where north is, we know where east is. London is east." He chuckled. "You see, to travel east by night it is only necessary to keep the North Star above our left shoulders. We can travel east for two nights, then, join one of the main highways on the next day's travel. All the main highways lead to London." He made a pleased smile and beamed at the group. "We could even start tonight."

Henry spoke for the first time that evening. "Then ye'll have to leave w'out me. I'm for a nip of brandy and then ta me bed." He rose and, holding a hand to his jaw, shuffled off.

As the door closed behind his old friend, Nicholas scowled and took a sip of his coffee. Then he rose from their bench and held a hand to her. "Shall we retire as well?"

Just those three words, and her hands went clammy.

"No." It came out more as a yelp. "I mean," Katherine struggled to regain her composure, "I could use a bit of air. 'Tis stuffy in here." She darted a glance at the groom. "Jeremy? Would you please accompany me outside? I would like to take a turn around the courtyard."

The young man looked at her in surprise, and then rose. "Certainly, mistress." He flashed a smile at Nicholas, who frowned back at him.

Katherine felt a momentary pique at the proprietary air of both of them. Turning to Nicholas she said, "I will be only a few moments."

"No, lass, I think not," he smiled. "'Twould be safer if I go with you."

Jeremy glared at Nicholas. "She will be perfectly safe with me."

"I'll not come to blows with you over this here and now." Nicholas smiled though there was a warning gleam in his eyes. "I need you to keep an eye on Henry. Make sure he only has a nip. Understand?"

Katherine bristled. She'd hoped to have a moment alone with Jeremy, away from Nicholas's forceful presence. She needed to think, to share her concerns with someone. Nicholas was proving to be an unreliable guide. His plan to follow the stars was harebrained at best. This sort of problem needed a common-sense solution. Yet, he would not listen to her good advice.

Hiding her frustration by picking up a few of the choicer table scraps, Katherine dropped them onto the sleeping cat in the basket. It was truly a marvel how much a cat could sleep, and under what circumstances. She rose, clutching the basket.

Nicholas followed her through the common room and out of the building.

Stepping outside, she shivered in the bracing night air, her still-damp clothing immediately picked up the chill.

The moon cast silver highlights all about. Nicholas hung back and watched, entertained, as Katherine took a turn in the courtyard. Her white cap showed brightly, an odd counterpoint to her dark cloak and the swish of silk that peeked out at the bottom. She swung the basket carrying his namesake as she walked. He was not surprised to hear an indignant meow. At that, she marched back to Nicholas, stopping just out of arms reach, and put the basket on the ground.

She spoke calmly, yet there was accusation in her eyes. "It should be a simple matter to get from Ashfield to London. But the way we are traveling, off the main thoroughfares, and now lost, 'twill surely take us an extra day at least. It gives my neighbor and my father an extra day to catch us. This is most unfortunate." Her shoulders were back now, her gaze strong as she faced him.

Nicholas flinched at the truth of her words. He could almost see sparks in her eyes. They were magnificent. *She* was magnificent in the moonlight.

"How could you get us lost?" She raised her chin against his scrutiny. Her lips formed into an unexpected and captivating pout.

Nicholas tried to suppress a smile as he felt himself drawn into the depths of her eyes. "We aren't lost. We know exactly where we are and where we're going."

Katherine turned from him. By the tilt of her head, he could tell his words had not mollified her.

"You make it sound so simple. But what of our journey tomorrow?"

Giving in to the urge, he walked to her, put his hands on her rigid shoulders, and turned her to face him.

She offered no resistance, but she still frowned, and the charming pout had vanished. Instead, her lips formed a firm line.

He made a coaxing smile, and was gratified to see her mouth relax a bit in response. Yet, she still looked at him fiercely.

"We can travel a good distance in the morning, rest in the afternoon, then be back on the road again in the evening. Think of it this way, lass, they will certainly not be looking for us here. So for now we are safe. Nor is it likely for them to come upon us at night. I think this little inconvenience may have served us well. We should be in London in just two days—three at the most." He chuckled. "London is a big city and not easy to misplace. We will find it."

She chewed her lip. He could not tell if he had convinced her or not. Still, with the silvery moonlight illuminating her upturned face, he felt a potent urge to kiss her, to see if what happened before would happen again.

The desire he'd repressed during the daylong ride took over. He drew her to him. At first, she pressed her hands against his chest to hold him back, but then she shuddered and curled her fingers into his waistcoat, tugging him to her. Eyes wide and luminous, she raised her lips.

The door to the inn flew open, and a large boisterous party spilled out.

Katherine pulled away. He reluctantly let her go. They watched the people say their farewells and depart into the dark night, the spell broken.

In the quiet that followed, Nicholas cleared his throat. "'Tis good the night is clear. Let me show you where the North Star is."

She tucked her hands inside her cloak and nodded, just out of arms reach. A perceptible wariness had come over her.

"There," he said, his good arm pointing to the brightest light above. "See that star?"

Katherine looked upward, pursing her lips. They no longer looked lush and inviting. Nicholas felt an odd sense of loss at their transformation.

She shook her head slightly.

"'Tis at the tail of Ursa Minor." He outlined the constellation with his forefinger.

"The Little bear," she murmured.

"So you know it."

"Not at all." A slight smile played upon her lips, softening them, making them appear kissable once again. "I have a small knowledge of Latin."

His arm dropped. "Latin?" he said, astonished. "You are quite the wonder, Katherine. A Puritan lass who knows Latin."

She sniffed. "They didn't want me to know it. Edward helped me, and I helped him as well. When they found out they punished us both." The words came out like a long held confession. "But I had learned enough by then to read some of the books in the library."

Nicholas nodded, remembering the dark heavy volumes that had occupied that room when he'd been a boy. Unlike Katherine, he'd resisted his Latin lessons. Later, during his travels, he'd been grateful his father had allowed the tutor to beat some of it into him. Sad really, that what he'd taken for granted she'd had to fight for.

"What books were so important to you, lass?"

Katherine shifted. "Medical books. Herbals. They belonged to the house. I don't think Grandfather or Father know they are there. Father reads to review his accounts, and Grandfather only reads his Bible. I always liked the pictures of the plants. I wanted to know the words that went with them. And I've made good use of the information." Her eyes met his. "It proved helpful when I tended your arm. I had never treated a lodged-ball wound before."

Nicholas nodded and looked away. He felt an annoying flash of remorse. His plan did not seem as right as it had the night before.

What would Katherine think when she found out about the letter?

What if Gerald Welles did not agree?

Then Nicholas would do right by the lass and deliver her to London and the waiting arms of her cousin as promised.

And then what?

No, it probably wouldn't be as easy as that. Very likely, this cousin would deliver her right back into the arms of the family she fled.

Funny how he hadn't thought about that before.

But he would have discharged his duty by doing what she'd asked of him. What more could she expect?

Nicholas realized he was scowling and eased his face into a smile. Where had he left off? Ah yes, showing the stars to a pretty lass, one who was a bit irked with him. By impressing her with his knowledge, he'd restore her confidence. She would realize he knew what he was talking about, and see the value of his plan to travel at night.

Raising his hand again, he pointed to the brightest star. "The reason it is called Ursa Minor is that the ancients saw a bear when they looked into the sky."

Katherine squinted in the direction he pointed and shook her head as she tightened her cloak about her. "I do not see it."

"It also looks somewhat like a ladle," Nicholas suggested. He took a step toward her and put his arm around her shoulder.

She stiffened at first, but then relaxed.

"See? Upside down? You have to connect the stars with an invisible line." He outlined the constellation with his forefinger.

Katherine shook her head.

The subtle scent of lavender put his senses on alert.

"They all look alike," she said.

"The north star is the bright one at the end of the handle." Moving his hands to either side of her face, he gently turned her head to where she should be looking. Leaning down so that his head was next to hers, he pointed.

He could feel her tremble, hear her breath catch. Lord he wanted to kiss her. Their lips were so close.

But she nodded and stepped away from him.

"I think I see it." She pointed in the correct direction. "That one seems to burn a bit brighter than the others, and it could possibly look like the end of a ladle with a bent handle. There."

"Right." Nicholas nodded. "Over there is Ursa Major." He outlined its shape with a finger.

"Big bear," she translated. "I see that. 'Tis also a ladle. They should have called it Big Ladle. There is clearly no bear."

"To the Ancients there was. In their mythology the big bear was Callisto, a woman loved by Jupiter. He transformed her into a bear to protect her from his jealous wife."

"That isn't a proper story at all," Katherine declared.

"Why is that?"

"'Tis not right for Jupiter to love a woman besides his wife. And, if he did love her, why did he make her into a bear?"

"Because he wanted to," Nicholas retorted. How could he impress her with his knowledge if she asked him ridiculous questions like that? He'd never even thought about it. He took a calming breath. "Over there is Cassiopeia." He pointed at another place in the sky. "See? It looks like a 'W'."

"Was she also a friend of Jupiter?" Katherine asked suspiciously.

"No." Nicholas almost barked. He tried to relax. "She was the

Queen of Ethiopia, and once claimed her daughter, Andromeda, to be more beautiful than a sea-goddess." He looked over at Katherine, her face tilted to the heavens. The moonlight made her skin alabaster. He could not stop himself from reaching a finger to run along her cheekbone. Instead of being hard and cold like marble, it was warm and soft. Like a woman.

She shivered, whether from the cold or his touch, he could not tell. But she did not move away from him.

"This made the sea-goddess very angry, so a sea-monster was sent to terrorize the people of Ethiopia and lay waste to the country. To save the land Cassiopeia had to give her daughter to the monster." He rested his hand back on Katherine's shoulder and gazed into her eyes, eyes that appeared dark, mysterious, and liquid.

Katherine swallowed visibly. "But what happened to Andromeda?"

"Cepheus, her father, chained her to a rock. There she was found and saved by Perseus, who killed the monster and obtained her as his wife."

"That is a much better story," she said. "Perseus was a gallant hero who saved her from an awful fate. I'm sure she had no objection to marrying him."

Nicholas dropped his hands. If Katherine was looking for a hero—or a husband—then she need look elsewhere. He was not her champion, and he did not like the direction this conversation was taking. He needed to finish making his point, and then be done with her.

"See how easy it will be to follow the stars?" He turned so the North Star was over his left shoulder and pointed ahead. "We will go that way to London."

She opened her mouth.

He continued on before she had a chance to speak. "Now I suggest you go in and prepare yourself for sleep. I will join you after I check on Henry. Do not take long."

Katherine snapped her mouth shut, surprised by his abrupt change of topic. She nodded, and without checking to see if he came with her, she scurried from the courtyard, picking up

Montford's basket on her way.

Inside their room, Katherine panicked. If she did not hurry, Nicholas might enter and find her undressed. Tossing her cloak on a chair, Katherine put down the basket and opened it.

Montford jumped free, leapt onto the black garment, and began to wash.

What had come over her? She had almost let him kiss her! Her fingers remembered the feel of his brocaded waistcoat and linen shirt as she'd grasped them. Katherine's heart pounded and she felt herself flush. In that moment, she had forgotten how disturbed she was that he'd led them astray. She had wanted to stay angry with him, yet in that moment he had changed her heart. How frustrating!

Katherine pulled off her petticoat and skirt, but no matter how she craned her arms behind her back, she could not manage to loosen the ties to the bodice. Without Nicholas's deft fingers, she could not get it off. But his help was out of the question. And if she did not ask his aid tonight, she would not need it again in the morning. So, she would just have to sleep in the dress. Vexed by the bodice and vexed by Nicholas, Katherine laid down on the straw mattress sure that sleep would not come easily.

It must have been several hours later. Katherine had fallen into troubled dreams of being pursued and running, running, running.

She woke up with a pounding heart, gasping for air. Her first realization, that she was not in her bedroom at Ashfield, was replaced almost immediately with the awareness of where she was when she saw Nicholas's large form stretched out before a fire burnt to embers. Then, the noise that must have wakened her repeated—a frightening sound.

Katherine could only remember hearing the like when she'd tended a woman in the throes of childbirth. Groans accompanied a rhythmic pounding that shook the wall behind her.

She must help.

Katherine jumped from the bed. Grabbing the satchel that contained her medical journals and carefully wrapped packets of herbs, she hurried to the door. The sounds grew louder, more insistent.

As she stepped into the hallway, a hand clamped onto her wrist.

CHAPTER NINE

Nicholas stood in the open doorway, his stance faintly menacing. His hair hung loose, his shirt open. Katherine could not see his eyes.

"There is a lady taken ill." She wiggled her wrist but he did not let go. A heart-wrenching groan emanated from the next room increasing Katherine's sense of urgency. "I must help her."

"The lady, if she is one, is not ill, Katherine." Nicholas's voice was rough with sleep and touched by a vein of impatience. "She would not welcome your interference now, believe me."

He pulled her back into the room and shut the door.

The wall shook in rhythm with the groans and pounding from the next room. As the noises grew louder and the woman's cries more urgent, Nicholas's eyes held hers.

Katherine tried, but she could not look away from his strong gaze. A blush rose across her cheeks, as excitement ran through her. Her breath came in gasps as the sounds reached a stunning crescendo, wrenching a small cry from her. Then everything ceased. Katherine shuddered. She stood in the heavy silence, still unable to take her eyes from Nicholas.

He pulled her to him. His chest grazed the front of her bodice. Her breasts tingled. His hand came to rest on the small of her back.

The satchel dropped with a clunk. Her hand rose, but instead of holding him off, it lay on his chest. Through the linen of his shirt, she felt the heat of him, the hairs on his chest, the rigid nub of a nipple, the steady beat of his heart.

Her head fell back, and she could see his eyes reflect the embers in the grate.

"They were mating, Katherine." His voice carried a thickness and urgency she'd not heard before.

She slowly shook her head.

"The most pleasant thing a man and woman can do together."

He released her wrist, and she drew back a step. "'Twas not the agony of pain you heard, but the agony of pleasure." He broke their gaze, and went to the fire. Katherine watched the sinewy movement of his well-muscled legs as he squatted down to tend it.

Mating.

A country girl, she had seen animals mate—rabbits, dogs, even horses; the male behind the female, growling and grunting in an almost violent display of lust. Once passing the stables, she had seen a hobbled mare screaming as a big stallion mounted her.

The most pleasant thing a man and a woman can do together.

With a shuddering breath, she shook her head. What he said was wrong. Men took their pleasure at the expense of women.

She narrowed her eyes and watched Nicholas as he added kindling to the fire, seeing him as the stallion. The image brought a sudden heat to her, and she looked away.

Yet, that did explain why her body had ached when he'd kissed her behind the copse. And why she felt taut as a bowstring remembering it.

Over the crackling of the newly kindled fire, she could hear the gentle tinkle of feminine laughter interspersed with the low rumbling of a man's voice, coming from the next room. The woman *did* sound happy.

Nicholas rose and turned in one smooth movement. Her breath caught. He pinned her with his eyes and advanced in her direction.

Katherine swallowed, feeling as helpless as the mare held by ropes. "It cannot be true," she whispered. "What happens between men and women is for making babes, which women bring forth in great pain. 'Tis no pleasure in it."

"What you say of birthing is true, but mating does not always make a babe." He gave her a knowing look. "Not if one is careful."

She looked at him, surprised.

"And if it is done right, it can bring great pleasure to a woman." He stepped closer and before she knew what was happening, he had loosed the strings of her cap, pulled it from her head, and tossed it into the flame.

Her hair slowly unfurled and descended in an avalanche. The weight of it hit her shoulders. A tender ache ran across her scalp. She put a hand to where her cap had been, and watched in disbelief as the fire consumed her headpiece.

Looking up, she saw a challenge in Nicholas's eyes. He took her shoulders in his strong hands, and slowly drew her to him.

She thought to push him away, but instead her fingers grasped his shirt.

His mouth swooped down, and his lips captured hers. As his arms wrapped around her, she melted into him.

A fierce heat rose up in her. Her hand moved up his chest and over his collarbone to his corded neck where she could feel the strong beat of his pulse.

His tongue teased her lips for entry. She felt a momentary quaver, a sense of alarm, at the knowledge that in his arms she lost all control. Then her mouth opened. As the kiss deepened, her pulse echoed in rhythm with his. A throbbing began in her women's place, and she heard herself whimper. With fear? Or pleasure?

For she felt both. His kiss consumed her, like brushwood in a fire.

His hand came to rest on her bodice. His fingers teased her nipple until her breast felt swollen and aching. Shock gave way to pleasure. She inhaled the warm familiar smell of him, of man and horse and coffee as his hand continued its exploration. Cradling her head with one hand, he pursued the kiss with more fervor. His other hand moved downward over her buttocks, kneading and pushing as he held her against the hardness at his groin. A shiver of alarm ran through her as she remembered the stallion and the screaming mare.

Katherine stiffened.

Nicholas groaned and set her from him.

With a shaking hand, she brushed a lock of hair from her face. She gulped and touched lips still tingling. Her words came low and labored. "I think I understand."

He looked at her, the planes of his face made harsh by the firelight. A mocking smile touched the corners of his mouth.

"No, you do not." He shook his head. "'Twas just the beginning of it."

Katherine slept no more that night. She lay awake listening to Nicholas breathe as he slumbered before the fire. Her body contained a restless energy. Her mind churned.

Again and again, the memory of his kiss and of his hands on her body returned, washed through her, enveloping her in a hot throbbing surge of sensation that left her shaking and on edge.

How could a kiss be so powerful? Leave her lost and aching and afraid?

Every time she closed her eyes, Nicholas's face would come to her: a pair of mocking blue eyes, a cleft chin, and a white streak lightening a head of black hair.

Tomorrow they would spend most of a day on the same horse. Katherine wondered how she could endure it.

Mating...the most pleasant thing a man and a woman can do together...

Her heart lurched, and she felt a strange emptiness in her belly. She remembered the challenge she'd seen in his eyes just before he kissed her. Was it a warning that soon, very soon, he would evoke wails and groans from her? That he would give her the pleasure a man could give a woman? A rush of heat ran through her, and she kicked off the covers.

The fire popped, and she heard him resettle before the hearth.

How could he sleep when she could not?

Katherine tossed irritably, then stilled, not wishing to wake him. Her breasts ached. Her woman's place throbbed. Tension built in her until she wanted to shriek.

How could she continue in his company?

Did he provide safety? Or danger?

Jeremy had offered his protection and he was no threat at all. He would follow her direction. Using the stars as their guide, now that she knew what to look for, they could make their way to London without further mishap. She could be free from Nicholas's overpowering presence and the temptation to discover things best left unknown.

Katherine took a deep breath and let it out slowly. She really had no choice.

Taking care to be quiet, she moved from the bed, aware of every creak of the ropes that supported the mattress. Standing very still, almost afraid to breathe, she surveyed the room. The satchel containing her medical supplies lay on the floor where she had dropped it; the other satchel was near the door. Skirt, petticoat, shoes and stockings were on the floor near the bed where she had left them. Her cloak lay on the chair where she'd tossed it.

Pity Nicholas slept so close to it.

Watching him sleep, alert for signs he was waking, Katherine slipped into her petticoat and skirt.

Montford lay with him, her back along Nicholas's front. Could she wake the cat without waking the man? As if in answer, Montford stretched out a paw, yawned, and nestled closer to Nicholas.

Montford had made her choice. Katherine closed her eyes and swallowed back a sob, then let out an even breath. Though it might break her heart, it would be easier to travel without her kitty. In any case, Katherine could not stay just because her cat would not come with her.

What of her cloak? She must have it or risk freezing.

Carefully testing each floorboard, Katherine eased toward the sleeping figures on the hearth until she stood behind the woolen garment. Holding her breath, she reached out only to snap her hand back when Nicholas stirred.

Her heart thundered. She waited, breathing only gasps of air, while Nicholas rolled onto his back, flinging his arm out to the side. Katherine watched in dismay as it came to rest on the hem of her cloak.

Could she slip the garment from under him without waking him? No. She could not risk it.

Frustrated, she scanned the room for a solution and spied Nicholas's cloak draped over the edge of the table. She would take that instead.

Tiptoeing on her bare feet, she moved about the chamber retrieving the items she would take with her.

Quietly working the door latch, she slipped into the blackness of the hallway. She paused a moment and put on Nicholas's cloak. Knee-length on him, it hung almost to her ankles. Trying to still her breathing and temper her heartbeat, she strained to hear any sound from the other side of the door.

All was quiet. So different from before, when she'd gone to aid a woman who did not need help, and Nicholas had stopped her.

Katherine gnawed her lower lip, still hot as if his mouth had just left hers. Steeling herself against the memory, she sneaked down the hall. Not until she peeked into the room off the stables where Jeremy and Henry slept, did she feel any measure of relief.

Henry snored loudly. She could probably shout to Jeremy and he would not hear her over the din. Instead, she crept to Jeremy's bedside and, putting a hand over his mouth, shook his shoulder.

He came awake all at once, grabbing her and thrusting her away. She landed on her bottom on the floor.

"Mistress?" he gulped in dismay, looking down at her. "Have I hurt ye?"

She shook her head. Lifting a cautionary finger to her lips, she nodded in Henry's direction.

Jeremy sat up. "Cromwell's own army would not wake our friend," he said, rubbing sleep from his eyes. "He drank so much brandy his words came out tangled. I had to help him to his bed." The groom yawned. "Why are you here, mistress? What is amiss?"

"All is fine, Jeremy." Katherine got up. "It is just that I have decided we must part company with our traveling companions. And 'tis less complicated to do so now than to wait until morning." She brushed off the back of Nicholas's cloak.

Jeremy searched her face in the darkness. "If he has harmed you in any way, I will call him out."

Katherine looked down. "He has not harmed me." She felt herself color, glad of the mask of darkness. It was not a lie, yet not exactly the truth either.

Jeremy nodded. When he spoke, his words came out softly. "I see you are wearing his coat. You have brought your belongings." He nodded to the two bags at her feet and her shoes and stockings. "But where is your cat? I cannot believe you have decided to leave Montford behind without good cause. What happened, mistress?"

"We lost a day of travel because we have an incompetent guide. I would prefer to go on without him," Katherine snapped, not wanting to explain her decision.

Jeremy looked unconvinced, but then he nodded. "I do not trust him, and have always felt we would be better off without him."

"We can travel at night as he suggested. Now that I know how to read the stars we can get to London without further mishap."

"I will saddle the better horse for us."

Katherine shook her head. "I will not ride. The horse is not ours, and I would not take what is not mine."

"It will lengthen our journey by several days. Yet, I understand why you do not ride." He nodded. "Aright, mistress. I shall be ready in a moment."

Katherine turned her back to him. As he dressed, she plaited her hair into one long rope, and put on her stockings and shoes.

Once out of the stables, Katherine paused to locate the North Star. Shrugging off the memory of Nicholas's hands upon her, his breath on her cheek, she forced herself forward. Fixing the bright star above her left shoulder, she led Jeremy from the courtyard, and through the town.

Katherine hugged Nicholas's coat against the chill. As they walked quietly through the empty lanes, his scent enveloped her, mingling with the smells of habitation. Their footfalls were loud in the hush of the still night. The weak light of the crescent moon provided scant illumination. A dog barked.

They had not been clear of the town long when Jeremy stopped and tossed down his satchel. "It has come to my mind, 'twould be best to return to Ashfield."

The loud chirping of a cricket filled the silence before Katherine answered. "I have already told you I will not go back. I would as soon travel alone as return to Ashfield with you."

"'Tis my duty to take you to your father."

Katherine shook her head. "I absolve you of all duty to me. Either come as my friend or come not at all."

"'Tis not so easy as that."

"Come Jeremy, or stay as you will." Katherine's voice was sharp and exasperated. "I do not wish to argue with you now. I go to London."

Jeremy reluctantly nodded. He reached for one of her bundles, and picked up his own. "To London," he agreed, but he did not sound happy.

Nicholas stretched. He could hear the bones in his back crack. Damn, but the floor was hard. It would surely be good to get back to London, to his rooms and his feather bed. This business of being a gentleman and taking the floor had little to recommend it.

He opened his eyes to see the early morning light creep in

through the window. A warm presence against his chest told him Montford had joined him during the night. He reached over and scratched her behind the ears. A loud purr erupted from the feline, and she extended a long languid leg.

He smiled, and gave her one last pat. As he sat up the cat fell sideways with a peculiar lack of grace. Sending him an irritated glare, she righted herself, and began to wash a spot just between her shoulders.

Nicholas chuckled then hushed when he realized he'd not heard a sound from Katherine. He glanced toward the bed but could not see her under the tumble of covers.

Who would have guessed his little Puritan would be so delectable? And so naïve. He could not remember ever being so innocent himself. And certainly never so frightened by a kiss. He had heard her fidget for quite awhile before he'd drifted off to sleep.

Against the protest of his joints, Nicholas stood. From this new perspective, it became immediately apparent Katherine was not there. He scowled. Where could she have gone?

To the kitchens?

Maybe to speak with the boy?

Nicholas frowned down at the other occupant of the room. "Where is your mistress?"

The cat paused in her morning ablutions and studied him gravely.

Raking a hand through his hair, Nicholas made a quick assessment of the room. Her cloak was here, but her satchels were missing.

"Do you think she has left us? I can understand her leaving without me. But without you? Or do you think—" Nicholas broke off as he realized he spoke to a cat. Placing his hands on his hips, he cast a glance heavenward. But then he looked back down at the wee beast. "Do you think she is just gone for the moment?"

Montford threw him a companionable glance and began to clean a paw.

Nicholas scowled. He could not take time with his toilet.

Stuffing his feet into his shoes, he looked about for his cloak, but it, too, was missing. Hastening to the door, he turned back to Montford before leaving.

Feeling ridiculous, nevertheless he shook a finger at the cat. "Do not go anywhere. If your lady returns, bid her stay."

Montford gazed back unblinking.

Moments later, Nicholas arrived at the room off the stables where Jeremy and Henry slept. Katherine had not been in the kitchen, nor the common room, nor standing about in the courtyard. But he'd not really thought to find her in any of those places. And Jeremy's pallet was empty.

He shook Henry awake. "They are gone, man."

Henry looked at him through reddened eyes. He raised a trembling hand to his head. "Have ye no care for me head, Nicky?" He sat up unsteadily, rubbing his jaw. "My tooth it is better, but me head pounds dreadful now."

"We must leave. Right now," Nicholas commanded. "Pull yourself together then have the horses brought round, unless they are also gone."

Gerald Welles looked up as the Ashfield butler interrupted his morning meal, yet another reminder that nothing had run smoothly since Katherine's departure.

"Yes?" he inquired through a mouth full of sausage.

"A letter. From the postal messenger." Old Blake proffered the folded paper as if he held a dead rodent.

"Well, give it here, man," Gerald wiped a greasy hand onto his shirt and reached for the missive. He'd expected word from Finch by now.

It had been two long days spent in prayer with Father. His knees hurt, and his back ached. Worse, the older man's sermons on sin and fornication had moved on from being directed at Katherine and Jeremy to Gerald.

He ran a thumbnail under the wax-seal. Holding the letter at a comfortable distance, he read the unfamiliar handwriting.

Master Gerald Welles,

Be it known your daughter, Katherine, is safe. She is enjoying good health and will be returned to you with her maidenhead intact, only when you release Ashfield and your claim upon it to me, the rightful owner.

As an act of good faith to your family for seeing this unjust situation righted, all amounts paid to Cromwell for the estate will be returned to you in the form of a dowry for your daughter.

Should you choose to turn down this offer, please know I intend to pursue my claim to Ashfield with an influential friend, also returned from exile, who I believe will be sympathetic to my plight.

You may respond to my man of business, Henry Fitzhughes, Abermarle Road, London.

I remain,

Nicholas Edward Henry Philip Montford, Earl of Ashton

Gerald put down his knife as he re-read the signature line.
Montford.
Earl.
Ashton.
The words popped out at him.

Katherine still had her maidenhead. Relief hit him hard and sure. Jeremy hadn't already got it, then. This was colossally good news.

Of course Gerald would not comply with any of the demands, even though the prospect of having Finch as a son-in-law had been losing its attraction ever since the deal had been set. He would use this to get back into Finch's good graces.

Gerald carefully folded the letter and set it aside. He smiled and took another mouthful of sausage.

CHAPTER TEN

As dawn's glow illuminated the murky shadows, green pastures and trees gradually emerged from the blackened gloom. In the light of the new day, Katherine's tired mind could no longer push away the doubts that had gnawed at her during the night.

Why *had* she left Nicholas?

Was it because he was an unreliable guide?

Or was it because she found him handsome and liked his kisses?

The most pleasant thing a man and woman can do together.

If she had stayed at the inn, would she have been tempted to discover if he spoke the truth?

Katherine shuddered. Her insides went fluttery as she recalled the feel of his lips on hers, of his tongue exploring her mouth, of his hands pulling her to him. The smell of exotic spice and coffee wafted from his cloak, reminding her of the comfort she'd found in his strong arms while riding atop the horse.

Trudging at Jeremy's side, she moved in a growing misery of aching legs and feet. Even though the groom had taken the heavier bag, her arms had long since grown weary of the other. Strands of hair had worked lose from her braid and hung limp in front of her eyes. She blew at them but they resettled before her nose.

Waves of exhaustion broke over her. A pebble had lodged itself in one shoe and she had not stopped to take it out. The growing irritation worked like a scourge of self-punishment. She felt a queer tightness in her chest and her eyes stung.

Reaching the apex of a hill, Katherine wavered. Fenced-in parcels of grazing sheep, cultivated fields, woodlands and farms dotted the landscape that stretched out before them. The road dipped downward and then up again as if it would go on forever. Would it lead to London and Cousin Alicia's house? Or had she got Nicholas's instructions wrong? Perhaps after days of travel they would find themselves in Wales.

And what if they did get to London and Cousin Alicia didn't want her?

Katherine's vision blurred and a moan rose from her throat. She dropped her satchel and fell to her knees on the dirt road. She pressed her hands to her eyes, but she could not stop the tears from spilling over and running hot down her cheeks. Strange choking noises finally erupted in a great sob.

"Mistress?"

At the note of alarm in Jeremy's voice, she bawled all the more.

"Are you all right?"

"No!" Pulling her hands from her eyes, Katherine saw a look of panic on his face. She took a deep breath to steady herself, but the sobs burst forth again. "Oh J-Jeremy," she wailed, "I am so s-sorry."

"Sorry?" he squeaked.

"For this f-fool's journey we are on."

Jeremy took a step toward her. "I think ye be needing food and rest."

Katherine shook her head. "I don't know where we are." She took a deep breath and let it out. "And if we do ever get to London, Cousin Alicia doesn't know I'm coming!"

Jeremy's jaw dropped.

Katherine wiped her eyes on Nicholas's cloak, catching another whiff of his special smell. A great longing hit her. She wished he'd been the kind of man she could have trusted. Or maybe that she hadn't been so afraid.

But she could not change that now.

"My cousin had said, when she was last at Ashfield, she hoped I could come for an extended visit." Katherine clenched her teeth and blinked hard so the tears would not come anew. "But she might have guests when we arrive. Or perhaps she has gone visiting herself and is not at home. Or perhaps I mistook the invitation."

She looked up at him. "An' it may not matter, since we could be lost, and we may never find her. Or even London, no matter how grand a place it is."

Jeremy took another small step toward her, raised his eyebrows and made a beckoning smile as if coaxing a stray animal. She half expected to see him stretch a hand forth with a choice bit of food on it.

"Let us rest, mistress. 'Twill seem different, no doubt, when our bellies are full."

Katherine sniffled.

Jeremy reached into his satchel and pulled out a half-loaf of brown bread. "Here. I have what we need."

In spite of the lint adhering to the crust, Katherine's mouth watered, and her stomach growled. Hysterical laughter rose in her chest and came out a strange giggle.

Jeremy helped her up.

They found a spot to eat and rest near a grove of ash trees, just out of sight of the road. Katherine took off Nicholas's cloak and spread it on the ground. Releasing her feet from the prison of her shoes, she tossed away the pebble and sank down beside Jeremy. She picked the fluff off the bread and took a bite. As she ate, a great lassitude stole over her. Robins chirped in the nearby trees. A caterpillar inched its way toward them across dew-laden weeds, its progress slow but purposeful, unaware of the obstacle they would present to its journey. Katherine wondered if their efforts were as futile as the bug's.

"How far do you think we have come?" she asked.

Jeremy hazarded a glance in her direction. "'Tis hard to say. I should think at least eight miles, but less than twelve." He flopped down on his back. Shielding his eyes from the rising sun, he added lightly, "Had we taken a horse, we'd be closer to London now."

Katherine shrugged at his rebuke. "Or, being lost, we could also be further away." She sighed. "And what of my father and our neighbor? Where do you think they are?"

"Far, far, from us, mistress. England is a very big country, and two people are very small. There is no reason to think they would find us after these many days." Jeremy rolled to his side. "Ouch," he rubbed his elbow. "What is this?"

Katherine had completely forgotten about the pocket on the inside of Nicholas's cape. Jeremy eagerly spilled its contents onto the cloak. She breathed easier when she saw no sign of the Raven's black cowl. She did not want to explain that now. Happily, the coins remained, which meant dinner could be bought when they reached a village or town.

Jeremy's eyes widened when he saw the odd cylindrical device she'd first seen in the cottage. "Why, I think 'tis a spyglass!" He picked it up and put one end to his eye. Then turning it around, he peered through the other end. "I have always wanted look through one of these." As he gazed through the strange object, his mouth curled into a smile.

Katherine followed the direction of his eye, but failed to see anything of interest, except perhaps the caterpillar she had noticed earlier. It had managed to find its way around them and still plodded onward.

"What does it do?" she asked.

"Look," Jeremy held the spyglass up to her eye. "Close t'other."

Katherine looked through the eyepiece and almost fell backward as the world rushed toward her. She pushed the instrument away. "It brings everything close. 'Tis dizzying."

"What do you suppose he is doing with this?" Jeremy raised it again to one eye.

Katherine could well imagine the uses of such a devise for a highwayman, but she just shook her head.

Leaving Jeremy to play with the spyglass, she yawned and lay down. With her stomach appeased, weariness overcame her. Nicholas's scent rose from the fine wool of his cloak and wrapped around her. She snuggled into the fabric and fell asleep.

"Damn the wench," Nicholas muttered. *And damn me for being an imbecile*, he added silently. Last night when she'd stepped into the hallway, he'd lost control of whatever good sense he possessed. Why couldn't he remember she was a missish Puritan and not one of the court flirts?

Nicholas glowered. If he had imagined just one month before, that he would be searching the countryside for a wayward Puritan heiress with the questionable help of his brandy-sick, but nevertheless faithful, retainer—and a cat—he would have thought it all a good joke. Yet today he failed to see the humor in it.

The situation was serious. He had to find her, and fast. With only the boy for protection, she would be easy plunder for any highwayman or ruffian she came across.

The sun had well passed its zenith when they turned into the courtyard at the *King's Tavern* in Marlborough, discouraged and tired after hours of fruitless searching. Nicholas threw his reins to the hostler as he dismounted, then untied the basket containing Montford, who protested with loud meows.

Henry swung from his horse. He landed unsteadily and winced. Raising shaking hands, he massaged his temples. "Nicky," he spoke in almost a groan. "No matter what I say or do, if ye care for me at all, do not let me take even a nip of brandy ever again."

Nicholas scowled. "I offered to leave you behind while I searched for the girl."

Henry pulled himself to his full height. "An' you remember what happened last time ye left me behind?" He shook his head, and grimaced from the motion. "Nah. I could not let ye go on your own."

"So it's to protect me that you have come along, my mighty

friend? I do feel much safer."

"Someone ought to protect ye from yerself, Nicky."

Nicholas gritted his teeth and strode to the tavern, leaving the older man to follow. On top of all else, he could now look forward to a lecture from Henry!

A portly innkeeper greeted him with deference. Nicholas waved aside use of a private room and sat down at a solid oak table.

All morning they had traversed narrow country lanes and major highways to the east of Devizes. If Nicholas had been able to leave Henry behind he'd have made better progress. But without knowing the direction Katherine and the boy had taken, he had no assurance that his search would lead him back to the inn. So Henry had, of necessity, come. And Nicholas had, of necessity, slowed the pace so the older man could keep up. He had not wanted to stop to eat now, but he could see his old friend needed sustenance and rest.

Henry fastened a bloodshot eye on him. "I am not truly settled in me own mind about Mistress Welles," he began. "We have not spoke on it, and 'tis not for me to express myself..." He trailed off as the potboy brought them two bowls of stew and a warm loaf of bread.

The innkeeper followed behind with two tankards, ale for Henry, and cider for Nicholas, who put a few bits of meat into the wicker basket, then set it on the ground.

"I know'd ye since ye was born. Ye've a good heart beatin' in your chest." Henry paused to take a draught of his ale. "So I cannot understand what you are doing with the woman."

"'Tis very simple. She's the heiress to my estate."

Henry closed his eyes and rubbed at his temples. "I know'd I should not have gone along with you playing at the Raven. I thought one or two such pranks would be a harmless diversion, and it should have been, until ye went off without me." He opened his eyes and let out a deep sigh. "But this is different. Kidnapping heiresses is a capital offense here in England. 'Tis not a lawless country like many ye have been to. And 'twill not serve your purpose with the King."

Nicholas put on his most innocent face. "Kidnap? I simply accompany her to London."

Henry's eyebrows rose to a point over his nose. "Ye can say that to yourself, and the magistrate when he asks you, but do not say that to me. 'Tis plain she would not have left her home had it not been for ye. And if anything happens to her or the boy, 'twill be yer fault."

"Which is why I mean to find them and keep them from harm," said Nicholas.

"But once found, will ye be taking them back where they belong?"

Nicholas grimaced. "Katherine does not 'belong' at Ashfield. Her father is forcing her into a marriage she does not want. And in truth I cannot blame her."

Henry shook his head and burped. "Finch is a bad'un, to be sure. A crueler lad I've never met, and always wanting what is not his. But, Nicky, 'tis not your problem."

A commotion at the doorway announced the arrival of newcomers. Nicholas looked up as three plumed cavaliers spilled into the room. He'd last seen them at court and recognized them immediately. Hugh Chiverton, the popinjay of the group, gave voluble instructions to the innkeeper, punctuating each sentence with a tap of his cane. Peter Langley stood beside him brushing the sleeves of his scarlet brocade waistcoat, his usual bored expression topped by a white periwig. The last of the three, George Talbot, slouched behind them, yawning into the ruffle of his shirtsleeve.

Nicholas looked down at his own attire. Rumpled from sleep, his shirt hung in disarray. He'd been in such a hurry to be off this morning, he'd not laced his doublet or put on a cravat. He certainly presented a different vision from when they'd last seen him at court.

"Ashton!"

Chiverton spied him before the others. Nicholas put on a smile as the three made their way to his table. Though impatient to find Katherine, he was none-the-less aware of the opportunity they provided to deliver him from Henry's sermon. He greeted

122

them warmly and agreed to join them in a private room, leaving Henry to finish his meal alone. Perhaps the older man could rest a few moments before they were on the road again.

The innkeeper brought them to a stuffy chamber dominated by a large table. The portly proprietor scurried about arranging benches and stools and throwing open the wooden shutters.

Talbot plopped down in a chair and was asleep in moments.

Chiverton spoke first. "What are you doing in this fine town? Could it be that you've received word of Talbot's grand fête and, like us, are on your way to his estate?"

Nicholas must have looked at him blankly because he continued, "No. I 'spose not. Ah well. I hear there will be sport of all kinds there." He cocked a wicked eyebrow. "Talbot's invited us all to celebrate the completion of his new waterworks."

"He's quite excited to unveil his new fountain." Langley spoke with his usual deliberate elocution. Waving in the direction of the sleeping man he added, "I'm sure if he could rouse himself he'd give you a personal invitation."

Chiverton laughed. "I understand our liege will be arriving tonight. Just a brief stop on his way to Bath. The Queen has gone for a cure," he added as an aside while fingering his laced cravat. "With the entertainment we have planned, I've no doubt our lusty King hisself will have need of Bath's restorative waters when he joins the Queen."

The landlord bustled in, followed by the potboy, both bearing trays of food and drink. They spread the contents on the table with great formality, but Talbot's loud snoring ruined the fine ceremony.

"What news from court?" Nicholas asked when they'd left.

Chiverton answered. "The Queen has been ill, delirious in fact. Rumor has it she believed herself to have given birth. Charles, in a touching display of husbandly affection, comforted her by telling her she had delivered two fine sons and a daughter. But 'twas a lie." He took a draught of his ale. "'Tis a pity that the king can beget bastards but not heirs."

Langley speared a piece of cheese with his knife, and raised it to his mouth. Fixing an eye on Nicholas he said, "Speaking of the

King, I understand Charles is none too pleased with you."

"Oh?"

"He mentioned on at least one occasion his displeasure that"—Langley's voice lowered several notes—"his dear friend Nicholas had quit London without so much as a by your leave."

Nicholas cursed silently. He had waited two long months after petitioning the King for the return of his birthright, but Charles, in his characteristic fashion, had been in no hurry to adjudicate the matter. Nor was Nicholas the only noble to petition the King after returning to England to discover his lands belonged to someone else.

Nicholas did not like to wait. So, he'd left the court, only meaning to be gone a few days, just long enough to see Ashfield and discover if it held up to his childhood memories. One thing had lead to another, and now he would have to make it right with the King. He would apologize for his absence and hope no one ever connected the short career of a highwayman named the Raven with Nicholas, the Earl of Ashton. And why would they? No one knew but Henry and Katherine.

Katherine.

Nicholas scowled. He would feel better if she were safe with him. It was time to retrieve Henry and take to the road while there were several hours of good daylight left. And if they did not find her by sundown, they would keep hunting through the night.

Nicholas came out of his thoughts to find himself the subject of discussion. Chiverton spoke to Langley. "Well I think his distraction, along with his state of dishevelment, points to the strong possibility that a new light-o'-love awaits him down the hall."

Nicholas made a shrug that neither confirmed nor denied his friend's suppositions. "As you say," he smiled and rose. "I must be off."

"Well, join us if you can. You might wish to take advantage of this informal occasion to put your face before Charles," said Chiverton. "I expect the night's entertainment will have a mollifying effect on his heart, and he will be all the readier to forgive you."

Langley grinned. "And you could always bring your latest light-skirt with you."

Nicholas restrained the urge to wipe the look off Langley's face with a well-aimed blow. Without saying whether he would come to the fête, he left the men and rejoined Henry in the common room, impatient to be gone from this place.

The nightmare played out again, with Katherine as powerless to wake, as she had been powerless to stop the accident when it happened. Frozen in horror, she watched the tragedy unfold with the alarm and dread of someone who knows what is to come.

Lazy clouds floated in a bright blue sky. Birds chirped in the trees. Edward rode the horse he'd just received for his fifteenth birthday.

Her heart swelled at the sight of him, so dashing.

Turning in his seat, he waved to her. He was going to jump the hedgerow. Horse and rider sprang up and hung aloft.

A cry caught in her throat. Her mind screamed 'no!'

For a moment, she thought they might clear the hurdle, but they had leapt too soon. The horse balked. In a terrifying crash, horse, bush, and rider came together. The heavy body of the horse fell back onto the hard earth, rolling over Edward, crushing the life out of her dearest brother.

They lay, a snarl of bodies, arms and legs at odd angles. The screams of the injured horse and Katherine's cries combined into a great keening wail that grew louder and louder.

Katherine tried to wrench herself back to consciousness. To escape from the torment of the disaster that had broken her heart and changed her life forever. To wake from the vision of Edward's shattered body, and the finality of his death. But, instead of ending at this point as the nightmare usually did, her dream continued.

She ran to him, to his twisted body and broken limbs. If she was gentle enough, careful enough, maybe she could put him right, and he would be healed. Life would flow in his veins again. Gazing into his sweet face, she was suddenly afraid. Would he fade away if she touched him, just as the edges of the dream were already fading?

He opened his eyes and smiled at her.

At the shock of their connection, a piercing joy filled her. Like a flower in sunlight, Katherine's heart opened.

"Edward, my dearest brother. You are not gone!" Tears of happiness ran down her cheeks.

"I am gone," he answered. "But I have come to speak with you now."

"Oh, Edward, I have missed you so."

"I am here, dearest sister, to tell you how sorry I am to have left you alone to deal with our father, and to beg your forgiveness for taking our mother. I have ever been a selfish boy."

"'Twas not your fault our mother died."

"I did call to her until she finally came. Nay, Katherine, do not try to minimize my faults. I wish to tell you, I have missed you well, and I love you so very much. I did not tell you that before I died. There was not time."

"I love you too, Edward. As I always have."

Tears still streaming, Katherine searched his face. "I do not blame you for leaving me, Edward. Yet, there is a great emptiness now that I have not been able to fill. There is none to care about my lessons, or cheer me up when I am sad."

Edward smiled. "There is Jeremy."

Katherine nodded. Edward's image was already dimming. She reached out to touch him, but he was gone.

She woke to find herself caressing Nicholas's wool coat. Her heart pounded and her cheeks were wet. Even though it had been a dream, her tears had been real.

Katherine dried her cheeks on the sleeve of her gown and sat up, taking a deep breath of the cool afternoon air. The sun was making its descent. It would be night in just a few short hours. They needed to get on the road soon. She flexed a stiff foot. Sore muscles protested all the way up her leg.

There is Jeremy.

Looking over at her companion, she examined him as if for the first time. His honey-colored hair hung straight to his shoulders, not much different in hue from hers, yet with enough color from the sun to make it appear almost golden.

In sleep, she could see his long, full eyelashes. His skin,

although streaked with dust from the road, glowed a creamy peach. She could not imagine he had ever seen a day's growth of beard. His cheeks were well formed, his jaw firm.

Leaving Devizes, she had told him to come with her as friend or not at all. She had not had a friend since Edward died, and she dearly needed one now.

"Jeremy?"

He rolled onto his back. Shielding his eyes from the setting sun he looked over at her. "Yes, mistress?"

"Are you awake?"

"I am now."

Katherine felt a smile tug at the corners of her mouth.

"I think 'tis time you called me Katherine."

"All right, Mistress Katherine."

Katherine's smile broadened. That wasn't what she had meant, but it was better.

"I should like very much," she said somewhat shyly, "for us to be friends."

"I should like that very much too, mistress, uh, Katherine." He beamed.

"Good." Katherine's heart warmed. "I would ask your counsel, friend. What do you think we should now do? And, since you are my friend, you must know that to even suggest one more time we return to Ashfield would make me cross."

"As your friend, I would not think of it." Jeremy smiled. "But, I would suggest we find our supper. From the road, I did spot church spires in the distance. If we walk toward them we will find a town or village. The coins you found in the pocket will purchase our dinner."

"'Tis good advice," Katherine agreed. Then a thought came to her. "I have known you long, Jeremy Haywood, yet I know little about you. Here we sit together, far from our home. I do not even know if you have a family you leave behind in another village unknown to me."

Jeremy blinked at her. "What do you mean?"

Katherine smiled. "A mother? Father? Sisters? Brothers? Or are you an orphan?"

"Nay, mistress." Jeremy looked away and picked leaves off the wool cloak while he spoke. "I am not an orphan. I lived with my mother until she died, and then I came to be groom at Ashfield. I have been on my own since then." He glanced at her. "Except for your good help, and that of your mother, when I was ill, or needed an injury tended."

"I am glad to know you do not leave loved ones behind. 'Twould not make me a good friend to take you from them." Katherine nodded. "I feel much recovered from the morning. You were right. I was tired and hungry."

"Aye," he smiled. "We will find London, and if your cousin is not there, or will not see you, I will take care of you, mistress, and see you do not come to harm."

Katherine smiled. Gentle relief filled her. It was good to have someone who would help her and not because they would get something in return. It was good to be able to trust someone. She reached over and squeezed his hand.

"I am happy to have you for my friend, Jeremy."

He smiled, and stood up, pulling her with him. "Shall we continue on, Katherine?"

CHAPTER ELEVEN

As night encroached, clouds disappeared into the darkening sky. A chill wind whipped at Katherine's braid until she tucked it into Nicholas's cloak. Hunger gripped her belly and set it rumbling in cadence with each step. As they got closer to the church spires, a signpost announced they had found the market town of Marlborough.

The broad avenue offered a choice of eating establishments. Katherine's mouth watered at a sign displaying a roasted goose. Standing in indecision, she and Jeremy were jostled more than once. Each time her grip tightened on the pocket holding the precious coins. She looked up again at the sign.

"Shall we sup here?" she asked Jeremy.

"Aye," he smiled. "I do not think I could go another step. We cannot tell out here whether the food be good, so we shall just have to find out."

Katherine pulled the latch, and they walked inside. The stench of unwashed bodies rose up to greet her, turning her stomach. She raised a hand to cover her nose. This tavern was not at all the class of those that they'd been to with Nicholas. She pulled the cloak tightly about her and cast a worried glance over her shoulder at her companion.

"I do not like this place." She spoke in a hushed tone.

"Nor I," he admitted quietly, "but eat we must, and our money will go farther than somewhere more grand." His gaze flitted over the crowded room. "We should draw little notice here."

Katherine nodded, her sense of practicality assuaging her doubt.

Resting a hand on her shoulder, Jeremy steered her through the boisterous crowd to an empty bench at a rough-hewn table.

Katherine sat down across from a couple locked in embrace. A hot flush ran up her neck to her cheeks, and she wrenched her gaze away. She handed Jeremy their coins.

He gave her hand a squeeze and walked off to purchase their meal.

A gap-toothed man grinned at her from the next table.

She shrugged deeper into Nicholas's cloak and looked down at her lap. A shiver of apprehension ran down her spine. Without Jeremy by her side, she felt vulnerable and defenseless. They would eat quickly, then leave just as fast.

Fortunately, it was not long before he returned. A dirty serving-maid trailed behind him, bearing meat pies and tankards of ale.

To Katherine's surprise, the food tasted good, and, for a change, it was venison instead of mutton. Grateful she had not seen the conditions under which it had been prepared, she savored each bite, ignoring the crowd and noise around her.

Jeremy ate without conversing.

Soon, Katherine's mind drifted off, settling on thoughts of Nicholas. Of the feel of his hands as he reached for her. The way his eyes had searched hers as he drew her into his embrace. The resonant timbre of his voice when he spoke.

The most pleasant thing a man and woman can do together.

Had that been just the night before?

Pulling herself forcefully from memories that were no safer than her surroundings, Katherine looked about. The couple across the table had untangled themselves. The woman giggled shyly and clutched her belly, heavy with child. Uncaring who watched, the man pulled the woman's breast from her bodice and rubbed her nipple. The woman moaned and smiled.

Katherine's face flushed. Clasping her hands together, she looked down at her lap and took a deep breath. Nicholas's scent, the musky smell of man and exotic spice, assailed her from his cloak. A physical jolt of longing hit her and with sudden certainty, she knew it had been a mistake to leave him. Not because of her aching feet and dirty clothes, or the hunger and exhaustion.

But because she wanted to be with him.

She closed her eyes. The image of his face came to her. His devastating smile and the twinkle in his eyes were so real she could almost hear the deep timbre of his voice, feel it settle in her spine, soothing her as it had during their long rides on the horse. An ache of yearning rose up, engulfing her, making her weak. Oh how she missed the feel of his comforting arms around her, even the sense of danger when he kissed her.

Had Nicholas also felt that danger? Katherine remembered the odd look he had given her after breaking the kiss last night. If he had not stopped, would she have been able to? If she had been less afraid—more bold—would she have clung to him, seeking his lips, his warmth, and demanded he show her *the most pleasant thing a man and woman can do together*?

Instead, she had grabbed her things and run away.

Run from Nicholas.

Run from herself.

Run from *wanting* that left her hot with longing, yet cold with desperation.

Katherine took a shuddering breath and clamped her lower lip between her teeth. She fought for control, as her thoughts ran unrestrained. She must go back to him, retrace her steps of the night before.

Would he still be at the inn in Devizes?

She swallowed. How to explain to Jeremy that they must return? He would surely think her softheaded, and perhaps that was true. She took a slow even breath and looked up.

Jeremy was looking away, his gaze fixed on something behind him. Turning back to her, he took her chin in his hand, and bent his head to hers. "Do not move," he cautioned softly. "I am afraid there is trouble here."

"We must leave." Katherine nodded, grateful to have a good excuse. "I am done eating and eager to be gone. Let us leave now." She pulled Nicholas's cloak together and began to rise.

"Do not move I said," Jeremy whispered in her ear. His hands clamped onto her arms, holding her still.

Katherine froze, the tone of his voice getting her full attention. She looked up at his stern face. His eyes bid her be quiet.

"What is it?" she asked, her voice the merest whisper.

"I'm afraid 'tis your neighbor and his henchman."

Fear clutched Katherine. The meat pie solidified into a solid lump in her stomach. This was not some vague danger encountered at an alehouse, but one directed at her in particular.

She leaned forward. "Are you sure?"

Jeremy made the briefest nod.

She took a measured breath to ease her panic. Without moving, she looked around as best she could, but Jeremy's head blocked most everything from view. To one side sat the man missing his teeth, at the other was the couple, still locked in embrace, oblivious to what was going on around them.

They gave her an idea.

Katherine put her hands on Jeremy's shoulders and pulled him to her. "Do not be alarmed," she whispered into his ear, "'tis the best way I can think they will pay us no mind."

"What are you doing, m-mistress?"

She snuggled closer to him. "I am pretending we are kissing," she nodded across the table, "like they are."

"Oh," he said in an unsteady whisper.

"Put your hands on me," she demanded softly.

Jeremy's arms loosely enfolded her shoulders as a hush fell over the room.

"I seek information." Richard Finch's voice echoed through the now silent room.

Katherine winced.

Jeremy gave her a comforting squeeze, and nestled her against his chest protectively.

"I look for a woman who travels with three men."

Snickers greeted this proclamation.

"One of the men has a streak of white in his hair."

Katherine's heart dropped. How had he learned of Nicholas? If he knew she traveled with Nicholas, did that also mean he knew Nicholas was the Raven?

"We must flee." Her voice rose in panic in Jeremy's ear.

"No," he whispered back, shaking his head slightly. His grip tightened around her. "'Twould be folly and serve only to draw their attention. Quiet and still, there is a chance they will not see us."

A shudder ran through Katherine. "I cannot bear this," she whispered.

Finch's heels clicked a slow march as he walked through the room. "The woman is small," he continued, "and dresses plainly. She is about twenty years of age. The other two men are servants, a stable boy, and an older man." His footsteps stopped uncomfortably close. The hairs on the nape of Katherine's neck stood up.

A cramp in her hand told her she had tightened her grip on Jeremy's shoulders. His hair brushed against her nose in a tickle.

"I offer a reward," Finch went on. He sounded to be standing behind her now. She could almost feel his eyes boring into her back. Her skin crawled. She had never been good at hiding games. Edward had always caught her because she couldn't stay still or quiet, knowing he would shout *aha* at any moment.

A titter threatened to escape her taut lips. Katherine bit hard on the inside of a cheek and closed her eyes, but the room and Finch's voice came up to surround her, choking her until she could not breathe. She took in a ragged gasp of air. Her heart pounded. Jeremy gave her a little shake causing her eyes to fly open.

She gasped.

Standing right behind Jeremy stood Jakes, staring straight at her. "It's them!" he cried.

Katherine and Jeremy jumped up. The bench fell over with a

crash. Hands clawed at her, and she pulled away.

Reaching for something—anything, she grabbed a wooden trencher from the table. Swinging it in a wide arc, it connected with someone in a bone-jarring thump. She heard a loud groan and hoped it wasn't Jeremy. Faces blurred as she whirled around.

"Get her!" It was Finch.

Hands grabbed her cloak from behind, yanking her back. The garment came off with a painful rip.

Just a few feet from her, Jeremy fought Jakes. A sob rose in Katherine's throat. What chance did her friend have against such a brute? His nose bloodied, face red with exertion, Jeremy's fists pounded the man who paid him no more mind than if he were a small dog yapping at his feet.

Finch struck Jeremy an effortless punch to the stomach. Her friend reeled back. Heaving and sputtering, he stumbled over a bench and crashed into a table. Katherine moved fast. In two steps, she stood behind Jakes. With a swift movement, the trencher connected with his head in a loud thwack.

But the brute did not waver.

Katherine sensed more than saw the crowd around her, crushing and holding her in. Loud voices rooted her and Jeremy on. Then her braid was yanked from behind and she was pulled back. Jakes punched Jeremy under the chin. The boy's head flew back and hit the floor with a loud crack. He lay still.

"Jeremy!" she cried, trying to move forward. Her assailant held her fast. Her scalp throbbed, and her eyes filled with tears from the pain. Her arm was seized from behind, then twisted. She could not move. An agonized cry escaped her lips.

"He cannot help you now." Finch's voice was quiet and deadly in her ear.

All of Katherine's temerity vanished. Her spirit crumpled like an old garment pulled from the line.

Jakes rubbed a fleshy hand across his forehead and spat. The sputum hit Jeremy on the face, but he did not stir.

"Where are the others?" Finch twisted her arm.

Her stomach clenched. "Others?"

He twisted harder.

Katherine's body strained backward. She bit her cheek hard to keep from crying out.

"Do not ever think me a fool," he intoned, applying more pressure. "I want the other two men."

A cry rose in her chest. Katherine capitulated before he wrenched her shoulder from her body. "I do not know. We parted company," she gasped. The pressure eased, but Finch did not let go. In front of her, Jakes kicked Jeremy hard in the ribs.

The boy made no sound.

The onlookers grumbled.

"Please…" Katherine entreated. "Do not hurt him more."

Finch attempted to steer her away, but the throng held them in. She was dimly aware of the disapproving scowls and protests directed at Finch and Jakes. Yet no one came to her aid.

"Enough," called Finch to his henchman. He tossed a handful of coins to the room. The mob fell into a wild melee as bits of silver and copper fell to the floor. Jeremy's wounded and broken body was lost to her view in the mad rush.

"Help him," Katherine called out. But no one paid her any mind. Instead, they scrambled after the money. "Please…" her voice broke off as Finch jerked her outside.

Stumbling through the cold drizzle, her senses withered. Jakes opened the door of the waiting coach and Finch shoved her in. She missed the step, and landed on her hands and knees on the vehicle's floor.

Climbing onto the seat, Katherine shrank back in the furthest corner and rubbed her bruised knees while the men talked outside. A shudder ran through her.

Did Jeremy lay dying? She brought her hands to her face. Her friendship had come at too high a price. If not for her, he would still be at Ashfield safe and secure, tending to the horses. Again and again he had offered to return her to her home, yet she had refused.

Why hadn't she let things be? After these days and nights of freedom and adventure, she would still marry Richard Finch. And he would make her suffer for her disobedience.

The coach listed violently as Finch climbed in and sat

opposite her. Katherine blinked back her tears. She must stay calm. Firm. Defiant.

His cold eyes glinted at her from under his curled white periwig. The sweet cloying scent from his perfumed gloves pervaded the close confines of the vehicle.

Katherine's stomach turned. She shivered. Without Nicholas's cloak, her satin dress provided scant protection against the night's chill and Finch's probing eyes. She raised her hands protectively above her décolleté bodice.

"You hide from me what you show to others?" His voice was harsh.

Katherine shook her head.

The coach jerked into motion. Her hands flew to the seat and she braced herself with her feet so she did not fall forward onto Finch. As the coach settled into a rhythmic sway, she returned her hands to shield her bosom.

Still, he leered at her. "Who would have thought you could look so enchanting? 'Tis plain you are not so plain after all." He made a bitter chuckle and removed his gloves, placing them neatly beside him.

Katherine thrust herself back into the leather seat. "Are we to Ashfield?" she asked, pleased at the steadiness of her voice, yet wishing it sounded stronger, more confident.

He did not answer. Instead, he leaned forward and grabbed her wrist, forcing her hand from its protective position. She pulled but he did not let go. Instead, his grasp tightened. The smile that hovered at the corner of his mouth disappeared, and his lips pursed together. He squinted, as he once again looked her up and down.

"You prefer a stable-boy to me?"

"I prefer to place my affections where I wish and not where I am told."

"Did you share your favors with him alone, or did you share yourself with the others?"

"My favors?" It took Katherine a moment to understand his meaning. Then she registered such fury she could not answer. She jerked back her wrist, but he did not let go.

"Answer me," he commanded. Even in darkness, the contempt in his eyes cut into her.

"I did not share 'my favors' with anyone!"

He moved next to her with sudden swiftness and placed his hand on her bodice. Katherine flinched beneath his touch. Something inside her snapped.

"No!" she cried and slapped his face with her free hand.

The sharp sound echoed in the small enclosure. Finch held a hand to his cheek. His eyes registered surprise no greater than her own.

Then he slapped her back.

Hard.

Tears stung her eyes as he captured her free hand and forced her hands behind her back. Katherine squirmed and shoved at him with her knees, but he twisted her wrists. She writhed. His eyes glinted as he increased the pressure, and she knew if she did not stop struggling, he would twist until her bones popped, so she went still.

His arms around her, he forced her into a position that thrust her breasts forward, into his chest. She could feel his breath, hot on her neck.

Katherine whimpered.

Finch's face hovered just inches from hers. "Why?"

Helpless, she swallowed sobs of frustration as he gripped both her hands in one of his. Her heart pounded so hard it seemed it would burst from her chest. She tried to still her trembling. "I don't understand."

He ran his finger over her lower lip. "Why the stable boy and not me?"

What a terrible misjudgment she had made, thinking she could hide by hugging Jeremy. She had not considered what Richard Finch would make of their embrace.

"Did you let him touch you here?" He pulled away from her slightly, and reached into her bodice. Nails scratched delicate skin as his hand moved down to cup her breast.

Katherine's stomach roiled. Bile rose in her throat. "No!"

"You lie." He yanked his hand from her bodice and slapped

her face again.

Her head flew back against the seat. She bit her lip to keep from crying out. Shaking her head, her face hot and smarting from the blow, she knew it mattered not what she said, he would hurt her anyway. He needed to. It was a bully's way to assuage his anger.

"Did you spread your legs for him?" He moved over her again, forcing her into an awkward angle, holding her immobile with his weight.

Katherine went cold at the realization that he did not just mean to hurt and scare her.

He meant to rape her.

To take from her that which she had been afraid to give Nicholas.

For a moment, she feared she might faint. Struggling to keep her wits, she shook her head and fought Finch with new urgency. With a vicious rip, he tore her satin neckline.

Her heart hammered crazily. She could scarcely breathe. Panic overwhelmed her. She must get out of the coach. Even if she hurt herself or died in the trying. She could not allow him to do this thing to her.

"Do you carry his brat?" he sneered, prodding her stomach with a long finger.

Katherine reacted like a wild thing. She bucked, and jerked, and her knee came up hard between his legs. He groaned and released her wrists. Pushing him away, she pitched herself headlong toward the door, but he grabbed her braid and pulled her back. She smothered a scream. The pain only added to her sense of urgency. She kicked at him savagely while reaching for the door latch.

Then, suddenly, the coach lurched to a halt. They tumbled together onto the floor, Katherine sprawled on top.

"Stand and deliver!"

Nicholas!

Over the pounding of her heart and the heaviness of her breathing, she recognized his voice with a rush of pure joy. She scrambled onto one of the padded seats, but so did Finch. He grabbed her and put his hand over her mouth.

"Do not say a word," he ordered.

She tried to bite his fingers, but he held her tight. Pushing her into the seat back, he levered his knee against her belly, then pounded on the wall of the coach with his free hand. "Drive on!" he yelled to Jakes.

Katherine pushed at him as the door flew open. Finch turned as a long arm reached inside and pointed the muzzle of a gun at his chest.

"Out," Nicholas commanded.

"I will not," Finch asserted. He knocked on the wall of the coach again. "Drive on!" he ordered once more. But the coach did not move.

"Your driver is incapacitated. I can tell you with great assurance that you will not be going anywhere anytime soon." Nicholas made a grim chuckle.

Katherine wriggled with renewed energy and managed to twist her mouth away from Finch's grasp. "Nicholas!" she cried.

The coach lurched as a black hooded figure appeared in the doorway, gun still pointed at Finch's heart. An elegant forefinger cocked the trigger. The chilling sound filled the small space.

"Let go of her," Nicholas ordered.

Finch released her wrists and raised himself off her. Katherine scrambled to Nicholas. The gun did not waver as he helped her up and swung her to the ground.

Katherine shivered. Raindrops fell onto her face and the exposed skin of her breast. She raised a limp hand to hold the pieces of her torn bodice together. A weakness ran through her; her hands shook. She drew a deep steadying breath of the chill air.

The coach had stopped at the bottom of a rise. Henry stood to the side of the vehicle, his blunderbuss aimed at Jakes.

Finch emerged from the coach with obvious reluctance. His wig askew, it lent a comical note to his usually fastidious appearance.

A hysterical giggle rose from Katherine's belly, and she covered her mouth with a shaking hand to prevent its escape. Big raindrops now splashed her face, as if to wash away her giddiness.

Nicholas removed his cowl. "We've a score to settle."

Finch looked from Katherine to Nicholas and back to Katherine again. "It's not just the boy, is it?" he said to her, sourly. "You are a highwayman's slut as well." He turned to Nicholas. "Who are you really, *Nicholas Raven*?"

"Someone who wishes you ill."

Nicholas handed Katherine the pistol. She took it with her free hand, wrist sagging under the weight of the heavy weapon. Raising it unsteadily, she pointed it at Finch.

"Do you know how to use it?" queried Nicholas.

She turned to him and shook her head.

He pushed the barrel back toward Finch. "Then be sure you are pointing it at him at all times, and never at me. Put your finger here," he repositioned the gun in her hand, "but do not pull back unless you mean to shoot, and if you do, intend to kill."

Finch blanched as the pistol wavered unsteadily in his direction. "I have no wish to fight," he said, and folded his arms across his chest.

"Then you will take a severe pounding," Nicholas replied. "It matters naught to me whether you defend yourself."

"The girl and I are to be wed. It is agreed. She can be nothing to you," Finch asserted.

Nicholas turned to Katherine, his face registering mock surprise. "Do you wish to wed this man?"

"No!" Her voice rang loudly into the night.

Nicholas faced Finch. "Then prepare to fight." He stood like a warrior, feet planted wide, hands on hips.

"Come, sir," Finch said. "I do not wish to quarrel with you."

"But I wish to quarrel with you. I do not care for the way you treat your bride." Nicholas's face drew into harsh lines. "And I do not care for the way you tie your cravat. You will fight me, whether you wish it or no."

In a fair fight, Finch would not stand a chance against Nicholas, but Katherine did not trust Finch one bit. She tightened her grip on the firearm and kept it trained on him.

Even under the dark, cloud-laden sky, Katherine could see Finch's eyes narrow as he studied Nicholas. "You are familiar to me," he said. "Yet I know not from whence."

"You will know me better after tonight," Nicholas said. "But you will not be happy with the knowledge."

With a shaking hand, Finch wiped at the raindrops landing on his face. He looked away and stood for a long moment, motionless except for the subtle movement of his jaw clenching and unclenching. Then he removed his periwig and made a great show of laying it inside the coach. His cravat followed, and his waistcoat. Suddenly, in one motion, he turned and lunged.

Katherine gasped as Nicholas stepped to the side. Finch fell past him to the ground, but was on his feet again in seconds. Katherine saw him pick up a jagged rock as he rose.

"Nicholas," she yelled in warning. "Look out!"

At her call, Nicholas hesitated. Katherine watched in horror as Finch connected. Blood streamed from a gash just above Nicholas's right eye.

Katherine shook in anger and frustration. She raised the gun, willing Finch to stand before it, but Nicholas stumbled into her view, so she let the heavy firearm drop, afraid she might shoot the wrong man.

Nicholas swung wild, missing Finch completely. Blood ran down his face.

Finch seemed to feel he had the upper hand. Fists raised, he swung at Nicholas's belly, but Nicholas intercepted Finch's thrust before it made impact.

Finch reeled back, his feet momentarily losing hold on the mucky ground. "Why?" he grunted.

"Someone needs to teach you a lesson," said Nicholas, landing a blow to Finch's jaw.

Finch's head snapped back but he recovered quickly. He feinted with his left then landed a well-placed jab on Nicholas's wounded shoulder with his right. The impact sent Nicholas back a couple steps. He gasped in pain.

"I owe you this for our previous encounter," Nicholas made a wild punch, missing Finch completely. "And this," his other fist slammed into Finch's nose.

He crumpled under the force of the blow.

Nicholas rubbed his knuckles. "That," he said, chest heaving from exertion, "was for Mistress Welles."

Finch held his broken beak between his hands. Blood ran through his fingers, down his arms.

Nicholas faced him. "The fight is over," he said with a grim chuckle. "You will stand over there," he pointed at a spot away from the coach. "And you," he waved at Jakes.

The rain had all but stopped now. Katherine's arm ached from holding the heavy firearm. She gratefully handed it to Nicholas. Close-up, the cut above his eye did not look so bad. She raised a shaking finger to trace the trail of blood on his cheek. If she had not known him, he would be menacing indeed. But standing next to her, breathing heavily, emanating his own particular scent, his presence was warm and reassuring. Katherine wanted to wrap herself up in it, away from the cold rain and bad experiences of this night.

Nicholas waved the gun at the two men. "Remove your clothes," he said to them, "and hand them to my partner." To Katherine he said, "Get inside the coach."

Katherine shook her head. She could not face the inside of that coach just yet.

"I cannot," she said a quaver in her voice. She looked around for an acceptable alternative. A whinny announced the presence of the horses. "I will stand over there," she said.

Nicholas nodded.

Some of Katherine's hair had come out of her braid. As she walked, she unraveled what remained of the plait, spreading her hair over her chest, like a shawl to hide her nakedness.

The horses stood beside a group of trees. In the murky darkness, it was a moment before she saw the basket tied to a saddle. "Montford," she cried. Untying the carrier, she took it into her arms.

Tears fell onto her hands, and she realized she was crying again. She had cried more in the last day than in all the months since Edward had died. Pulling the sleepy cat from inside the basket, she held her tightly. Montford purred in a warm vibration.

As her tears continued to flow, Katherine began to shake. Her teeth started to chatter, and she felt dizzy. Her stomach turned. She tried to call for Nicholas. She needed to tell him about Jeremy, that they must go back and get him, but her voice remained wedged solidly in her throat. She heard a loud rushing in her ears. The ground came up and then the earth blurred and tilted sideways.

As the moon broke through the clouds, heralding the end of the downpour, Nicholas watched Finch and Jakes fumble with their clothing. He enjoyed their clumsiness and embarrassment, knowing it was nothing compared to the humiliation they would feel when they were discovered.

Henry had come up to him, and now stood with his back to the men.

"Do you know the punishment in Algiers for rape?" Nicholas queried his friend idly, aiming his pistol at Finch.

"I do not, Nicky."

"Castration."

Finch's fingers lost their hold on his cravat.

"You're not in Algiers anymore, Nicky."

"Pity…" Nicholas's voice trailed off.

Henry cleared his throat. "Where do you think the boy is?" he asked.

Nicholas shook his head. "I had forgotten about the lad."

"I can not imagine he would let his mistress come to any harm if he could prevent it," Henry reasoned. "He would not have left her, I know it. Something is amiss."

Nicholas scowled. "No he would not." He turned to the two men. "Where is the boy?"

Neither answered.

"I am sure we will find out soon enough," Nicholas muttered.

An uneasy silence fell upon the group. The men continued to

disrobe. Finally, they stood naked. Even in the moonlight Nicholas could see Finch's nose turning an angry purple. Jakes stood awkwardly, his hands covering his privates. Henry walked over to the two men and leveled his gun at Jakes. "Where is Jeremy?"

Jakes drew his lips together in a hard line.

Henry lowered his weapon so that it pointed at Jakes' groin. "I'll only ask you one more time," he said calmly as he cocked the trigger.

Jakes' mouth fell open. "Back in Marlborough, he be. At a tavern called *The Goose*, I think. We left him there."

A wicked gleam lit Finch's eyes. "We did indeed, after finding them kissing," he hissed out the last word.

Katherine. A flash of hot jealousy ran through Nicholas. He looked back in the direction she had gone.

At first, he could not see her, but then a glint of moonlight reflected off the satin of her clothing, showing she lay upon the ground.

He left Henry with his blunderbuss still trained on the two men and hastened to Katherine's side. She had swooned. Her skin was the color of new plaster and felt cold to his touch. Her breathing was shallow. Montford had curled up in the blanket of her hair. Nicholas scooped the cat into the basket, then pulled Katherine into his arms, and carried them back to where Henry stood.

"Hurry man, let us be gone. Send off our horses. These two as well," he nodded toward Finch and Jakes. "Quick!"

While Henry ordered the men off with his gun then shooed the horses in the opposite direction, Nicholas laid Katherine on a seat inside the coach. Kneeling on the floorboards, he brushed his fingers across her clammy forehead.

She lay so still.

Too still.

He needed to get her to safety and warmth. A roaring fire would thaw the ice that filled her veins. But he couldn't bring an unconscious woman to an inn without drawing unwanted attention. And though he'd gained the advantage with Finch for now, he must do his best not to leave a trail to lead the man back to them. Where could he bring an unconscious woman with little remark?

Nicholas scowled and ran his fingers between her cold limp ones. Drawing them to his lips, he tried to blow some warmth into them.

Then an idea presented itself. Nicholas blessed his good fortune at running into his friends that afternoon. It would be perfect. With all eyes on the King, who would notice them?

He cast open the door as the coach swayed while Henry took the drivers seat. "Lydney Hall," he called to his friend. "I believe 'tis not far from here. If we come back part of the way we came, 'twill be quite visible to the right."

CHAPTER TWELVE

Lydney Hall stood in silent grandeur at the top of a gentle rise. Under the moody midnight sky, Nicholas recognized the silhouette of hipped roof, dormer windows, crowning balustrade and cupola. Tall chimney stacks bespoke warmth inside.

His goal now in sight, Nicholas considered the danger to himself. Lydney Hall would keep Katherine from peril, but bring him close to it. Once awake and among his acquaintances, she could discover the truth about him. Armed with the knowledge of his deceit, she could expose him as the Raven.

And he would not blame her if she did.

He braced himself and Katherine as the carriage careened up the tree bordered drive, slowing only as it gained the circle before the great house. He pulled the unconscious woman into his arms and kicked open the door.

"What about the boy?" Henry yelled from the coachman's seat.

Nicholas paused but a moment to nod up to Henry. "Find him," he barked.

Henry nodded. With a shouted command to the horses, the coach was off, sending a spray of dirty water in its wake.

Nicholas forded a mud puddle and mounted the marble steps in a few long strides. A butler opened the heavy door.

"M'lord." He bowed as if it were an everyday affair for a nobleman to arrive with an unconscious woman in his arms.

Nicholas gave the servant his best withering stare. "Tell your master, the Earl of Ashton has arrived," he said and strode into the entry hall, ignoring the man's offer to deliver him to his host.

Distant chatter and sounds of gaiety came from the right. He stood for a moment trying to remember the arrangement of rooms in the vast residence he had only visited once before.

Of recent construction, Lydney Hall provided a modicum of privacy to its residents unheard of in older homes, such as Ashfield. Rooms opened off corridors, not off each other. A central staircase led to the first floor gallery. At least he remembered the bedroom suites were upstairs. Taking the steps two at a time, he paused a moment on the upper landing.

Was everyone downstairs enjoying the festivities? Talbot would be busy regaling his guests and no doubt partaking of the pleasures brought from London. Had the King arrived? Nicholas shook off the sense of dread he felt at walking straight in to the lion's den. With a bit of luck, he should be quite safe here while the revelers debauched downstairs.

Closed doors ran down the hallway. There should be several empty bedrooms. He just had to find one that no one would wish to use until he was well done with it.

Nicholas put his ear against a door and listened. There were no telltale sounds coming from inside. If he opened the door, would he discover a couple in the throws of lovemaking?

He would just have to take his chances.

Cracking open the door, he cautiously peered within. It was dark and no one called out for him to close it. He shouldered the door open and went inside. It was empty. At least for now, they would be alone.

Kicking the door closed, he crossed to the hearth. Laying Katherine on the woolen rug, he stoked the embers until he had excited a cheery roar.

In the light of the fire, she seemed less wan. Golden lights danced in her hair. Pink slowly returned to her cheeks, yet she did not stir. Her bodice lay open where it had ripped, exposing a perfect pale breast, topped by a rosy nipple. He longed to touch it and had the sudden thought that he might return her to consciousness by doing so.

But that would not do.

Instead, he found a crock of water beside the tester bed. Kneeling beside her, he splashed her face with droplets of the cold liquid. She stirred and her eyelids blinked open.

Nicholas let out a great sigh. Relief washed over him as her eyes focused on his. A gentle smile played across her mouth. He reached for her hand and brought it to his lips.

"Where am I?" she said, her voice throaty.

"Safe."

This seemed to satisfy her. She closed her eyes. Swallowing with apparent difficulty, she shifted, exposing her other breast to his view. Scratches ran along her tender flesh. A hot flash of anger ran through Nicholas. He had not made Finch pay enough by half for the damage done, nor was he sure of the extent of the fiend's violation.

Drawing her up, supporting her back with one arm, he held the water jug to her lips. She opened her eyes and sipped. A large drop escaped, making a sensuous journey, first slipping down her chin, then over the crest to slide down the smooth plane of her neck. There it hovered a brief moment, gathering itself together before surmounting her collarbone. Finally, it crept bit by bit down the valley between her breasts to disappear into the remnants of her tattered clothing.

Katherine reached a weak hand to trace the path of the moisture, and flinched. Grabbing at the pieces of her bodice, she tried to hold it together, sitting up at the same time. Averting her face to the fire, she held her lower lip between her teeth in the way she did when troubled.

A hand gripped at Nicholas's heart. Even though it was Finch who had hurt her, it was no less Nicholas's own fault. He had helped her run from Finch, but instead of aiding and protecting her, Nicholas had frightened her, forcing her to flee again. Berating himself for his callous behavior, he resolved to treat her as a sister from now on.

"I am just now remembering," she said, her voice low and rough.

"I am very sorry," he said, and brushed an errant hair back from her face, tucking it behind her ear. His fingers seemed too big for the simple task. "'Twould be best to forget."

A great shudder ran through her. "He was very angry. He wanted to hurt me." She spoke to the fire, not to him.

Wanted. A sudden jolt of happiness pierced through Nicholas. Finch had not ravished her then. "Ah, lass," he spoke into her ear, "he is a bad one to be sure. You are safe now. 'Tis best not to dwell on't."

Even as the fire roared, she shivered. Then her shivers turned to sobs. Nicholas put a clumsy hand on her shoulder. Why was it he felt so comfortable evoking passion in a woman but so awkward giving solace?

She turned to him and threw her arms around his neck. He held her close as shudders wracked her small frame, and she clung to him with fierce desperation. Her bare breasts pressed against his chest through his linen shirt, awakening a physical need so strong he almost groaned aloud. He cursed inwardly and shifted to relieve the tightness in his breeches, while searching for chaste thoughts to fill his mind.

Katherine's sobs eased, and she quieted. "I would die rather than marry him." Raising a shaky hand, she looked into his eyes. Delicate fingers trailed along the stubble on his cheek.

Nicholas pulled back, fearing she could see the lust in his heart. But he could not look away. Her eyes glistened. Her lips parted, and she ran her tongue slowly over her bottom lip.

Katherine dragged her hands down his chest and grasped his shirt. "I would rather kiss you than anything else," she said, her voice almost a whisper.

Nicholas's good intentions melted away as she brought her lips to his.

It was a kiss of wild despair, a kiss of need. Artless. Passionate. What it lacked in artifice it more than made up for with intensity. His arms tightened around her, and he crushed her to him. The fire beside them sparked. Fever ran through his veins. He ran a hand over her curves as she clung to him.

A voice in his head said he should hold back, what had happened with Finch had muddled her senses, she could not know what she was doing and if he had any sense of honor, he would tell her. She was not some trollop he found in an inn, or an experienced lady at court who knew the game of love, but a simple country girl, grateful for her rescue. He'd taken her from her home, promised her safety but given her none. He'd teased her, taunted her, and tormented her with kisses; given her the first taste of arousal. He was a scoundrel and a knave.

And he'd just decided to treat her as a sister.

Nicholas sucked in a deep breath, hoping it would moderate his pounding heart and throbbing loins. "I am no hero."

Her breath caught. She went still in his arms, looking up at him in surprise.

"I know you are grateful," he said. "But it is not necessary to express it in this fashion."

"I do feel gratitude, but I do not kiss you for it." Katherine traced a finger along his ear, sending tender sensations all through him. Her eyes focused on the fastenings of his linen shirt. "I kiss you because it pleases me." Her fingers trailed down from his ear to run feather-light over his lips and down his shirt to the fabric tie at the neck. "I should not have run away." A light smile played upon her lips. "I was afraid of your kisses." She tugged the knot apart exposing his chest, and put her hand inside his open shirt, onto his hot bare skin, settling over his heart.

The air sizzled between them. Nicholas's chest burned where her hand rested. His heart throbbed almost painfully, as did his loins. He let out a long breath.

"I am not afraid anymore." She looked into his eyes and smiled an innocent seductive smile that made his heart twist.

"Ah, lass, do you have any idea what you do to me?"

"I think it must be very like what you do to me." She leaned forward, raising her lips to his. "Please do it some more."

Nicholas groaned. He was a knave to be sure. She needed comfort, but she asked for passion. So he would give it to her.

He lowered his mouth until it met hers.

Heat ran through Katherine as Nicholas's lips played with hers, alternately soft and demanding. Never had she wanted anything as much as she wanted to be with him, just like this.

She marveled at his many textures. The smooth firm muscles of his shoulders, the hard tendons in his neck, the softness of his lips and tongue, the roughness of his shirt as it brushed her tender nipples.

It seemed each moment since she first came upon him, had inevitably led to this one, this moment that would change the course of her life forever.

He buried his hands in her hair. She gasped as his lips left hers to trail over her chin and down her throat. Each tantalizing movement of his mouth sent shivers of heat surging through her.

Easing her from his lap to the floor, he settled beside her. His hair brushed across the tender skin of her breasts as his tongue traced the line of her collarbone, not tickling exactly but sending delicious thrills over her sensitive skin—thrills that grew as his mouth moved to cover her nipple. Her breath caught as he suckled on one breast while caressing the other. Her breasts thrust forward, aching, needing, seeking more. Little moaning sounds rose from her throat as waves of pleasure ran through her.

His mouth came up to hers. His teeth grazed her upper lip. He suckled on it as he drew up her skirt. Inch by agonizing inch, the hem rose, passing her ankles, her calves, and then her knees. The kiss deepened, became more urgent.

She felt the shock as his fingers touched the bare skin behind her knee and moved up the delicate skin inside her thighs. They slid under the satin fabric, moving in a slow torture until they reached the apex of her legs, touching her through the flimsy material of her drawers, in a place she'd never been touched before.

Katherine clamped her legs together.

"Do you wish me to stop?" Nicholas's voice was thick and rough. He took his hand away.

Katherine let out her breath in a shudder, trying to ease the tension building inside her. She wanted him to continue, more than she had ever wanted anything.

She shook her head, and eased her thighs apart.

Nicholas put a hand on her knee and spoke, the words almost too loud after the music of their breathing. "A woman may feel pain the first time she joins with a man. I am sorry for it, and I will do my best not to hurt you."

Katherine swallowed. "I trust you."

Nicholas stroked her thigh and gave her an odd smile. "Do you now?"

He reached for her hips, and drew her to his body. The hardness at his groin pressed against her most sensitive place. His breeches did little to disguise its size and nature.

Could he possibly fit inside her? It probably *would* hurt. She frowned.

"You are sure, lass?"

Feeling shy, then bold, she hovered for a moment in indecision until the boldness won out. Katherine smiled. She would not run away this time.

Reaching up, she ran her fingers through the white streak in his hair, and then moved onto her side, facing him. She ran a stocking clad foot along his leg.

Nicholas groaned. His hand trailed up her thigh, to her waist. He untied her drawers, easing them down her hips, and bringing his hand to brush against the curls at her most intimate place.

Katherine's breath caught.

He kissed her, lightly at first. As his tongue slipped into her mouth, his finger slid inside her.

She arched up against his hand, opening her legs to him, wider, wider. As he moved his finger in and out, slowly at first then faster, she moved with him. Her body burned in unspeakable places. A strange moaning rent the air. It was a moment before Katherine realized she was making the noise, like the woman at the inn.

The most pleasant thing a man and woman can do together.

And it was true. Pleasure she had never imagined rolled over her and built. She gasped and moaned, clutching at his arms, and his shoulders.

He moved her onto her back. Her breath caught as she felt his finger leave. He pulled her skirt up to her waist, removed her drawers, and moved his body between her legs. Loosening the laces of his breeches. His man's part sprang free. Thick and full, he took the length in his hand, and positioned it where his finger had been.

Katherine held her breath as he pushed into the slick tight opening of her woman's place, until she was stretched to a point beyond comfort. She looked to see his face screwed up in fierce concentration.

"Nicholas?" she gasped.

"Hmmm?" he groaned.

"You *are* hurting me."

He stilled, bracing himself on his arms above her. "Do you wish me to stop?"

She saw regret in his eyes, but acceptance as well.

She shook her head. "No. I cannot but wonder, though, how much more could fit without tearing me apart."

His eyes twinkled. "You will be amazed at what a good fit we will make, though there will be some pain when I break your maidenhead." He went down on one arm, rolling her onto her side facing him, and started to play with her nipple, rubbing and tantalizing it into a hard pebble.

Katherine sucked in her breath and moaned as the tightness eased.

"There is naught to be done about it, lass." Nicholas spoke into her ear. His breath, hot and sensual, sent chills through her.

Her muscles clutched his long male length, and then relaxed.

He exhaled a hot breath against the side of her neck and pushed into her, the penetration deepening, feeling strange but not uncomfortable.

"The pain will not last." He kneaded her breast, teasing the nipple with his thumb, then ran his hand down her hip to her buttocks, holding her tight as he pressed into her. "I promise." His voice was a husky whisper across her lips.

He kissed her. His tongue teased until she forgot everything but the feel of it as it danced with hers and the feel of his lips as they played upon hers with increasing urgency. His hand massaged her bottom and she felt herself stretch to accept him as he pushed deeper and deeper inside. She felt hopelessly full of him, yet a strange tension began to build where they joined, and she wiggled to ease it, a movement that allowed even more of him entry. Katherine moaned her pleasure, clutching at him, arching against the throbbing torment.

He moved her onto her back, holding his weight up on two arms. She could feel his strength restrained, hovering above her. Their eyes met as he pressed forward, stretching her to a point well beyond comfort.

Suddenly he thrust into her. Deep. Hard.

Katherine felt as if she were torn apart. She tried to hold in her cry, but could not. "No! It cannot be like this, there is no pleasure for me. You are too big. We do not fit."

"Just this time, for this short while." He grunted between clenched teeth, holding himself in place as she squirmed against him. He groaned.

She whimpered, but the pain was easing. Balancing on one arm, he reached between them and began to stroke and tease her most sensitive place, until she was slick and hot, and burning with need. Pleasure radiated to her fingers and her toes. As he began again to move his man's part in and out of her, her muscles relaxed against his invasion. Tension coiled up inside her. She tightened her legs around him.

"That's right," he said. His hair fell about her. He moved his mouth over hers again.

She tasted coffee as his tongue pleasured hers. His smell filled her senses. His body rocked hers in an even rhythm, and an almost intolerable pleasure built within her. As he moved, she held him tight, mindless to anything but the extraordinary sensation growing within.

"Yes, lass," Nicholas whispered in her ear. "Yes."

His warm breath and the velvet timbre of his voice combined with the pressure building inside her. She tugged at his shirt until she had exposed his naked chest to her tender breasts. He lowered himself onto her and grasped her buttocks, pulling her to him until he was deep inside.

They moved together in a union of heated need and longing. He thrusted into her until she could bear it no longer. She writhed against him, crying out his name. As fierce pleasure pierced through her, she came undone. Nicholas held her as she whimpered her release.

Awareness came back slowly. Nicholas lay beside her, his man's part still big and hard inside her. Her body ached and throbbed. Nicholas pressed gentle kisses along her brow.

She swallowed, and looked away, embarrassed. "Did it feel this good for you?" she asked.

"Not yet."

"Yet?"

He nodded.

"There is more?"

Nicholas grinned. "Now it is my turn." He rolled her onto her back again, and rose up above her. With almost painful slowness the full length of him filled her. Then he withdrew, leaving her empty.

She slid her hands along his back, the muscles hot and slick with sweat. Her arms traveled over his shoulders and the puckered scab from his bullet wound, and then down arms that rose like columns to each side of her, veins distended from the effort of holding his body aloft.

His face drew into intense concentration.

She wrapped her hands around his wrists, holding on as he thrust into her, deep and hard. The feeling of pressure, of being a tightly wound spring grew, replacing her lethargy. She thrust up to meet him. Just as she felt herself begin to shatter once more, he let out a groan. His face contorted as if in great pain. He jerked, as spasms ran through him, all the way to his man's part.

Understanding flitted through her mind. It was not pain as she had ever known it, but the wrenching ecstasy of the deepest pleasure. Then their cries joined together, her completion all the sweeter this time for sharing his.

❧

They lay together, her back to his front, faces to the fire, like two pieces of a puzzle. In spite of their difference in size, it was a perfect fit. Nicholas wished they could lie thus forever, basking in the afterglow, bodies sated, languid.

But his mind, filled with self-loathing and self-recrimination, would not let him fully enjoy the moment. In an endless chant it intoned: *what have I done?*

If his other crimes against the lass had not been enough, by taking her maidenhead he had ruined her. And he now had no leverage over her father, since he could no longer return her intact. And, in dishonoring her, he had dishonored the pledge he'd made to his father.

Voices in the hallway abruptly penetrated his thoughts. He heard the low rumble of a man's voice accompanied by the higher pitch of woman's laughter. Would they try to enter this room? He tensed, arms tightening around Katherine, aware that discovery would not only expose his identity but compromise her as well. Then a door down the hallway opened and closed and all was quiet again.

Katherine turned in his arms, lips pursed, a frown marring her lovely forehead. "What of Jeremy?"

"Ah, my wanton, now you remember your friend," Nicholas could not keep himself from teasing, then at the look of utter consternation that swept her brow, he added hastily, "Henry has gone to get him."

"Montford?"

"I must have left her in the coach. Henry will bring her back."

"Tis remiss of me to forget them," Katherine shook her head. "I have paid attention to naught but you." She looked around the large room, taking in the stately bed at one end, and a roaring fire before them. There were several nice pieces of furniture. "Are we at an inn? It does not look like one. I had not thought to ask."

"No," he replied, brushing a thumb over her brow. "'Tis the estate of an acquaintance. Perhaps you can see some of it in the morning," *when the other guests are all sleeping.* "'Tis safe here, to be sure." *For you.*

He massaged her neck and the back of her shoulders and she dozed off. Time stretched on with only an occasional pop from the fire. It would have been perfect were it not for the troubling thoughts that kept him awake, bubbling up as if from some witch's cauldron in his mind. Or perhaps it was the embers of a conscience finally sparked into existence.

No doubt Henry would think so.

Katherine stirred. Montford had joined her sometime during the night and lay on her chest, purring. Katherine hung for a bit in that delicious between-place, not asleep or awake; a languid sensual creature enjoying the comfort of a good feather bed, the warmth of a down coverlet, the lingering smell of a man.

Nicholas.

The sudden vivid recollection of the night brought a flash of heat surging from the ends of her toes to the very roots of her hair. All at once, she realized she lay naked. And alone.

Flooded with equal parts of relief and dismay, Katherine opened her eyes to take greater stock of her surroundings. Last night she had paid them little mind.

Katherine sat up. Throwing Montford off her chest and hugging the coverlet, she peered through the dimness at the large bedroom. A chest sat along the opposite wall. Dying embers of a fire burned in the large fireplace.

The ruins of her clothing lay discarded on the floor. At some point during the night—she could hardly remember when—Nicholas had divested the remnants of her clothes and helped her onto the lush mattress. She'd sunk into a deep sleep, so deep she had not heard him leave. Nor heard Montford and her satchels arrive.

Katherine slid from the bed. She padded cross the soft wool rug to the draped window. Tugging back a corner of the dark velvet, she peered through the glass. The sun beamed brightly on the outside tableaux. Any vestiges of the night's rain had burned off.

A well-groomed garden stretched out in a long vista. Here and there a gardener stooped, a spot of brown against the variegated greens. At the end of a long row of topiary chess pieces, sat a large fountain. Water cascaded in ribbons from what looked like a giant sea creature, maybe a dolphin such as she had read about.

Suddenly aware she was naked, Katherine stepped away from the glass.

She donned her shift. The clothing Nicholas had given her was ruined, so she dug the horrid black dress out of her bag, put it on, and finger-combed her hair. With no pins or cap it hung loose to her waist, undoubtedly making her look like a young girl.

The thought brought her up short. Heat flooded through her. She was a woman now. A tenderness between her legs and traces of blood on her thighs testified to her loss of childhood. A smile played upon her lips. Would any part of her be the same? Somehow she doubted that.

Montford started scratching at the floor.

"No puss, not here."

Katherine pulled her shoes on over her stockings. She grabbed up the kitten and walked to the door. Taking a deep breath, not knowing what she would find on the other side of this portal, but knowing she had no choice but to find out, she opened the door.

An empty hallway greeted her.

Katherine exhaled with relief. Giving Montford a pat and cradling her to her chest, Katherine started down the hall toward what appeared to be a staircase landing.

All of a sudden, Montford growled, stuck her claws into Katherine's chest and jumped atop a tall cabinet. At the same time, Katherine heard the riotous sounds of dogs barking. The commotion got louder and then they were there—six spaniels running and jumping. A tall man who looked a bit like Nicholas followed them. She had a quick impression of a dark complexion lightened by sparkling eyes, and plentiful shining black hair that curled into great rings. He looked at her with perhaps as much surprise and stupefaction as she looked at him.

And then Montford vaulted over them all and shot down the stairs. Katherine tore after her, with the barking spaniels and the unfortunate man behind.

CHAPTER THIRTEEN

Nicholas hunted a maze of corridors, peering into chamber after chamber, each devoted to some trifling domestic activity. Startled servants made a hasty bow or curtsy as he passed. Finally, he found Katherine in what he guessed, from the drying plants that hung from the ceiling, was the stillroom.

He stood in the doorway, an observer unobserved. Jeremy lay on a pallet stretched before a fire with Katherine beside him, his hand clasped between hers. A hot flair of jealousy ripped through Nicholas but he stayed quiet, unwilling for them to notice him until he had his emotions under control.

Katherine's face was away from him. He wanted to see her expression, especially her mouth. Would it look soft and well kissed from last night, or would she be nibbling her lower lip in that adorable way of hers?

The conspiratorial hush of their voices disturbed him. What could they be saying to each other?

In the dim light of morning, he'd risen in haste, urgently aware of the need to be on the road before the household awoke. He'd been gone but a few moments to bid Henry prepare their departure and returned to an empty room. His heart had plunged clear to the bottom of his boots, and his first thought had been she'd run off again. But then he'd seen her bundles and been reassured on the one hand. On the other hand, what he'd heard from a servant had not been reassuring.

The man told him of the Puritan and her cat who had been run off by the King and his spaniels.

The vision this conjured in his mind should have been quite comical, yet this morning he could not even smile at it. All he could think was he'd missed detection by a hair's breadth. Running into the King would be disastrous, putting him in the awkward position of having to beg Charles's forgiveness and explain his absence now, instead of later in London after he had come up with a good story. Nor did he want to think of Katherine discovering his duplicity.

Nicholas took a deep breath and let it out. Suppose they did get away undetected, and then to London...what was he to do with her? Would she be safe from Finch at this cousin's home?

And why did he not want to think of sending her off at all?

Nicholas made an impatient shrug. What good would it do to think ahead? Experience had taught him to focus on the present, to seize the opportunity each moment brought. Right now he needed to get Katherine away from Lydney Hall.

He cleared his throat and stepped into the room. "'Tis a most charming reunion but it must conclude. We must be off, Katherine."

Katherine and Jeremy looked at him in surprise. A flush ran across Katherine's face before she turned away. The black dress covered her trim figure, disguising it. Perhaps it was not such a bad garment after all.

Her hair hung straight down. Still tousled from sleep it made her appear very young. But when she turned back, he saw the determination on her brow and the stern brilliance of her eyes. This was the Katherine he knew.

"But Nicholas," she protested. "Jeremy cannot travel until he is healed."

"Then he must stay." Nicholas said. "Henry will bring him along when he is well. You and I must hasten before Finch would find us."

Katherine bit her lower lip.

He had not meant to frighten the lass, merely set her to moving, so he tempered his next words. "After the events of last night, I think he will look the more."

This time Katherine blushed, and he realized she had mistaken his meaning. "He will be looking for both of us now."

Jeremy looked from one to the other. "I am able to travel," he said, but he grimaced when he attempted to sit up. His left eye was black and blue, and his upper lip puffed out. A length of linen bound his chest, no doubt Katherine's work. In truth, he looked awful.

"'Tis clear the boy cannot sit."

"In a coach, with pillows to cushion the ride, he will be all right," said Katherine.

Nicholas met her fierce protective gaze, and knew it was this quality in Katherine that had saved his life. During his years in the East, he had come to understand the barbaric nature of English medical treatments. Had he been subjected to bleeding, clysters, purging and the like, he easily could have died. He owed his life not only to her conscientious treatment, but to her good sense as well.

Did the boy need her healing magic? Suppose Nicholas took her away, and Jeremy worsened?

A coach *would* speed up the journey. Once on main roads they could even reach London by nightfall.

"Aright, lass. You have convinced me. I will arrange for a driver and have Henry prepare the coach, for it will need a bit of black paint on the doors to hide the crest. Then we will be on our way." Nicholas approached Katherine and held his hand out to her.

Katherine gave him a brilliant smile, and slid her hand into his. Reassuring warmth banished the last threads of jealousy and irritation, and Nicholas smiled back. He tightened his grasp and helped her rise, not relinquishing her hand once she was up.

"There is a pretty garden I saw from a window," she said. "I would very much like to see it before we leave. And Montford requires a visit out of doors as well."

As much as he wished it, he could not forbid her to go. It was unlikely she would run into anyone but gardeners outside at this hour. Still, one could never be sure. "Do not speak to strangers," Nicholas admonished giving her fingers a last squeeze before letting go. "I will join you there in a moment."

Katherine nodded and watched him leave. After her encounter with Finch, she appreciated Nicholas's protective attitude more than she had before. She plucked Montford off Jeremy's lap, bid her friend rest until it was time to leave, and exited through a side door.

As she explored the gardens, the crisp morning air caressed her skin, banishing the heat of the stillroom. Sunlight played upon the dew, turning the droplets to diamonds scattered on a field of grass.

Montford stalked a butterfly.

A gardener, trimming an already neatly manicured hedge, tipped his hat to her as she walked by.

Thoughts of danger seemed out of place in such well-tended surroundings. However unlikely it was that Finch would jump out at her from behind a perfectly pruned tree, it was nerve-wracking to think he could be nearby. Prickles ran along the back of her neck as she sensed someone watching her. Katherine glanced about. A flicker of something moved inside a second story window. A mild rush of alarm ran through her.

What had become of Finch and Jakes? Had they managed to get a ride from a passing carriage? Had they found shelter and clothing nearby, or were they now running naked about the countryside, hiding from every rider and coach that passed them? A giggle rose in her throat.

She arrived at the magnificent fountain. The sound of falling water helped soothe her mind and ease her anxiety. Small orange fish flitted through the water. And there, reflected on the surface of the pool, was a Katherine she'd not seen before. The undulating ripples of water lent her a fluid, dreamy look. She appeared softer, even pretty. Katherine smiled at her likeness and it smiled back.

Montford rubbed against her ankles.

Katherine picked up the kitten and placed her on the rim of

the pool where she hunched down and watched the fish, her tail switching back and forth. Finally, as a fish swam too close to the surface, Montford plunged a paw into the water and jumped back shaking it off. Clearly mortified, she commenced cleaning.

Katherine laughed.

A hand clutched her shoulder from behind.

She screamed and whirled around, arms raised to ward off her attacker.

And all at once, she fell into Nicholas's strong embrace.

"Whoa, Katherine," he said, his low resonant voice easing her panic and coming to rest inside her heart.

She threw her arms around his neck and held him tight, her head nuzzling his chest.

He rubbed her back in a comforting manner, but then his hand drifted lower and he pulled her to him. The fright that had coursed through her turned to excitement. Her breath caught as she turned her head up to meet lips that she knew by instinct would be searching for hers.

Their mouths met in a slow sensual joining, a dance of meeting and parting, then tongues together. Katherine lost awareness of all but Nicholas, his fire, his strength. He smelled of exotic spices and tasted like coffee. She melted into him, the ache of pleasure starting at her core.

As Nicholas pulled his lips away, Katherine moaned.

His hand eased from behind her head, moving across her cheek. His forefinger traced her lips in a reverent, tender, and utterly sensual caress.

"I did not mean to startle you. But if this is your response, perhaps I would do it again." His eyes twinkled.

Katherine grinned.

Nicholas trailed his finger down her neck to her shoulder.

"I did not hear you," she said. "I had been thinking about our need for haste. That made me jumpy."

"Ah, lass. We should be leaving and not lingering here, no matter how pleasant. By the time we have helped Jeremy to the coach, Henry will have it ready."

Katherine smiled and looked down just in time to see

Montford jump from the fountain and scamper across the grass, an orange tail sticking out of her mouth.

Getting Jeremy to the coach had been a slow painful journey, even though it was no great distance. Katherine had begun to think it was a mistake to insist he come along, but then Henry produced a small brown bottle of laudanum.

"Makes me very sick, it does, but should do just the thing for our friend," he said.

Jeremy complained at the bitter taste, but swallowed down a dose anyway.

Nicholas had arranged for the loan of four magnificent black horses and a driver. Even with the crest painted out, Katherine felt a rush of alarm when she got inside. But instead of Richard Finch, it was her friend Jeremy facing her on the other seat.

She helped him into a comfortable position across the bench, propped up on pillows. His gangly legs folded like a grasshopper's against the wall of the vehicle. She was surprised when Nicholas did not join them. Instead, he mounted a magnificent dark brown horse. Henry joined the driver in front after handing her the basket containing Montford.

Jeremy's mouth drew tight, and his pallor worsened the moment they got underway. She felt for him with every jolt of the coach as it bounced down the long drive, and prayed he would be sleeping soon.

Not long after joining the highway, Jeremy's breathing settled into a rhythmic pattern and his head nodded with the movement of the vehicle.

As the countryside swept past, Katherine gazed out the glass window. Each time she caught a glimpse of Nicholas her heart clutched.

London.

The word echoed in Katherine's head, filling her with a mix of elation and disappointment. *Then what?* They would part, of course. She to Cousin Alicia's. And Nicholas? He had said he had business to attend, also that his highwayman days were behind him. Would she see him again once they reached London?

A similar thought plagued Nicholas, riding alongside the coach. He had told Henry he would act as an outrider, but, in truth, he needed some distance from the lass and the turmoil she'd set him in.

Last night, Katherine had drifted into a sleep punctuated with the most delightful light snores, but he'd slept little. A strange restiveness had come over him. He had watched her by the light of the dying embers, enveloped in her lavender smell—and more: the earthy smell of coupling. An aphrodisiac. It had taken restraint to leave her be and not ply her with further lovemaking. She'd been through much that night, and her body, unaccustomed to a man, would surely feel sore in the morning.

He'd spent much of the night watching her and thinking; his sleepless mind would not allow his body the peace of passion's aftermath.

With the dawning light of the new day, he knew he'd likely failed his father. By taking Katherine's maidenhead, he'd lost any room he had to negotiate with her father. And though he could continue to petition the King, he'd raised his liege's ire and that did not bode well for a decision in his favor.

So why did he feel a strange freedom?

Could it be that released from the promise that had driven his actions and controlled the direction of his life, he might finally be his own man?

But who was that?

Nicholas the Raven?

Nicholas the privateer?

Nicholas the Seventh Earl of Ashton?

Or could it be a Nicholas he hadn't yet met? Perhaps a Nicholas who simply wanted the love of a good woman and the happiness of watching his children grow.

What an unsettling thought.

They broke their journey at Wokingham. Grateful to be out of the confines of the bouncing coach, Katherine breathed deep the crisp sunny air, while stretching muscles that ached from inactivity. They left Jeremy snoring and went in search of food.

It was market day. Stalls displayed goods from fancy ribbons and root vegetables, to baked items. Nicholas bought her a slice of woodcock pie and some cider. They stood in companionable silence, eating the good food and enjoying the sights and sounds around them.

A crowd strolled by, some people stopped to make purchases, others just haggled before moving on without buying anything. Behind the gaiety, burned out shells of buildings stood deserted and collapsing, leftovers from the destruction of the Puritan revolt.

An elegant woman paraded past them. Dressed in bright colors, she'd painted her face white and her lips red. Her hair fell in powdered ringlets around each ear, and was raised into an elaborate fashion in the back. Katherine tried not to stare, but found herself fascinated by the woman, who paid her no mind though she eyed Nicholas.

The pie formed into a lump in Katherine's stomach. She brushed crumbs off the bodice of her awful black dress, suddenly conscious of her hair still hanging loose. Although she had finger-combed it in the coach, it was still a mess. At that moment, she felt plain and drab again.

She was painfully aware of Nicholas watching the woman walk by. But then he turned to her, and smiled.

Searching for something to say to cover up her awkward feelings, she said, "I am sorry about the pretty dress."

"Don't worry about that. We will find another."

"I did not mean—"

"I know," he gave her hand a squeeze, brought it to his lips and kissed her knuckles. Katherine's stomach relaxed and she felt warm all over.

The stylish lady had stopped to talk with a gentleman, certainly someone she must know well, Katherine surmised, as the gentleman whispered in the woman's ear. The lady giggled and, taking his arm, they walked off together.

"There," said Nicholas, pulling her attention back to him, "is a woman who sells her favors."

Katherine frowned, unsure of his meaning.

"She trades her body for money. A night of pleasure—or in this case an afternoon—for a few shillings, or perhaps half a sovereign if she is lucky and the man is well pleased."

"Oh." Katherine looked at the woman again. She had never seen a harlot before. Grandfather had preached against them with grandiloquence, decrying them as instruments of the devil along with gluttony and lace and at least a dozen other sins.

She watched the woman hang on the man's arm, now well away from them. How had Katherine not seen it? She had mistaken tawdriness for elegance, commerce for companionship.

Yet she could not condemn the woman. Did not most women end up being bartered in one way or another?

"It is not so different in marriage. Women who marry also trade themselves," she lowered her voice. "Men may think marriage is for joining properties and uniting bloodlines, but to the person being traded, it seems as if one's body is being sold, and not just for an afternoon or evening."

"As you put it, I find I must agree with you, although I had not thought on it before. Ah, lass, see the people over there?" Nicholas pointed to a crowd at the far end of the marketplace. "'Tis a wedding party, I think. Come; let us see what the bride makes of her situation."

They walked along hand in hand until they had almost joined the revelers. Clearly, the gathering was a happy one. The bride wore flowers in her hair: a garland of rosemary and red roses, intertwined with pink and yellow ribbons. She cast a radiant smile on the lanky flush-faced man beside her, who could only be the groom.

The music began. A drum and tambourine set a rapid rhythm, while a pipe and two stringed instruments played a melody. Couples formed into lines with the bride and groom at the head and began to dance. There was much laughing and clapping.

Katherine found herself entranced. Music was not unknown

to her; nevertheless, it was a rare treat.

Nicholas tapped the beat with his booted foot and motioned for her to join him in the dance.

"I could not," she said. "I do not know how."

"You have never danced?" Nicholas looked surprised, and then smiled at her. "I suppose not. Let me show you."

Katherine shook her head. "I do not think I could, but I do enjoy listening and watching."

"Come," said Nicholas. He tugged on her hand and smiled in such a charming way that she allowed him to draw her into an open space.

As strains of music filled the air, he helped her find the beat and tap her feet to it. Then, when she had the rhythm, he showed her how to move.

Standing behind her and to the side, he held both her hands. It was a more intimate pose than that of the other dancers. But, when he showed her the first step and she stumbled, Katherine was grateful his strong arms kept her from falling. She concentrated so hard trying to follow his example, keeping her feet untangled, and not losing her balance again, that when Nicholas stopped, she was surprised to discover the music had ended.

Suddenly self-conscious, she looked around, but most of the revelers were having so much fun they ignored the uninvited couple. Here and there she met a curious glance.

Another dance began. This time the pace was slower, and Katherine had less trouble following Nicholas's feet. She eased into the rhythm as they made little hops and jumps together, stepping this way and that in a simple repetition. Katherine relaxed into his tall strength, enjoying his warmth and the way their bodies moved together.

She looked up from his feet into his twinkling eyes. Her breath caught. She missed a step and would have fallen again had he not twirled her into his arms.

They stood thus, and the crowd and noise and even the music dissolved away as Katherine was aware of only Nicholas, his eyes, now serious and full of need, his full lips descending to hers.

His kiss was hungry, demanding, and thorough. She tasted coffee, sweet, not bitter as his tongue teased hers, and his lips sucked hers, seeming to extract her very essence. His hand cradled the back of her head, his fingers tangled in her hair. She wrapped her arms around his neck, holding on for support, and he crushed her to him. His need consumed her. Her body strained against her clothing. Her breasts tightened, her nipples tingled. A hot ache started in her woman's place. Then, he lifted his mouth, his arms loosened. He drew away.

Dazed, Katherine took a half-step back. Applause and cheering broke out all around them. She blushed, and hid behind the veil of her hair, while Nicholas bowed to the crowd. Then the musicians struck up a new tune and the dancing began again.

They left the wedding party, walking hand-in-hand down the crowded street. A bittersweet longing came over Katherine. She tightened her hold on Nicholas's hand. They would be on the way to London soon. There they would part. She would smile and thank him for the safe journey. They might kiss good-bye. And then he would be gone from her life, after being in it for such a short time.

Yet his presence had changed everything.

She could only be glad she had found him, nursed him to health. He had more than returned the boon, saving her twice now from Finch.

She had not known she would lose her heart to him.

But she had. Thinking of life without him brought tears to the back of her eyes and her nose prickled. The colors around her dimmed on her sad sigh.

Nicholas stopped at a ribbon seller and helped Katherine select several lengths of ribbon. He pressed her to choose as many as she wanted, and then added red, blue, and green ribbons to the pile of peach, pale green, and yellow she had picked. He wrapped the green ribbon several times around her left wrist, tying an elaborate bow then raised that hand to his lips in an elegant courtly gesture. His gaiety made it so hard to be sad. Katherine smiled and curtseyed in return, not caring that she must look ridiculous in the drab black dress.

They proceeded through the town in a leisurely walk. They arrived back at the coach to find Henry and the driver finishing their meals. The horses had been fed and watered. Jeremy still slept—a deep healing sleep, Katherine hoped. Montford lay curled up in the crook of his neck on a pillow.

A hostler brought forward Nicholas's horse. Katherine stepped into the coach, turning to watch Nicholas swing himself up.

Out of nowhere, a goose scurried right in front of him, closely pursued by a barking dog. The horse reared up, kicking its forelegs high into the air. Nicholas, caught halfway into his seat, threw himself forward. In an awkward movement, he swung his leg over the saddle.

Katherine's heart pounded. Her breath caught. Once again, she saw Edward smiling and waving at her before falling from the horse with that terrible heart-rending thud.

She gasped and jumped down from the coach. Henry grabbed her and held her back.

"Whoa," Nicholas commanded. He pulled the reins to force the horse's head down, but the alarmed horse resisted. Nicholas struggled to stay seated as the horse reared again and again. Finally, the beast settled, and dropped its head as if embarrassed over the whole incident.

Nicholas leapt to the ground throwing the reins to the hostler and came to her.

Henry released his hold, and Katherine flung herself into his arms.

"I was so afraid," she whispered, holding him tight around the middle, inhaling his scent, feeling the reassurance of his heartbeat against her body. "So afraid…"

He pulled back from her. Holding her face in his hands, he looked into her eyes. She covered his hands with hers and made a deep shuddering sigh.

"I am all right," he said.

"'Twas like Edward," she gulped. "I could not bear it."

"Ah, lass. Such sadness for you. But it would take more than a skittish moment like that to throw me from a horse." He raised her chin and smiled at her. "I have escaped much danger in my life. Do not fear for me."

Then he kissed her.

A kiss of comfort and solace.

A very public kiss that Henry and the driver could see.

And Jeremy, who stared at her from the open coach door.

CHAPTER FOURTEEN

As the coach sped along the High Road, Katherine stared out the window. Riding beside them, man and horse moved together as one. It was no surprise Nicholas had handled the horse so well. Silly of her to make a public spectacle over it.

Cheeks still hot with embarrassment, she took a deep breath and then let it out. She needed someone to confide in. Edward, she would have told everything—well, most everything. The Edward in her dream had said *there is Jeremy.* Could she share her secrets with him?

She could only hope that lingering traces of drowsy syrup would make him a kind and indulgent listener, receptive to her explanation.

"I have come to care for Nicholas," she said making a quick sideways glance at her friend.

He frowned. "But you ran away from him. So I thought maybe you did not like him after all."

"I did not know my own mind. I was afraid of how I had come to feel. Of how he made me feel." Her voice dropped to a whisper. "I have become very fond of him."

Not willing to look at Jeremy, Katherine gazed outside the window once again. She toyed with the ribbon on her sleeve. "He is really quite kind."

She peeked at her friend.

He was nodding to himself, a puzzled look on his brow. "Well, he is a better man than Finch. Yet I do not think he is a good enough man for you." He looked at her. "What d'ye really know about him?"

Katherine released a long sigh. It was worse than he knew. "I know a lot about him," she said. "He drinks coffee and does not like to be serious. He gets lost upon the road and sits a horse very well. He has odd friends..." she thought of the man-of-many-spaniels she'd run into in the hall, "and he is an outlaw," she finished, almost cringing as she spoke the word aloud.

"Outlaw?" Jeremy's eyebrows rose along with his voice.

Katherine nodded. "The Raven."

"That scoundrel?" Jeremy sounded doubtful. "You said he was *not* the Raven."

"I did not *exactly* say that. But, I did lead you to believe he was not. I should not have done that, but I did not think you would let me leave Ashfield if you knew who he was."

"You are right. I would have done everything in my power to make you stay, e'en though 'twas not my place to stop you." He gave her a glazed and puzzled look. "You aided a known criminal who might hang for stealing clothing instead of valuables? A foolish man."

Katherine made a timid smile. "I would agree 'twas foolish, but 'twas his idea of a jest."

"To risk life and limb for a joke is ill-conceived." Jeremy yawned and shook his head at the same time.

"'Twas not wise of him, no. And he did come to harm, 'tis true. But he has recovered, and now he says 'tis behind him and he will no longer be the Raven." Katherine frowned. "Except for last night. Did you wonder whose emblem Henry painted out?"

Jeremy frowned.

"'Tis the Finch coach we travel in," Katherine explained. "And 'twas Finch and his man Jakes that were left without their clothing—or their coach—last eve."

Jeremy snorted then broke into a loud guffaw. He clenched his teeth as a look of pain crossed his face. "Ye are right, Mistress

Katherine. 'Tis funny."

Katherine tried to smile. "He has saved me twice now, and I will miss him overmuch when we part." She felt the sting of tears starting behind her eyes. "Every revolution of the coach wheels takes me closer to that moment, and I cannot bear it."

Jeremy smiled faintly. "Every revolution of the coach wheels pains me as well, but for a different reason." He reached a hand across to her. She put hers in it and he tightened his fingers around hers.

Katherine squeezed back. No matter what else, something good and lasting had come from this adventure.

She had a friend.

Nicholas watched the sun slip down the sky, bringing London closer with its descent. The increasing proximity brought a familiar loathing. Crowded buildings, stinking streets, and the incredible din of too many people living too close together always made him feel trapped and claustrophobic.

The traffic had been increasing since Wokingham. First drovers and their herds blocked the road; then oxcarts, wagons, and country-folk returning home had slowed their progress. He had not minded. Each impediment put off the moment he would relinquish Katherine to her cousin's care. He found himself disliking this cousin immensely, and he had not met her yet.

Each barrier also served to postpone his appearance at court when he would have to beg the King's forgiveness. Nicholas wrinkled his nose. He could almost smell the over-perfumed atmosphere already. The elaborate decorum, obsequious courtiers, and the empty, idle flirtations held less allure than when he'd first arrived on England's shore. Was it only four months ago? What had been exciting—the prospect of assuming his proper status in the world—he now viewed with distaste. He'd fled the court to Dorsetshire as much from boredom as a wish to see his childhood home again. And were he to be completely honest with himself, which was something he found himself doing this day with alarming frequency, he'd found Ashfield smaller and less attractive in person than in its exalted place in his memory.

Continuing this importunate strain of honesty, he acknowledged to himself that, since awakening to find Katherine pinned beneath him in that damp cottage, he'd been happier than he could remember.

Now this idyll was to end.

From the safety of the coach, Katherine viewed the great city at twilight with both awe and mild alarm. The clatter of the wooden and iron wheels on the cobblestones combined with the din of the street criers, becoming louder and more insistent until she put her hands over her ears. Jeremy slept, having taken another dose of laudanum not long after leaving Wokingham.

She peered out the window, fascinated by the pageant of brightly dressed cavaliers, beggars in rags, even bleating sheep and goats. London was much busier, dirtier, and louder than she'd imagined.

When it seemed her teeth would rattle loose, the carriage came to a stop and the door opened.

Nicholas extended his hand to help her out.

Reluctant to leave the security of the vehicle, Katherine spent an extra long moment composing herself before taking his hand. She carefully stepped down, avoiding a foul-looking puddle. Holding up her skirts to keep them from the filth on the ground, she sniffed the noxious air. It could not be healthy. She had not truly appreciated country air before this moment. Katherine raised a hand to cover her mouth and nose, with the fleeting thought that if she could barely manage a few minutes without feeling sickened by this place, how could she ever hope to make it her home?

"The hour grows late. We shall sup here," Nicholas announced.

Katherine nodded, feeling a sudden giddiness as he took her

hand, knowing their separation would be put off for a few more hours. The sign suspended above the diamond-shaped windowpanes read the *Hawk and Pheasant*. At least the steps leading to the door of the timber-and-plaster building appeared to have been cleaned recently.

Nicholas swept her inside. A curt command to the proprietor got them a private parlor. The walls were bare save for a small dirty tapestry near the door. Katherine could not make out the picture. Two unmatched chairs and an oak table occupied the center of the room. A brazier in one corner provided some warmth.

They crossed to the window. Through the uneven panes, patches of color moved in the fading light—people on the street outside. The windows muffled a good deal of the noise, yet the street criers' calls were loud enough to be heard.

"What do you think of the great city of London?" Nicholas asked.

"I do not think much of it," Katherine said almost apologetically. "The sounds, the smells, 'tis too much all at once."

Nicholas laughed.

"I suppose I will adjust to it, as I am to live here." Katherine tried not to sound as sad and forlorn as she felt.

Nicholas took her hand and raised it to his lips.

His mouth on her tender finger-pads sent streams of fire through her.

Still holding her hand, he twirled her around. With no music but the sounds from outside the window, they danced as they had at the wedding. Nicholas gave her a final turn and took her in his arms.

They stood together for some time, senses heightened, aware only of each other. Soon life would go on as if all was the same, although it would never be. But now, this moment belonged to them, to savor, to push away the future.

A soft rap on the door broke them apart. Nicholas bid the servers enter. Plate after plate arrived until they overfilled the small table. Two candles provided gentle illumination.

Despite the appealing aroma, and the novelty of sweets and

savories she had never seen, Katherine found herself without an appetite and just nibbled at her food.

Nicholas picked up an orange. He looked over at her, an impish look on his face. "Shall I amuse you, my lady?"

Katherine frowned, unsure of his meaning.

He bid her be seated, and then tossed the orange into the air while grabbing two more off the table. In a moment, all three were airborne. Nicholas juggled the fruit with great dexterity—a hand behind his back, one under his arm, even under his leg, without dropping any. Then, in a quick flourish, he doffed his hat and each fruit, in turn, fell into it. He bowed.

Katherine clapped her hands. "La, Sir, you are most talented."

Nicholas took an orange from his cap and sliced it into neat crescents. He handed one to Katherine, and took one into his teeth, pulling the soft inner flesh away from the peel.

Katherine savored the orange—a treat rarely come to Ashfield. Nicholas handed her another piece, and they ate companionably until the whole fruit was gone. She licked the juice off her fingers.

Jeremy's words in the coach came back to her. There was so much about Nicholas she did not know. "You have oft mentioned the East, yet you have not explained how you came to know it," she said.

Nicholas sat down and surveyed the evening's fare. "I spent time in Algiers, Morocco, the Levant, but never traveled farther east than Persia. There I found people who think and behave differently than English people. My fellow English would say I spent my years among barbarians. These 'barbarians' are just as certain that we English are outlandish." He smiled at her. "I have not yet determined who is right. One thing is certain, I developed a liking for the food and drink, especially coffee." He picked up a mulberry tart and took a bite. "I learned the most about the East at sea. An Arab seaman taught me Eastern notions, as well as navigation. We would lie on the deck late into the night, watching the stars and discussing such things."

Katherine continued her questioning. "Your family left England during the revolt?"

"My family did not favor Cromwell and the Puritan regime, as you know. When they captured the King at Oxford, we fled."

Katherine nodded, and then another question occurred to her. "Tell me about the grand place we stayed last night. How did we come to be there?"

Nicholas took another bite of the tart. "Lydney Hall is the home of a friend of mine."

"You did not introduce me to him," Katherine said, disappointed. "But I did meet a man in the hallway walking a group dogs. Or maybe they were walking him, I'm not sure. They led that poor man a merry chase. They were trying to catch Montford, but she did escape." Katherine giggled. "That man would not want to see me again—certainly he would not want to see my cat. Was that your friend?"

"I believe he is a different friend." Nicholas swallowed down the last bit of mulberry tart. The time has come, he thought, I could tell all now, but when she hears the truth and learns the lie, the interest in her eyes will turn to accusation. I would not like that. So, perhaps I could answer with a part-truth, the part that won't upset her.

Nicholas cleared his throat. "I have a title. Cromwell took my lands. You may call me Baron Eddington, if you wish, but I'd rather you call me Nicholas," he smiled at her.

Katherine's eyes had widened at the announcement of his secondary title. "So *Baron* Nicholas Eddington of no property, what is it that you do when you aren't robbing Puritans of their clothing?"

"I have contacts in Holland," he explained. "'Tis quite simple to procure lace and wines and other items whose import has been prohibited by the English government. There are many who will pay handsomely for such."

"You are a smuggler?" Katherine pursed her lips.

He wanted to kiss them back into softness. "I am a trader," he shrugged. "Now that you know my secrets, perhaps you could share yours? You have not told me where this cousin of yours lives."

Even in the candlelight, he could see Katherine flush prettily before she looked away. He had hit the mark without even aiming. The lass had at least one secret she had not shared with him, and it was about this cousin.

"What is her name?"

Katherine fidgeted with an orange peel. "My mother's cousin, Alicia Pemberton, lives on Fenchurch Street, but I know not where that is." Katherine looked at him, eyes wary. She cleared her throat as if something was stuck. "She does not exactly know I am coming, so 'tis possible she will not be there."

Nicholas picked up an oyster on the half-shell. Katherine's secret was not such a big one after all. "Then she will not worry on the lateness of your arrival if you do not appear today." Resting the rough shell against his lower lip, he tilted it so that the oyster and its juices spilled into his mouth. Just a few light chews and it slid deliciously down his throat.

Katherine smiled. She looked beautiful in the candlelight.

"What a lot of food," she said as if she'd just noticed. She picked up an oyster and sniffed it.

"It smells salty, and looks most strange." She cast a dubious look at it. "What is it?"

Nicholas shook his head. "It is an oyster, fresh from the sea. A bit of lemon has been added to the juices to bring out the flavor of the ocean."

"Not cooked?"

Nicholas shook his head.

Katherine eyed the seafood with suspicion and sniffed it again. "I have never seen the ocean."

"'Tis a mighty place. At the shoreline, the water is noisy and powerful, but away from land it is quiet, and solitary. There is a vast tranquility, unless, of course, there is a storm. Then you can fear for your life." He took a bite of bread and chewed for a moment. "You asked me where I call my home. For the past five years my home has been the sea."

"I would like to see it someday."

"Sometime I shall show you," he said. "But first, try the oyster. Since ancient times some have thought they arouse or enhance sexual desire." He picked up another oyster and ate it.

Katherine frowned at her oyster. Then she looked at him.

He nodded.

She put the shell to her lips and sucked in the raw seafood. Her eyes grew wide as she chewed—"Gently, gently," he told her—and then she swallowed it down.

Her eyes big, her lips pursed, she looked like Montford after eating the fish at the water-works.

Nicholas laughed.

Then Katherine began to laugh too, peals of sweet laughter, until there were tears streaming out of her eyes. She held her sides, gasping for air and making a giggling wheeze.

"You looked at me in such an odd way," she said when she could, "and it tasted so unusual, not at all like something that would make me want to mate with you." She blushed. "I would never need oysters," she added.

"Ah lass, physical attraction can be a powerful spell. You have caught me no less than, it seems, I have caught you."

"What are we to do?" she whispered.

Nicholas rose and held out his hand to her. "'Tis clear we must ask the innkeeper for a bed."

It was a small room with a small fire, mismatched furniture, and a threadbare carpet. But it was clean, and the bed was big, and the rope supports tight. Once the door was latched, Katherine flung herself into the warmth of Nicholas's arms. Hot joy overwhelmed her. She had this last night with him.

His mouth swooped down, capturing hers, his tongue seeking, plundering.

She fumbled with the buttons of his brocade waistcoat, urgent fingers always so capable, now unable to accomplish such a simple task, until at last she had it open. In hurried jerks, she thrust the garment over his shoulders and down his arms. She yanked his linen shirt up from his breeches and ran her hands along the hot smooth skin of his back, then slid a hand around his waist and brought it to rest on his heart which beat in a hard steady thrum.

He walked her backwards to the bed. Without moving his mouth from hers, or relaxing his hold, he came down with her onto the thin flock mattress, rolling onto his back so she rested on top.

Katherine wrenched her mouth from his, and propped herself up on her arms. "I cannot understand this need. 'Tis like a beast within me. 'Tis frightening to find I cannot stop myself from touching you, from wanting you inside me." She ran her fingers through his hair, spreading it out in a halo around him.

Nicholas stroked her cheeks, tucking her hair behind her ears. "We must use care tonight, lass. Your newly plucked maidenhead may keep you sore for a bit. I would not wish to hurt you."

"I do not want to be cautious," she said fiercely, shaking her head so her hair fell all about them. "All my life I have been cautious. I wish to be incautious. I wish to be heedless, even reckless. To act like there is no tomorrow; there is only now. Here. Only you and me."

Nicholas groaned, pulled her head down, and kissed her, a soft delicate brush of the lips that sent fire through her. He traced her eyebrows and nose with his fingertips, before returning his mouth to hers for a long, tender joining. They both sighed when the kiss ended.

"Patience, lass. Your nether lips are like flower petals. If we overuse them, they will bruise. We must go slowly, and you must lead, but the pleasure will be just as sweet."

Nicholas got up and helped her to rise. She watched him divest himself of his clothing while she fumbled with her stays. Frustrated with impatience, she snarled the laces, and Nicholas had to help her with the knot.

As her clothes dropped into a pile on the floor, Katherine could not keep her eyes off Nicholas's impressive form. He stood at an angle to her, a golden-bronze figure in the firelight, long muscular torso and compact hips above strong well-formed thighs and calves. Even his feet were beautiful. Everything about him was perfect, except for the red puckered place on his arm where he had been shot. She went to him, and kissed that spot, to thank it for bringing them together.

Against her bidding, her eyes drew downward to his man's part, pointing straight out like a sword. Katherine gasped, but he smiled, a charming Nicholas smile, and she relaxed. He reached his hand to her, and she took it, warm and reassuring in hers.

He pulled her onto the bed. They lay on their sides, facing each other. He stroked her arms and back, leaving trails of heat in spite of the chill air. His hands caressed her breasts. She moaned as her nipples went hard. He teased each in turn before his hands trailed down her stomach, to the curly hairs that covered her woman's place. He examined her with such intensity, and touched her with such care, that she felt a sob catch in her throat at the loveliness and exquisite pleasure of it.

She rubbed his chest, marveling at the hard strength in him. As she traced his nipples, his muscles tensed, and his breathing grew rough.

"Although we must go slowly, I find I cannot wait. I want you now," he almost groaned the words out. "But 'twill go better for you if you are on top of me."

"I-I don't know what to do," she whispered.

"Shhh," Nicholas soothed. "I shall show you." He ran his hands over her breasts, to her hips, coaxing her onto him. "You must put me inside you, and then ride me, like I am a horse."

Katherine took in a deep breath as the image of the stallion and the mare came back to her. This time the thought flickered through her mind that perhaps the mare did not scream from pain, but from lust.

She rose above him, awkward at first, but then gained courage as he smiled at her. He parted her nether lips, and she positioned herself over him, gasping at the feeling of fullness as she eased herself down his hard erection. Her tenderness urged her to move slowly as he slid deeper and deeper. His face wore an expression of concentration. He traced his fingers along her stomach, over her breasts, and down her sides, and she started laughing because it tickled. It felt so odd to laugh with him inside her, her muscles clenching his hard length.

He closed his eyes and groaned.

Katherine sobered. "Are you alright? Have I hurt you?"

Nicholas shook his head. "Nay, but your laughter squeezes me so. 'Tis a good feeling, lass. A very good feeling."

Their eyes locked. Her breath caught as he took a fistful of her hair in each hand. Wrapping it around his wrists, he drew her face down to his and kissed her rough and thorough, his tongue teasing hers until she relaxed and became accustomed to the feel of him inside her. He tasted of coffee, and she knew she would never smell that particular drink without thinking of him. He ran his hands to her hips and back along her buttocks, urging her to accept more of him.

As he began to move in slow easy motions, a rush of heat surged through her. She braced her arms on either side of him, and found the angle made his motions feel even more exquisite than before. Her breasts hung before him. He took one in each hand, squeezing them and teasing her nipples. Katherine breathed in short little puffs, unable to take a full breath. Her body began to throb, as a pulsing pleasure built within her.

Going up on one arm, Nicholas took a breast in his mouth, alternately teasing the nipple with his teeth, and sucking hard.

She moaned her pleasure.

He lay back, ran a hand to the apex of her thighs, and began stroking in time with her movement.

Tight heat began to build inside her. Nicholas clenched his teeth, and he groaned. He put an arm around her, and rolled her onto her back. She wrapped her legs around him as he thrust, hard, deep, and quick. Katherine writhed, reaching to meet him, consumed by the power of their joining. A profound tension built inside her and then it exploded. She shrieked, and Nicholas cried out his release.

He went down onto his side, bringing her with him, holding her close. She trembled.

He brushed the hair from her mouth, where it stuck, hot from the heat of their passion.

"Why do you cry, lass?" He wiped a tear from her cheek. "Did I hurt you? I had meant to go slow."

"No. I...I do not know," she whispered. "That is, I did not

know I was crying." She shuddered, overwhelmed by a rush of emotion she did not understand. The tears came in earnest.

He wrapped her into his arms and held her tight until she stopped.

"'Tis so wonderful," she said. "I could never imagine anything so pleasing. I do not know why I cry when I am so happy."

He took the end of the sheet beneath them and wiped at her face, then kissed where the tears had been.

"'I am greatly relieved," he said, eyes twinkling. "But I wish to know, if you cry when you are happy, do you laugh when you are sad? Mayhap instead of trying to make you laugh all these days, I should have been trying to make you cry."

Katherine giggled.

"Ah lass, when you laugh I come undone." He found her hand, raised it to his lips, and sucked on the end of each finger, one by one. "You taste of orange."

"Mmmmm," Katherine moaned softly. Her body still hummed. She wanted his hands all over her and him inside her again. Her breasts swelled and she throbbed. Katherine did not think she could possibly sleep. From the ends of her toes to the tips of her fingers, she quivered with life. She ran a finger along the cleft on his chin, and kissed him there. She wanted this night to go on forever—so that she could remember it forever.

A sudden crash outside in the hallway made them both jump. Nicholas leaped from the bed. His pistol materialized in his hand. He faced the door. A loud voice cursed just outside, and Nicholas relaxed.

"'Tis but a drunkard who cannot find his room," he said, putting down the gun and joining her on the bed. "There are many villains in London. One must be ever on the alert."

"I noted your sword at the ready," Katherine smiled.

"My sword?"

Katherine nodded and looked pointedly at his erection.

Nicholas laughed. "My sword likes to be ever alert, but as to whether it would protect you or ravish you, I think 'twould be the latter."

Katherine smiled. Then she shivered. She felt safe in this

room, but somewhere outside was Richard Finch. She had no doubt he already searched for them.

"Do you think *he* has tracked us to London?" she said, unwilling to say Finch's name. "In my mind, I see him behind me, ready to grab me. Or I sense him hiding somewhere near. I know he isn't there, but 'tis unnerving."

Nicholas put his arms around her and held her tight. "Ah, lass. He cannot be here. I think it most likely he has slinked off to his home, hiding behind each tree and bush all the way." Nicholas chuckled, and she felt it rumble in his chest. "'Twould be hard for him to follow us here so quickly without his coach or his clothing."

Katherine chewed on the inside of her lip.

Nicholas continued. "I do not think we have seen the last of him. But I think we are safe from having to view his arrogant face for many days." He pulled a sheet over them, and tucked her into the curve of his arm.

"Tonight you may sleep without fear, lass. Should any further commotion threaten our peace and security, my sword and I will protect you."

Then he kissed her again.

They had made love once more. This time without haste, prolonging each moment, in a slow deliberate joining of body and soul that wrung exquisite, exhausted pleasure.

Nicholas had quickly fallen into a sound sleep, but Katherine could not. She lay tucked into his embrace, his hand cupping her breast, and her head resting on his arm. For what must have been hours, she found herself in that strange place between waking and sleeping, where one did not precisely dream, nor completely lose awareness of their surroundings. Nicholas's rhythmic breathing in one ear, and the steady sound of his pulse in the other, disconcerted and soothed her. Just as his presence had always alarmed and charmed her.

A month ago, entrenched in the daily grind of Ashfield, she

would never have imagined lying naked beside a man.

A month ago, she had not known Nicholas.

He had turned her life upside down. Or perhaps he had made it right-side up.

The night watchman called out, "Past two of the clock and a cold windy morning." Katherine sighed and wiggled her toes. Even at night, the noise of London persisted—the sign rattled outside, drunkards yelled in the street below, dogs barked. The floor outside their door creaked as guests passed by. She could hear their conversations, and wondered if anyone outside had been able to hear their lovemaking. With an embarrassed sigh, she snuggled into Nicholas's protective form, and he gave her a squeeze.

In the wee morning hours, as the sky lightened, she wondered how she would ever manage at Cousin Alicia's when she had such need of Nicholas's touch, his smile, his humor. He had turned her drab, gray world into one that had color, sound, and movement. He had shown her passion and tenderness. How was she to give that up? Her growing need for him had already changed her. If she was not careful, she would beg him to keep her.

Katherine shifted on the thin mattress and let out a long heaving sigh.

He had said naught of the future but that he would show her the ocean. It was the kind of remark tossed out in conversation. An empty promise. Not a promise on which to build a lifetime.

A new day would dawn on the morrow, bringing with it clarity, reason, and hopefully her usual good sense.

She edged away from Nicholas's warm body.

He made a light snore, and settled her back close to him.

Nicholas awoke refreshed and with a plan. It had come to him during the night. In the clear light of morning, he rejoiced at its simplicity.

Katherine slept soundly, tucked into his warmth. Her head lay a heavy weight on his arm. She snored light puffs of air. He craned his neck to look at her. Tears stained her face. Had she cried during the night?

He blew into her ear.

She brushed at the place he had blown and made a gentle snort. This time he kissed her there, and began to suckle on the lobe.

Katherine moaned and opened an eye.

"Good morn," he said.

She yawned and closed her eyes again.

"You must get up. 'Twill be a big day for us." He gave her a jiggle. "Arise, Lady Katherine. Today we shall be wed."

CHAPTER FIFTEEN

Katherine's eyes popped open.

She could not have heard him correctly. *Marry? Today?*

How could that be?

She lurched up, holding the bedclothes to her chest. "What did you say?"

Nicholas beamed at her. "Today you will be my bride." He plucked her fingers from the sheet and brought them to his lips, planting a tender kiss on her knuckles. "I have compromised your honor, so I shall marry you. You shall be safe from Finch and your father. And my heir will be protected if you carry him."

Katherine swallowed. She would be safe, a babe would be safe. It was a show of his good honor that he wished to marry her. Yet, she felt a great disappointment at his words, as though she'd received a drenching of cold water. She wanted more from him than duty.

She wanted love.

Avoiding his eyes, she began to finger-comb and plait the tangled mess of her hair. He had once said he would require passion in a mate.

But passion was not love.

And he had not asked her if she would be his wife. Nay, he had told her they would marry. Yet, had he asked her, how could she say 'no' when she loved him so?

For she did. God help her she did.

She looked up, and their eyes locked.

"Have you naught to say?" Nicholas asked.

"You have taken me by surprise," she said. "I could not speak at first. Truly, Nicholas, I thank you for your wish to save my honor and protect me. 'Tis very good of you, and I am very grateful. Yet, I would hope there is more to such a request as this?"

He sat up and looked at her oddly. "No, I do not marry you just to save your honor." He ran a hand through his hair. "Katherine, I often act on my instincts. It is my way." He took her hand and drew slow circles on her palm with his forefinger. "I know 'tis not romantic to say so, but my instinct is to marry you. It is the right thing for both of us." He smiled. "I find myself wanting to take care of you. You already take good care of me in so many ways. You inflame me, Katherine."

His voice had gone husky. He leaned to her and put his lips on hers. Their tongues met in a deep, passionate kiss that sent a hot thrill through her. When they broke apart, they both were breathing hard.

"What say you, dearest Katherine?"

Katherine smiled. "Yes, Nicholas, though you have not actually asked me, I say 'yes I will marry you,' and without my father's consent. But however can we do it today?"

"One can do anything in London, even find a clergyman who will marry an impatient groom and bride without a special license, banns, or questions." He got out of bed and began to dress. "You bide here while I make the arrangements. I will have your breakfast and have the cat sent up in the meantime."

Katherine slowly plaited her hair and watched Nicholas dress, admiring the long lines and flexing muscles of his hard body.

"You will have to get up, lass, to lock the door after me," he said when he was done.

Still holding the night rail to cover herself, Katherine rose and followed him. He captured her in his arms, raising her chin for a deep kiss.

"I will be back as soon as I am able." His eyes smiled into hers. "Ah, Katherine, you look so tired." He gave her a squeeze then raised his hands to her shoulders. "But do not go back to sleep. Be ready when I return?" He raised an eyebrow.

Katherine nodded, and gave him an uncertain smile as he departed.

Standing alone in the quiet room, Katherine did not know whether to laugh or cry.

Marry Nicholas?

Become a Baron's wife?

Plain Katherine would be Lady Katherine. The thought brought a giggle to her lips, but then she sobered as her disappointment returned.

It had not mattered that John Perkins did not love her, because she did not love him. But she did love Nicholas. A declaration of love on his part would have filled her heart with joy.

She dropped the sheet and began to dress. Struggling with her stays, she chided herself for being fanciful. Then she looked at her black dress and pursed her lips. Black did not bode well for a marriage. But there was naught she could do about it.

Just as she could not make him love her if he did not.

Two hours and a short hackney ride later, the bride and groom stood in St. James, Duke's Place, a church noted for thousands of 'special' weddings. An aged parson stood before them, reading from the *Book of Common Prayer*.

Jeremy and Henry stood behind them as groomsmen. Jeremy, looking battered, but approving, supported himself on one-side with a stick. Henry propped him up on the other. Montford sat in the crook of Henry's elbow. The kitten, Katherine's only female attendant, wore a bit of ribbon about her neck that she noisily tried to chew off.

Katherine had not been able to fashion a true bridal garland, but had created a coronet with her braid and ribbons, hoping the bright colors would offset the dour black dress.

The clergyman intoned the words in a singsong of sounds that had apparently lost meaning—and clarity—after so many recitals. Katherine found herself almost unable to understand him, but she smiled and held Nicholas's hand through the proceeding. Waves of exhaustion rolled over her. A sense of unreality grew until she wondered if she was in a dream standing next to Baron Nicholas the outlaw, *her* outlaw, and marrying him.

Finally, Nicholas said "yes" at what seemed to be the appropriate time and prompted her so she said "yes" as well.

It was over.

Nicholas gave her a long lingering kiss that singed the roots of her hair, but stopped short of her heart.

Jeremy and Henry shook Nicholas's hand in turn.

The parson wrote their names in his parish register. "Make haste and bed the wench," he admonished Nicholas. "The marriage can be annulled if 'tis not consummated."

Katherine blinked. The minister had clearly misconstrued the nature of the wedding and Nicholas's purpose in making her his bride. Although clandestine, it was not an abduction.

But a niggling doubt remained. Would Nicholas's instincts and his willingness to protect her be a good enough foundation for a good and satisfying marriage?

She would not think about that right now. Katherine squared her shoulders. Taking her husband's proffered arm, she strode beside him out of the vestibule to the waiting hackney.

The quiet group gathered in the small parlor back at the *Hawk and Pheasant*. Nicholas sipped his coffee and studied the lot of them. Jeremy balanced on his stick with one hand and ate a chicken leg with the other. Henry eyed the candied fruit but did not take one. Katherine sat on a stool by the open window. In the diffused light, the blue circles under her eyes stood out.

Nicholas felt a crush of disappointment. Where was the gaiety? Song and dance? Where were the smiles? They acted as if they had just come from a funeral, not a wedding.

"Shall we sing a song?" he volunteered.

Jeremy looked back at him in mild alarm. Henry coughed and shook his head. Katherine yawned.

"Then shall we dance?" he asked Katherine.

"Dance?" she said. "Thank you, Nicholas, but I think I am too tired to dance." She turned away from him, resting her chin on her hands on the windowsill.

"I would dance if I could," said Jeremy. "But I cannot." He tapped the stick. "I do not even think I can stand much longer." He limped to the chair next to Nicholas. "May I sit?"

Nicholas nodded permission, and Jeremy awkwardly sat down.

"I cannot say I have been to many weddings," Jeremy said, "but I did think this one to be prodigious quick. Did the hackney ride not last longer than the ceremony?"

Nicholas smiled. "I believe it did."

"Nor could I understand most of the words. I think I heard 'matrimony' once or twice—at least 'twas a relief to know the parson performed a wedding and not a christening."

Nicholas chuckled. "Even had he, 'tis true and legal for he listed it properly in the parish records."

"If it's all the same to ye," Henry broke into their conversation, giving Nicholas a glum look. "I'm going to find a strong drink. Me tooth requires it." He nodded at Nicholas and then to Katherine where she sat quietly at the window, her back to them. "I wish ye both the best, of course," he said and left.

Nicholas's attention drifted to his lady, to the elegant line of her neck, the relaxed slant of her shoulders. She had been so quiet since the ceremony. Mayhap she did not know what to do with a husband anymore than he knew what to do with a wife. Except for bed-sport, of course. He smiled. They could look forward to long hours of that.

Jeremy cleared his throat. "I want to tell you I am truly pleased you and Mistress Katherine have wed."

Nicholas took a gulp of the hot coffee. He might as well tell the lad as much as he had told Katherine. "'Tis *Lady* Katherine now. She married a Baron."

Jeremy's head snapped up and he looked Nicholas in the eye. "Then why did ye not say so before?"

Nicholas had discovered long ago, that when lying it was best to stay as close to the truth as possible. "It means naught to me."

Jeremy looked at him seriously. "Yesterday she told me you are an outlaw."

"An outlaw no more, lad. Soon I will be a seaman, as I was for many years past." Nicholas took another drink of coffee. "And you, my friend groom? What shall you be now that you are in London and your Lady no longer requires you? Will you stay with the horses or try for something more grand?"

Jeremy smiled. "There are many ways a man can improve his lot in London."

A man? Nicholas smiled. "How old are you?"

Sitting up as straight as possible, using the stick for balance, Jeremy said, "I'll be nineteen in less than a fortnight."

"Ah, so old then? I 'spose you are a man, my friend. I urge you caution in this grand town. There are many ways a man can find trouble here, or trouble can find him."

"I am not all that trusting, as you may recall, but I thank you for the warning," said Jeremy. "What plans do you have? Would you take my mistress, I mean my Lady, to sea?"

Nicholas frowned. "We have not yet decided." Nay, he thought, he had not even thought on it, or talked to the lass about it. He looked over where she sat at the window.

"My bride has been very quiet. Think you she has fallen asleep?" He rose and walked over to her. Katherine's eyes were closed. She let out quiet snores. Her hair, beribboned atop her head, looked like a crown. Several wisps straggled out, one dangled before her mouth, quivering in and out with her breath. Her skin looked translucent in the sunlight, and Nicholas realized how tumultuous the last days had been for her. He fingered the love-token in his pocket. Instead of giving it to her at the wedding feast, he would wait until she awoke.

He nodded to Jeremy, carefully gathered Katherine into his arms and carried her from the parlor.

Nicholas lay on the bed, watching Katherine sleep. Four hours earlier, he had carried her into their room, over the threshold as custom dictated, and put her down on the mattress. After loosening her gown and stays, he had stretched out opposite her. His mind had begun to churn, and he'd not had a moment's peace since.

He had satisfied his pledge to his father: Ashfield was his, as was its mistress.

But what was he to do with them?

He'd never thought to have a wife. Katherine would surely make an admirable helpmeet. She knew how to manage an estate. She could run a staff of servants, but he didn't have an estate, and was not likely to have one—even hers—for many years. He had no servants, save Henry. Although it was arguable *he* might need some managing, there would not be much else for her to do.

And though her future was now out of danger, he was not yet clear of it. In London, there was always the possibility he would be recognized by a passing friend, and she would learn the truth about him.

On the other hand, if he were to tell her all of it—his full title, why he'd returned to England, and what Ashfield was to him—then he wouldn't have to worry about her finding out some other way.

And she would never trust him again.

But perhaps, if he told her just right, she would understand.

Nicholas leaned forward. "Katherine," he said softly, yet loud enough for her to hear had she been awake. "I need to tell you something." She did not stir, much to his relief. "I have sinned against you. Since the beginning of our acquaintance, I have lied to you about who I am. I chose to help you so that I could help myself. And now I sit here asking your forgiveness while you sleep because I have not the courage to ask it while you are awake."

Katherine shifted, and Nicholas's heart dropped. "Are you awake, lass?" he asked, swallowing uncomfortably. But she did not respond.

Relieved, Nicholas sat back on the end of the bed. As far as rehearsals went, it was adequate. Maybe next time he told her it would go as well.

Katherine drifted awake. Through the trailing ends of a dream she became aware first of the rough broadcloth coverlet against her cheek, and then of the hazy twilight that filtered through the window. She rolled onto her back to see Nicholas sitting across from her on their bed, his expression unusually melancholy.

A thrill ran through her as the day came back to her in a rush. She and Nicholas were married! She had pledged herself to the man of her heart. Katherine smiled, remembering the unintelligible singsong ceremony. At least, she hoped that's what she'd done.

"My lady awakens," he said, his deep resonant voice curling into her heart. "She deigns to smile upon me. 'Tis like the sun when it rises in the morning."

"Good afternoon, dear husband," her pulse quickened when she said the word. "I did not intend to sleep through my wedding day. Or have I dreamt it all...?" Katherine's voice trailed off. She leaned forward, and reached a finger to Nicholas's cheek. Warm and scratchy from the day's growth of beard, he was real and not imagined. "I did not dream, you, did I? Standing by my side? Saying you will be my husband?"

Nicholas smiled and took her hand in his warm grip. "Nay, 'twas not a dream. You are my wife; I am your husband. And as such, I would ask a boon."

"Whatever is in my power I would grant." Katherine smiled.

"'Tis a simple request." He relinquished her hand. "Give me your Chinese coin."

Surprised, Katherine reached inside her neckline, noticing

that Nicholas had loosened her clothing while she slept. An unaccustomed familiarity, but it spoke of the new intimacies in her life, and she felt touched by his care for her. She pulled the ribbon over her head and handed the coin to him.

He held it cupped in his hand for a moment, examining it as if he could read the foreign characters.

"A token to seal our troth," he said and opened his other hand to reveal a fine gold chain.

"A gift?" Katherine asked. Her heart rose and then fell. "But I have naught for you."

"*You* are my present." Nicholas leaned toward her. She raised her lips to meet his; a light gentle kiss, but its warmth reached her heart.

Katherine made a contented sigh and watched his big fingers struggle with the knot on the ribbon, finally getting it undone. He strung the Chinese coin on the delicate chain and clasped it behind her neck. When he had it fastened, he ran his fingers along the links where they rested on her skin.

She threw her arms around his neck. She was not ready to tell him she loved him, but she could tell him some of how she felt. She put her forehead against his. "You make me very happy. I did not know what 'twas to be happy until you came into my life."

Nicholas gave her a half smile and stroked her hair. "Ah lass," he said. "Then I am happy too."

Over the next days, Nicholas and Katherine shared the fine details of their lives like children exchanging confidences. Nicholas had many opportunities to divest himself of his lie, but he let each one go by. Often Katherine's giggles would fill the room, a sound so joyous he did not have the will to make it stop. He told himself he didn't want to ruin this honeymoon period, to see Katherine's smiles turn to frowns, but he knew in his heart it was because he was a coward. He had wedged himself into a tight spot, and he could not extricate himself with grace.

Or honor.

Although for most of his life he had been able to shrug off his worries, he now found it impossible. So he hid them as best he could behind a wall of hot sensuality. Late at night, he'd lie awake watching Katherine sleep, realizing he had been hoist by his own petard.

He enjoyed this time with the bittersweet appreciation of a man awaiting the hangman. They could not stay cocooned in this room forever. Sometime they would have to venture out. Sometime he would have to tell her the truth, before she found out from someone else.

On the afternoon of their third day as husband and wife, Nicholas found himself in bed watching her as she stood by the small window wearing nothing save his lucky coin on the gold chain he had given her. Her hair, unbound and gloriously tangled from love-play, hung long and silky down her back.

He eyed the square set of her shoulders, her firm derrière, the elegance of her small bare feet, while he again told himself *it is time*.

The words floated through his mind, disjoined. He opened his mouth to speak, but shut it quickly before any of the words could slip out. He did not want to bungle it. There had to be some explanation she would understand. He had just not thought of it yet.

"Nicholas?"

He propped his head on his hand. "Hmmmm?"

"I have come to the realization that you did not tell me the truth."

A flash of alarm, like hot fire, ran through him. How had she found out? She had not been from his sight in days. Had he spoken in his sleep? Had she been reading his mind?

He cleared his throat. "I truly did not mean to cause you any pain," he said.

"Oh no," she reassured him. "You have not hurt me, although I confess to having a slight soreness." Her smile trembled. "You have shown me the greatest bliss."

Relief washed over Nicholas like a wave of cold surf. A chill ran through him with the dawning realization that causing Katherine pain would pain him as well.

He patted the spot, still warm, next to him.

Katherine walked toward him and sat down.

"What did I do?" he asked, not sure he really wanted to know.

"You did not tell me the truth," her voice quavered. She put a warm hand on his cheek. "Mating 'tis not the most pleasant thing a man and a woman can do together. 'Tis so much more than that, Nicholas. When I eat a comfit, or my stitches turn out right, *that* is pleasant." She turned away from him, but he could still see a light stain of pink touch her cheeks.

"When we join as man and woman 'tis the greatest joy. Yet I cannot believe it is usually so." She frowned. "I heard talk, servants' talk, that made me think that some find it not even pleasant at all."

"No, 'tis not always so," he agreed. "Although I cannot tell you why. There is some special alchemy between us. Together we make gold." Light goose flesh ran down her arms, and he rubbed them before pulling her into his embrace.

Katherine snuggled into his warmth. "What would have happened to my life had I not walked into that storm and found you in the cottage? Would I now be married to Finch? Would you have survived?" Katherine shivered. "How frightening to think that had the storm started just a few minutes earlier, or father delayed our meeting by even half an hour, I would not have left my home. I would never have found you."

Nicholas tightened his arms around her. "It cannot be chance that we met, dear Katherine."

Katherine smiled. "I shall never feel the same way about thunderstorms again. I shall always find them romantic."

Nicholas laughed. "I find you romantic. The way you bite your lip, the way you make little noises when you sleep, even the way you look at me when I have done something that annoys you."

Katherine giggled.

"'Tis not funny," Nicholas protested. "Ah lass, I fear I am losing my reason—whatever reason I did have. All I want is for you to be here beside me, and for me to be inside you." He gave her a last squeeze before he sat up and covered her with a blanket. "But, we must give your tender parts a rest now."

"I would like a bath and my supper."

"Then I will brave the dangerous outer reaches and find us provisions. And some hot water."

Before his body could convince his mind to stay, Nicholas pulled on some clothes.

When he returned with food, and attendants delivering the tub and water, Katherine was hiding under the sheets.

"You can come out now," Nicholas called to her as the door shut, and he latched it behind them. "Shall I feed you as you bathe? How very dissolute that would be, eh?" He smiled. "I think you would like it."

He helped her into the tub and found that, instead of feeding her, he could not keep his hands off her. He lathered and rinsed her as if she were a great lady and he her servant. He washed her hair, her shoulders, her breasts, her feet, leaving her tender parts to soak.

"Will you not get in?" Katherine made a playful splash.

He would have liked to join her, but that would be folly. His breeches had already become uncomfortably tight, and his breathing ragged, from the exquisite process of bathing her. He trailed kisses across the slippery expanse of her forehead and down her nose before he came to her lips, pliable, waiting for him, opening to his tongue, so unlike their first kiss, and yet so similar in that it left him stunned and winded. He reluctantly pulled away.

"Ah, sweet Katherine, perhaps 'tis best I stop and eat some of the food they have brought, else you find yourself my dinner."

Katherine giggled. Her face a dewy radiance from the heated water, he wondered how he could have ever thought her plain. Her newfound sensuality called to him like a siren.

"If you will not join me, then, perhaps 'tis time for me to get out," she said, rising from the bath and pulling a linen towel around her to dry. He wondered what it would be like to watch Katherine grow heavy with child. His child. Suddenly a great yearning rose up in him for something he had never known he wanted.

She pulled her muslin shift over her head. The loose fabric fell in a curtain to her ankles.

"I have not been outside this door in so many days I have lost count," she smiled and walked to him, the outline of her small figure clear through the translucent fabric.

Nicholas felt a prickle of unease.

"I know there is much to do in London. I have never seen a play," she said somewhat wistfully.

He reached his hand to hers, and she took it. He pulled her to his lap. Rubbing his head against the soft muslin fabric, he inhaled her scent of woman and lavender. Her wet hair trailed against his shirt. "I have forgot there is another world besides this room and the kitchen." He nuzzled her neck. "I have seen several plays, and I have found them to be greatly overrated," he said, wishing the lie were true. He could not keep Katherine cocooned in the room much longer. They were both becoming prisoners of his deceit.

"Katherine, I must tell you something."

"Yes, Nicholas?" She readjusted herself in his lap.

Another rush of desire coursed through him. He wanted her again, god help him. Nicholas ran a hand up inside her smock, along the silky skin of her leg up her thigh to her nest of curls.

"I...I..." Nicholas took a deep breath and was assaulted by her sweet smell. He swallowed and took the coward's way out, yet again, as the wrong words spilled forth. Words that did not tell her the truth. Words that postponed the telling until another painful moment. "I am more and more reluctant to attend to the business that brought me here to London. I am finding it hard to attend to anything but you." That, at least, was true.

Katherine made an indrawn breath and opened her legs to him. She put her arm around his neck. While he teased her with his finger, she made the most wonderful little sounds. He raised his mouth to her, and she kissed him, a strong powerful joining of souls. He wanted to lift her in his arms and take her back to the bed.

She rested her head against his shoulder, breathing heavily. "I think I cannot eat with your hand there. I cannot think of food. But I do think I must eat. I am hungry for you, my husband, and for my dinner."

Husband. A strange sounding word. Certainly one Nicholas had never thought to hear himself called. But it sounded so right when Katherine said it. A warm, pleasant word. An endearment.

Nicholas reluctantly pulled his hand away and picked up a piece of bread. "Yea, wife, I will make sure you have energy to match mine anon. But tonight we shall rest." He took a bite and then handed the bread to Katherine to eat. They sat companionably cozy and fed each other a sensual meal of bread and cheese and kisses.

When they had eaten their fill, Nicholas carried Katherine to their bed. They lay in each other's arms, tired and sated from the meal.

Katherine ran her hands over him. He knew he could have her, but that she needed rest, as her body needed rest from his. He had never slept the night through with a woman without physically joining with her. The prospect was a novelty, and it moved him almost as much as Katherine's innocent joy in sexual discovery.

They lay together, Katherine's back to his front, her head nestled on his good arm. Her breathing was hypnotic, and Nicholas found himself floating off sleep.

"I love you."

The words were a sigh, so soft that at first he thought he had not heard her correctly. No one had said those words to him in a very long time. Not since his mother died.

They warmed him.

Then they chilled him when he realized that telling Katherine the truth would destroy more than the precious happiness they shared.

It would destroy her love.

And that might destroy him.

❧

Early the next morning, Nicholas emerged from their room. He had not slept well that night, so afraid of losing something he did not fully have. Katherine had slept, snuggled beside him, the sound of her even breaths giving him some relief from his recriminations. He left her sleeping in a tangle of bedclothes. He needed to get away from her. All resolve fell away in her presence. In his own company, he could muster his will to beseech her forgiveness.

Sending Jeremy up to guard the door, he joined Henry in the common room.

His old friend nursed a mug of ale. His eyes were bloodshot, and his swollen jaw made his face appear lopsided.

"A good morning to you," Nicholas greeted him.

"Nay, I think not," Henry said. His hand shook as he reached for his mug. "Me tooth hurts fierce, it does. I didna sleep a wink. I would be drinking the laudanum if it didna make me so puking sick. If I were a horse, ye would do me the favor to take me out and shoot me."

"That I could not do," said Nicholas, sitting across from him. "But I could find a barber to pull the tooth."

Henry put his mug on the table with a clunk. "Shootin' me would be much kinder."

A serving maid brought Nicholas his breakfast and the two men sat in silence. While Nicholas ate, Henry nursed his mug.

"Lady Ashton is well?"

"You well know my mother has been dead these twenty years," Nicholas pretended to misunderstand him.

"Nay, Nicky, I speak of yer wife, or have ye forgot ye married the lass." Henry burped, and then graced Nicholas with a smile. "I ne'er did think I'd see ye married. But glad I am, as long as ye treat her good and kind. Mayhap this marriage will see ye settled down, no longer drifting from place to place. And I would not be surprised to see you with a wee babe in yer arms a nine-month from now."

Nicholas scowled. "I do not forget I have a wife. But, she does not yet know she is Lady Ashton, and I do not care for your prodding me on't."

"Ye did say ye would tell her."

"I did tell her once, to see how it would go." At Henry's puzzled look, he added, "I spoke while she slept. She did not mind that time. I think she will mind when I tell her again. But I must find the right moment."

"The moment will be right when ye make it right. 'Tis like me tooth. The longer ye wait, the worse it will be."

Nicholas nodded. What Henry said was true. Today he could shoulder his responsibilities and do the right thing by both of them. He would start with Henry's tooth.

He ordered a full bottle of brandy and set it between them. Henry eyed the bottle, and then looked up at his old friend.

Nicholas sighed and poured Henry a slug of brandy. "You need not scowl at me so. Because of our marriage, Katherine's lot is much improved. Now that she is wed, Finch should leave her alone."

"How is he to know this? An' d'ye think he will give up so easily? He was never a one to do that before. He'll fight ye on't, ye can be sure about that."

"I shall write to her father tonight," Nicholas said, uncomfortably remembering the last missive he'd sent the man. Henry did not know about that.

"What are yer plans?"

"Other than telling Katherine the truth, I have none," Nicholas sighed. "Until then, we cannot go out safely for fear I shall be recognized. I begin to think we should quit London anyway. Mayhap 'tis time to quit England. 'Tis not really my home, after all."

He found himself clenching his teeth against a tide of emotion. "Ashfield was not as I recalled. It seemed lesser than that grand manse my father spoke of, and smaller than I remembered." He sighed. "I am not a squire or a courtier. I mislike court and idle conversation. There is not much here for me." He found himself restating what he had told Katherine. "My home is the sea."

"Will she go w'ye?" It was the same question Jeremy had

asked him.

"And you?" asked Nicholas, seeking to avoid an answer by asking a question. "Will you settle here with a good English maid, or perhaps a well-to-do widow?" he chuckled.

"Mayhap I could settle at the bottom of a brandy bottle. My cup is empty." Henry held it upside down and not even a drop splashed onto the table between them.

Nicholas filled his cup. Drunk as a piper, it would be much easier to get Henry—and the offending tooth—to a barber.

Katherine cracked open an eye. Golden sunlight streamed through the window. Montford lay curled at her feet, but there was no great body beside her. Nicholas was gone.

She stretched from the ends of her fingers to her toes—a great feline stretch—and smiled, happy to greet the new day and its myriad possibilities.

First, she must find her husband and her breakfast.

Katherine rose. She eyed her horrible black dress. Its somber tone belied the happiness of her life, but she had naught else to wear. Perhaps she could liven it up with some ribbons. Later. Not this morning. She needed to get out of this room, among good company. She had not seen Jeremy and Henry for many days. Although they would know what she and Nicholas had been doing, she would have to face them sometime.

She used the chamber pot and pulled on her clothing. Leaving Montford asleep, Katherine opened the door to the hallway and almost fell over Jeremy who lay before it.

"What are you doing here?" she exclaimed. Could he have been there the whole time? What had he heard?

"The Master bid me guard the door." He yawned and pulled a straggling lock of hair out of his face as he got up. "I had not thought to fall asleep. But 'tis a busy place and I have not been able to get much rest. 'Tis quieter here than downstairs."

Katherine relaxed. "I'm sorry, Jeremy. I did not mean to be shrill. Is Nicholas below? 'Tis hungry I am."

"Aye, he is with Henry, poor fellow. His tooth is paining him fierce as ever."

At Katherine's entrance, Nicholas stood. He came to her and kissed her, right there in the common room for all to see. Katherine could feel herself blush, but she did not care overmuch.

He spoke into her ear. "I am working on a plan."

His warm breath sent tingles down Katherine's spine, and she nodded.

"I am plying Henry with brandy," Nicholas continued. "He is on his third cup since I have joined him, and he was already a bit inebriated when I arrived. He is almost drunk enough to have the tooth pulled." He kissed her on the ear, and Katherine giggled.

"I need you to stay with him while I arrange for a barber. I will not be away long."

Katherine smiled. If it had been her plan, she would have made sure that Henry knew what was to come, but Nicholas knew his friend best, and she would abide by his wisdom. They kissed again, and she watched him walk from the room, his tall wide-shouldered form filling her with happiness.

Henry nodded as she sat down in the place vacated by Nicholas. "'Tis good to see ye, m'lady."

"Thank you, Henry," Katherine smiled.

"Shall I get you something to break your fast? Perhaps a bit of meat-pie?" Jeremy asked her.

"Yes, please." Katherine's stomach made a loud grumble of assent.

Jeremy made a slight bow and walked off.

She smiled at Henry.

He smiled back.

It was the first cheerful look she had seen him make since Devizes, and the swelling on his jaw gave it a humorous touch. They sat in silence for a few minutes, two people who did not know what to say to each other.

"'Tis a good lad ye married," Henry finally said, a slight slur to his words. "I knowed him since he was a wee boy, and though his actions may be a bit rash, his heart is good. Ye may need to be a bit extra patient with him from time to time, but I think he'll respond to your good nature."

"Thank you, Henry. I did not know you have known him so long."

"We have known each other in good times and some very bad ones too. Nicky does not like to dwell on the hardships in his life. The old Earl, God rest his soul, could never gi'up the past. But mayhap that 'twas good after all since it brought Nicky to England and to you." He clapped a hand on the table and made a lopsided grin at her.

Katherine frowned. Henry was very drunk and made no sense. "The old Earl...?"

Henry nodded. "His da. Forever pining after Ashfield he was, and for his Lady who was buried there. He left his heart with her, he did. And when they murdered the King...after that he drank his way through many bottles until he died." Henry looked at his bottle and took a slug of brandy. "It hurt the lad very bad to see his da like that. He doesna like it when I drink neither. Which I do now because of me tooth, which feels better." He looked around the room and chuckled. "Everything feels better now."

Katherine stiffened. Could he be saying what she thought he was? Or were his words the incoherent ramblings of a drunkard?

"How is it you have known him so long?" she asked, her voice barely controlled. She braced herself, not wanting to hear his answer.

"Steward to Ashfield I was, as my father before me, and his before that," Henry said making a careful effort not to slur, and then burped.

Shock hit Katherine like one of her father's slaps. For a moment, she could not breathe as heat, and then a bitter cold enclosed her.

Nicholas.
Ashfield.
The old Earl.

She shivered, and her voice shook. "Montford." Answers to questions she had not known to ask fell into place before she could stop them. She nodded. "The Earl of Ashton."

Henry nodded, and gave her another lopsided grin.

"Nicholas is the Earl of Ashton," she said in dawning disbelief.

Henry's smile faded to a mild frown.

Katherine stood up. Her seat fell back with a bang.

Henry flinched and put up a hand to cover his ear.

"Katherine," Nicholas called to her. She turned to see him striding into the room. "Is aught amiss?" He smiled his charming smile, yet she found herself looking upon a stranger, not her beloved Nicholas, Sir Outlaw. This was a man called the Earl of Ashton.

Tears filled her eyes. She blinked hard. "Amiss?" she said backing away from him. "I have just heard I married a man who did not tell me who he is. But 'tis no matter, for now I see you for who *you* are: a scoundrel and a knave. A man with no honor and no conscience. 'Twould have been a favor to leave me with my father, at least he did not lie to me. You pretended to be my friend so you could get what you really wanted." Katherine's voice became a whisper. "And that was not me."

"That is not so," Nicholas protested, walking toward her once again.

"Stay back," Katherine admonished. "Do you deny you married me for my property?"

Nicholas looked uncomfortable. "'Twas only one reason."

"'Twas the only reason you did not tell me. And without any of the others, 'twas reason enough." Katherine put her hand to her throat. She felt as if she were choking, and took in ragged gulps of air. Her fingers tangled in the gold chain. Grasping it in her palm, she ripped it off, easily breaking the fine links. She looked at the love-token hanging in her hand for a long sad moment, then opened her fingers and let it fall to the ground. A sob escaped her lips.

"'Tis sorry I am, my Lady" Henry called after her.

Katherine looked back at him. "Thank you, Henry, but I am

not your Lady, nor anyone else's." She bit hard on her cheeks to keep from crying. "I am but a country squire's daughter." She focused on Nicholas. "But at least I am who I say I am."

"If you would give me a chance to explain," Nicholas said, as if trying to persuade a small child.

Katherine crossed her arms over her chest. "Since I found you in the storm you have had that chance, every minute of every day when we have been together. But I will give you one last opportunity to explain. If you can."

He held out his hands. "I meant to tell you. I planned to do so."

"'Tis not an explanation, Nicholas. 'Tis a lie."

"I would have told you this afternoon."

"Am I to believe you? You must think me a silly, foolish girl." The tears she had been holding back spilled down her cheeks, and she angrily wiped them away. "But I am not so foolish as to believe you anymore. I am not that stupid."

Nicholas had dropped his hands. "I . . . I am sorry."

"No more than I." And with that, Katherine went to the door. Opening it, she did not look back, but stepped onto the top stair. Shaking from shock and emotion, she took a deep breath of the fetid London air, and walked forward into the noisy, bustling street before her.

CHAPTER SIXTEEN

Katherine had no money for a hansom cab or sedan chair, and she'd just thrown away the only thing of value she owned. She had left Montford behind as well. But she would not go back. She could not go back. All she could do was find her way to Cousin Alicia's house.

Fenchurch Street could not be that hard to locate.

However, it turned out she was wrong. Katherine soon found that the streets in London twisted and turned and, although there were numerous signboards, the names of the actual streets were nowhere to be found.

If she'd had a purse it would have been stolen within the first few minutes. She felt so many hands on her body that she stopped crying out, merely hurried faster each time she was touched.

Nor was that the only danger. Twice she found herself in dank alleyways rife with unsavory characters and smells. Once she'd come across a man urinating on a wall. On the wider thoroughfares, she dodged coaches, horse riders, dung carts, and slops tossed out of second story windows, before realizing she had a better chance of avoiding the filth if she walked right alongside the buildings, under their projecting upper stories.

Feeling dirtier and dirtier with each new block, she trudged on. The overwhelming numbness from Nicholas's betrayal was replaced by a state of alarm, when she realized she'd passed a row of shops before, perhaps more than once before. A wary exhaustion seeped through her bones. She could not keep walking without knowing where she headed.

Tired and discouraged, she stopped a rag-picker to ask directions. Once he realized she was not a paying customer he brushed her off and walked on, as did an ink-seller. At last a kindly chimney sweep stopped. After making sure she wanted Fenchurch Street, not Avenue or Place, he gave her very thorough directions of how many blocks to go, where to turn, how many doors to count and how many steps to climb.

As the sun began to sink behind the buildings, Katherine began to fear she had misunderstood the man, or miscounted the blocks. Finally, she turned a corner onto a quiet street and spied a blue door, five doors down, set in a tall brick residence.

That must be it.

Her pace picked up. Taking a deep breath and brushing off the front of her dress, Katherine climbed the steps.

She pounded with the knocker and then waited, heart quaking, hands trembling. Finally, the door was wrenched open and a butler, wig askew, peered out at her.

Katherine pulled herself up to her full height and tucked a strand of hair behind her ear.

"Mistress Alicia Pemberton, please," she said. "Do let her know cousin Katherine Welles has arrived."

He peered at her first with one eye and then the other, as if not at all sure she wasn't playing a prank on him.

"This is the Pemberton household, is it not?" Katherine inquired.

He cleared his throat. "It is."

"Then please convey my message," she said, almost stomping her foot with impatience and pent up frustration.

The man nodded with a frown. Then he closed the door, leaving her to wait outside.

Several long minutes passed before the door flew open and Alicia appeared. She stared at Katherine in disbelief and opened her arms. Katherine stepped into her warm embrace, dissolving into tears. The pain of Nicholas's treachery overwhelmed her, and her heart felt it would burst. She sobbed her agony until her head seemed full of wool, and she could barely breathe.

"Oh my!" Alicia exclaimed. "Where is your coach? Have you come by yourself? You must tell me all, but I am afraid it will have to wait until we have supped, and the children are abed. Then I want to hear it." She stepped back. Three-year-old Anne peeked out from behind Alicia's skirt and smiled with her thumb in her mouth.

Dogs barked as Katherine was ushered inside. The other children clambered about. Pandemonium and cheerful good feelings engulfed her, and Katherine's heart eased, just a bit.

She was shown to Alicia's room, where she washed her hands and face at the washstand, combed and put her hair into a knot, and felt marginally better. She breathed deep. She would be safe from Nicholas's deceit here. Safe from Finch and her father. At least she hoped so.

Dinner was a chaotic affair. Although the food was tasty, Katherine could not eat. She watched four-and-a-half-year-old Robbie, and six-year-old Hal both feed bits of their dinner to dogs lurking under the table, wishing she could do the same.

Serious Alice, the eldest at eight, sat next to Katherine. She spoke little, regarding the proceedings with a tolerant yet resigned indifference.

Alicia somehow managed to keep order, supervise the courses, and feed Ollie, the youngest at eighteen months, all at the same time. The children's abigail attacked her meal with gusto, ignoring the commotion around her.

James Pemberton arrived part way into the meal and nodded to her, as if it were no surprise at all to see her at the table.

Soon the children were in bed, and Katherine had to decide how much to tell Alicia. She was afraid of the pain that would come with putting words to what had happened. Ensconced in the warm and loving Pemberton household, she wanted to pretend she had never known Nicholas, never loved him.

They sat in a small sitting room. A fire burned in the hearth.

Alicia took out her needlework and, without looking at Katherine or addressing her on the subject, waited for her story.

Katherine fished in Alicia's mending bag for something to occupy her hands. As she plied her needle, she started to talk. Soon her hands were flying along with her tongue. It all came out, every bit of it. At the end of the recital, a blanket of calm came over her. She glanced at Alicia to see her cousin had put down her mending.

"Do you love him?" Alicia asked.

Katherine bit back tears. "I thought I did. Now I do not know how I feel. I have been so stupid."

"Not stupid, I think. Blinded by your heart." Alicia replied, her needle back to work again. "What do you want to do?"

Katherine made a knot in the thread, and broke it. She held up the little dress, Anne's she supposed, to see if her handiwork showed. "I do not know what I want, except to ease my heart, and I do not know how to do that." She put down the garment and fished for another. Alicia stayed her hand.

"Then let us off to bed," she smiled. "A good sleep works wonders for a tattered heart."

In a borrowed nightgown and cap, Katherine found herself bedding with the sour-faced abigail. The woman snored, but not loud enough to block out the riot of thoughts and images Katherine could not hide from in the dark—Nicholas's face with his tender, lying lips; his deceitful, laughing eyes.

She would begin her new life on the morrow. A simple life with a loving family. The life she had always wanted. But it seemed so empty compared to the brief time she'd shared with Nicholas. Would that she had never found him, never asked him the favor of taking her to London, never been faced with his betrayal. Or the betrayal of her own heart.

She should never have let her heart rule her good reason.

And she would never let that happen again. From now on, she would close her heart away. Her good sense would be her guide.

Katherine gritted her teeth and clenched her eyelids against a fresh onslaught of tears. She buried her face in the bedclothes to still her sobs, but they kept coming. Pain wracked her body, settling in her chest, and Katherine knew her heart was truly breaking.

"You are sure she is aright?" Jeremy asked.

Nicholas gulped down a swig of brandy and nodded. The potent brew burned a trail down his throat, settling warm in his stomach, yet he remained chilled outside.

He had not started out to follow Katherine across London. He had meant to join her on the outside steps—to talk to her, reason with her, beg her forgiveness. He had been alarmed when she'd walked off down the street, so he had followed to make sure she did not come to harm. She had not looked back. Not even once. Had she done so, she would have seen him.

The lass had courage, more courage than he had ever suspected. And, it seemed, more courage than he had.

Nicholas scowled and looked down at the rough table. Cradling his head in his hand, he acknowledged he should not have let it come to this. He should have told her his name when she first asked him.

Nicholas took another gulp of brandy.

As the afternoon had grown late, he thought she might turn back and seek the safety of the *Hawk and Pheasant*.

Instead, she had approached a doorway and spoke to someone inside. After some waiting, a woman, presumably her cousin, had appeared and embraced her soundly. Even from a distance, he could see his lass sobbing. It seized his heart and made him feel the worst sort of scoundrel.

She went inside, and the door shut behind her.

He could not leave. Some force kept him there, just down the street, at a good vantage point where he could see but not be seen. He had stayed for some time. He'd told himself it was because he wondered if she would come out again. He told himself it was because he was too angry with Henry to return. He told himself it was because he liked the feeling of the night as it settled like a blanket over London.

Nicholas drained his cup.

But, in his heart, he knew it was because he needed to be near her. Lord help him, he was in a mess. He had married her and then lost her.

Some hours later, he had taken a hackney back to the inn and found Henry passed out in the common room. Jeremy, too weak to carry him out, sat beside him like a guard.

Now, Nicholas wished for nothing else but to drown himself in strong drink, but it did little to soothe the ache in his heart.

He banged his cup on the table and bellowed for more.

Jeremy flinched.

Henry startled, then settled back to sleep again.

Nicholas glowered. It was too bad he could not beat an already insensate man. He would have to wait until the morrow for the reckoning.

Nicholas awoke on a bench in the common room the next morning. Pulling himself to sitting, he reflected morosely on the need of a man for a place where he could sleep without his neck or his back getting a kink in it. Then he cursed himself for the drink that made his head ache and his mouth feel as dry as the Algerian desert.

Jeremy lay stretched out on the table, snoring.

Henry had made his way onto the floor during the night and slept beside a brown mongrel.

Nicholas nudged him with his booted foot.

"Get up, man," he said none too kindly. "'Tis time to make coffee."

Henry groaned.

Nicholas felt a moment of remorse, but it passed. He reached down and shook Henry by the shoulder.

Henry lurched up, grabbed his head and shut his eyes hard. "Ye may as well kill me, as make me gi'up and get t'work. Me head's poundin' as hard as me heart and me stomach..." He paused before he spoke. "Ye do not want to know about me stomach."

Nicholas banged a heavy fist on the table.

Jeremy awoke with a start. He looked at Nicholas and flinched.

"You may find me a cup of coffee," Nicholas informed him.

Jeremy looked doubtful.

"You will take this mug," Nicholas picked one up from the table and poured its remaining contents onto the floor, "to a coffee house nearby and ask them to fill it."

Nicholas threw a few coins on the table.

Jeremy picked them up and rose to do his bidding.

"Ye do not have to take it out on the boy," Henry said after he had left. "The murder I see in yer eyes is meant for me." He rose, first onto one knee and then the other, finally drawing himself up to standing. Clasping his shaking hands before him, he looked at Nicholas. "'Tis yer pardon I beg most humbly, *m'lord Earl.*"

"But...?"

"Yes, but," Henry continued, "ye had no business lyin' to her. Ye should have told her the truth before ye married her, so she would know who she did wed."

Nicholas scowled. He did not need this tongue lashing from his old friend. His conscience already pained him, as did his head.

"I had no business tellin' her, ye be thinkin', and ye be right. But I will not be responsible fer keeping yer lies straight agin." Henry sank down onto the bench across from Nicholas. "Me head pounds no less than me tooth now, if that gives ye any satisfaction."

"Little enough."

It was some time before Jeremy returned with coffee that had cooled in transit. Nicholas took a big gulp and sat the mug down on the table. He let the flavor roll around in his mouth. The bitter drink complemented his feelings. As usual, the brew served to clear some of the cobwebs from his mind.

Henry was right. He should have told her, but he had not,

and now he must do what he could to fix this mess he had made.

Nicholas took a last swallow of coffee. "We will go to her," he announced.

The short squat man had been standing outside the house with the blue door for two days now: day and night, and now day again. He had seen the young woman arrive and go inside, and noted the man who followed her, who'd stayed in the shadows and then left several hours later. Because of the man, he'd had to wait before he could hire a messenger boy. But finally when the man left, Jakes had sent word.

Katherine Welles has arrived.

What a canny one, his master was. He'd knowed she would come, and so she had. And now his master waited down the street, with two strong men. When the woman left the house they would take her into the waiting coach and bring her back home where she belonged.

Jakes made a satisfied sigh and waited for the moment when he could make the signal.

Inside the Pemberton household, pandemonium ensued. Ollie teethed on a wooden spoon while Robbie and Hal fought over who would get to sit next to Katherine at breakfast. Anne sucked her thumb. Katherine spooned bowls of porridge at the sideboard. Alice sat primly, watching her mother separate the two boys and place them in chairs on opposite sides of the table.

When everyone else was seated, Alicia took her place. The children stilled as their mother said a quick prayer of thanks. Except for baby Ollie, they said "amen" in unison. Then all was bedlam again.

Moments later the butler, wig askew as usual, came to speak to Alicia. She nodded to Katherine.

"A gentleman is here to see you," she said over the din. "Perhaps you should see what he would say."

Katherine felt a hot flush run over her and the porridge stuck in her throat. It had to be Nicholas, but she would not see him. "I would prefer to stay here," she said, taking a sip of small ale.

"Mum, mum," a maid came running in. "Theys a'fightin' in the street, they is. The three men that came and the three that came after."

Katherine's spoon hit the table with a clatter, and she jumped up. Before she knew how she got there, she was at the window at the front of the house. Pulling back a drape, she stared in horror at the street. Her pulse quickened and her breath jumped all the way to her throat when she saw Nicholas in a sword fight, while Jeremy—not yet recovered from his last beating—and Henry fought hand-to-hand with two thugs in a full melee.

Hal and Robbie came up and pushed their way to the window, shoving each other to get a better view through the thick glass.

Katherine heard the sickening sound of flesh connecting with flesh and the harsh ring of metal upon metal. She gasped when she realized it was Richard Finch who fought Nicholas.

Jeremy took a swing at one thug but missed, getting slammed on the head in return. He dropped to the ground.

Katherine clapped her hand over her mouth. Would no one come to his aid? She ran to the door.

Alicia grabbed her by the arm and pulled her back. "You cannot go out. You could be hurt, or distract your husband and his friends. You are not the help they need. I have sent for the constable."

"What of James?"

"You know he is not here."

"The butler?"

"He is who I sent for the constable." Alicia took Katherine's shoulders and shook her to get her full attention. Her usually amiable countenance was pulled tight. "'Tis but us, the maids, the abigail, and the children. We are of no help to them. You must understand this, cousin."

Katherine pulled her gaze from Alicia. Her eyes darted around the room. "Do you have a gun?"

Alicia tightened her grip on Katherine. "No." She shook her head. "Do not think of that."

The only weapon Katherine could see was the fire fork. She looked back at her cousin and spoke quietly but firmly. "Let go of me Alicia. I must do what I can to stop this. 'Tis because of me that they fight. I will not allow it to continue."

"When men fight you cannot stop them."

"I must try."

Alicia released her grip. Katherine went to the hearth and grabbed up the heavy implement. Hurrying to the door, she swung it open just in time to see a ruffian grab Henry's head and yank it down, slamming it into an up thrust knee. Henry took a mighty whack to the jaw and crumbled to the ground.

Katherine thought she might be sick. She clutched her belly, almost dropping the large fork.

Two men now fought. Swords clashing, Nicholas and Finch seemed evenly matched. Katherine could not see their faces, but the intensity of their concentration was evident in their stance and the careful control of their thrusts and parries. There were no wild movements, no cries of triumph or dismay.

She did not want to divert Nicholas's attention from Finch, so she stayed in place. But when he moved, she felt as if she moved with him; when Finch's thrusts came close, she felt as if he almost hit her.

Nicholas lunged.

Her breath caught.

Finch slid just out of range, but not fast enough. It looked like he might have been injured.

Katherine's heart made a painful flutter. Then she saw Jakes for the first time.

He came up behind Nicholas holding a stout club.

Still lugging the fire fork, Katherine rushed forward, but she was not in time.

Jakes brought the bludgeon down on Nicholas's head.

Katherine shrieked.

Nicholas collapsed in a heap.

Katherine moaned. The iron weapon fell from her hands with a loud clang. She sagged and would have fallen if Alicia had not caught her and held her up.

The two brutes rolled Nicholas onto his stomach, bound his hands behind him, and tied his feet together.

Finch took the club from Jakes. He looked up and down the street.

In dawning horror, Katherine saw him raise the weapon. He brought it down on Nicholas, swift and hard. Once. Twice. Each strike harder than the last.

Katherine raised her hands to her ears against a horrible wailing which she realized was the sound of her own cries. She clamped her mouth shut, holding her lower lip tight with her teeth.

Where was help? She lurched away from Alicia and grabbed up the fire fork and started forward again.

Finch held the club aloft. His eyes focused on Katherine. He raised it further as if in warning.

She froze.

Still looking at her, he nodded and brought down the weapon, swift and sure.

Nicholas's unconscious body took the force of the blow.

"No!" Katherine fell to her knees.

Finch smirked, clearly enjoying her misery and intending to hurt Nicholas all the more because of her presence. He raised the club.

Katherine shuddered and closed her eyes. Her stomach lurched anew. She tasted blood and realized she'd bit into her lip.

Loud yells came from a distance. Feet pounded on the cobblestones.

Alicia's voice came to her, calm and steady. Katherine could feel her cousin's capable hands take hold of her and urge her up. "The constables are here now. You must come inside."

Supporting Katherine, she led her to the door.

Katherine grabbed hold of the doorframe. "I cannot leave them. I must do something." She wiped her tears on the end of her apron.

"We can do nothing for your husband until the authorities have sorted this out. As soon as possible we will see to him and the others, I promise."

Of course, Alicia was right. Katherine allowed her cousin to escort her inside. Heart pounding, she returned to the window. Although she couldn't hear Finch, it was clear from his gestures he explained what had happened in a way that put his actions in a positive light. The stance of the newcomers changed from challenging to interested, and Katherine knew they believed whatever lies they were told.

He didn't need to lie. The truth about Nicholas would put him in jail.

Katherine convulsed as a sob hit her. The clatter of wheels on the cobblestones outside broke into her misery, and she opened her eyes to see a coach pull up.

One of the constables helped Jakes lift Nicholas and dump him into the vehicle. Finch climbed in. The constable and Jakes got up front with the driver. The thugs took their place at the rear, and they were off, leaving Jeremy and Henry behind.

Katherine's heart constricted when the vehicle rumbled out of view.

Alicia pulled her into a hug as uncontrollable sobs wracked her frame. Katherine breathed in her cousin's comforting smell of lemon verbena and porridge while her anguish cried its way down to a sodden whimper.

Outside the window, the butler and the remaining constable helped Jeremy and Henry to their feet and brought them inside.

Katherine broke from Alicia's embrace and they walked to the kitchen. She dried her face before joining the men who sat— a sorry twosome—on stools before the fire. New bruises would join Jeremy's old ones, but he had not fought long enough to be injured as badly as the older man.

Henry held his jaw like it might fall off if he let go. It took some convincing before he allowed Alicia to probe, but the mighty blow had loosened the offending tooth to such a great degree that a trip to the barber was no longer necessary.

While Alicia prepared to remove the molar, Katherine tended to Jeremy, cleaning away dirt and applying bandages and salve. They did not speak; Katherine could not. The tears would return if she gave them a chance and she did not want to cry, not for Nicholas and not now. She took a deep breath and willed her pain to wait until she was alone.

Jeremy took her hand and squeezed.

Alicia assembled a pair of pliers and several clean pieces of linen on the table beside Henry.

"Ready?" she asked.

He nodded and made two fists in his lap.

Katherine avoided his gaze, and slid her free hand over his calloused one. He opened his palm and took her fingers in a firm grip.

The three of them formed a chain, a bond of shared experience, compassion, and strength.

Alicia murmured, leaning into Henry.

The room was quiet and still as they all held their breaths. Henry's grasp grew stronger and stronger. Katherine's fingers turned red.

Alicia made a swift yank. Henry's head jerked forward and the tooth came out.

Henry groaned, whether from pain or relief Katherine could not tell. She and Jeremy both exhaled.

Henry gave her a short nod and unfolded his fingers, flexing them and rubbing hers while she pulled her hand away.

Jeremy let go her other hand.

Katherine felt bereft without their contact.

"'Tis good the tooth came away so easily and in one piece," Alicia ran a hand across her forehead. "I had some worry it would not."

As Henry started to rise, she stayed him with her hands on his shoulders. "You must sit here for the nonce," she instructed. "Keep the linen in your mouth and do not talk for the next few minutes. I would not want you fainting in my kitchen."

She looked up, a sudden frown on her brow. "What do you suppose the children are doing? 'Tis very quiet. That does not bode well. I cannot imagine the abigail has them under control. I fear they are up to some mischief."

"Go," said Katherine. "I will clean up."

Alicia nodded. But she took the wad of bloody linen from Henry's mouth and had him bite down on a new one before she left.

Henry balefully eyed the tooth. "Thith a sma thing to meke tho muth twouble fo a man."

Katherine shook her head. "Do not speak."

"Buh I muth thay I yam thoddy, m'Lady."

"Please do not apologize, Henry. And when 'tis all right for you to speak again, you must address me as you did once, as Katherine, or Mistress."

Henry grunted.

Jeremy nodded. "I am sorry as well, Mistress, for what has happened here today."

"'Twas not your doing, Jeremy. 'Tis for me to apologize. I am sorry for the pain I have caused you, twice now. And you, too." She put a hand on Henry's shoulder. "I am to blame."

Henry patted the hand on his shoulder.

Jeremy spoke. "'Twas not your fault, Mistress."

"I can only think you say this because you are a true friend." She sighed, letting her hand drop from Henry's shoulder. "You left Ashfield because of me. You have been in two fights because of me. That does not make me a good friend, I fear. And now what? Where will you go? What will you do? I cannot think my cousin will mind if you both stay here while you recuperate."

"I had thought to find myself work at a stables, or mayhap at an inn as a hostler." Jeremy put his hand to his chest and grimaced. "Mayhap I shall wait a bit."

Henry brought himself slowly to standing, as if testing each bone and muscle in the process. Shoulders back, he spat the wad of linen into his hand. "I shall see to my master," he said and threw the bloody mess into the fire.

A sob caught in Katherine's throat. She blinked hard and took a deep breath to keep back the emotion that threatened to overwhelm her.

Henry eyed her as if he understood. "You take care of the lad until he is well enough."

When he had shuffled out, Jeremy spoke. "I will protect you now," he said. "Master Finch knows where to find you. Perhaps he will leave you alone now you are married, but I think not. We do not know how or why he came to be here."

Katherine frowned. She had assumed he had found Nicholas and followed him here, waiting for the right moment to get his revenge for the earlier humiliation. But, what if he'd been laying in wait and Nicholas came along, walking into a trap really meant for her? A shiver ran through her.

She was trapped. More trapped than she had ever been at Ashfield. Raw pain stabbed through her, and she blinked hard to push back the tears that came with it.

At least she had a friend, someone she could trust, who had never failed to have her best interests at heart.

She turned back to him. "Jeremy, I cannot thank you enough for your loyalty. My heart aches so, yet your friendship gives me ease. Someday I will find a way to repay your kindness."

Jeremy made an awkward smile.

Katherine spent the next days in a numb fog. She held off her emotions by making lists and marking things off as they got done. She wiped dirty noses and insisted on clean hands before meals. She haggled with the fish seller and prevailed upon the costermonger to provide fresher vegetables.

For the first time in her life, Katherine found scant satisfaction in regular domestic chores. Washing, ironing and baking assumed the proportions of tyranny. No matter how well they got done, they would need to be repeated in just a matter of days. Long, endless days. With the joy wrenched from her life, how was she to make her way through them?

The Pembertons provided the warm and happy household she had always longed for, but her new life did not fill her heart. Instead, that organ ached with a constant piercing throb. In idle moments, Nicholas's face would come to her, with his twinkling eyes, and full expressive mouth, causing other parts of her to ache as well. Then the pain of his betrayal would hit her in a hot rush, leaving her stunned and hurt, but still wanting.

Of him, there was no news.

Even though Alicia had insisted Jeremy stay with them while he healed, Katherine saw little of him. He spent his days exploring London. She wondered if he saw Nicholas and did not tell her, but she had not the courage to ask.

One afternoon Jeremy returned bearing a small basket.

"Montford!" Katherine cried then clapped a hand over her mouth at the name.

She did not want to care what had happened to Nicholas, but she did. Wouldn't he be able to talk his way out of the charges and use his noble status to secure his release? He was an expert charmer, but would that work in jail? Even if it didn't, he had no compunction against using people to get what he wanted. Katherine felt certain that, like Montford, he would land on his feet.

But what if he did not?

This question tormented her in the dark, quiet hours before dawn, when the pain of his betrayal and the humiliation of her misplaced love was fresh and sharp. Tired and weak, she could not push away her worries. Would they brand him on the face and send him to the colonies? Or might they see his actions as treason, and hang him until dead?

And why was it not a crime that he had broken her heart?

But Katherine already knew the answer to that: because men ruled the world, and they had no hearts.

CHAPTER SEVENTEEN

Hal and Robbie ran into the kitchen, almost knocking into Katherine in their haste to find her.

"A man is here to see you," Hal announced breathlessly.

"One of the sword fighting men," Robbie added.

Katherine wiped flour from her hands onto her apron.

Nicholas?

Here?

Her heart fluttered and then crashed into her stomach. She raised a hand to her breast. Had he come to apologize? Ask her forgiveness? But how had he gotten away from Finch and the authorities?

"I will be there anon," she told the boys.

They scurried off to tell the butler.

Disappointment washed over her when she entered the sitting room. Then fear took its place. It was not Nicholas's tall muscular form that greeted her, but Richard Finch's smaller one. He stood in the center of the room, dressed immaculately, periwig perched atop his head. His face had been powdered white, no doubt in a futile effort to disguise his bruised and swollen nose.

"Let me speak plainly," he said as soon as she entered the room. "Your lover is in Newgate awaiting trial. The blackguard said you married him. Did you know he could very well hang for the crime of abduction?"

Katherine trembled at the shock of Finch's accusation.

He stepped toward her. "So you did not know. 'Tis a very serious crime. As a highwayman he could lose an ear, be branded on the cheek, or be sentenced to hard labor. It is possible he would hang. But for abduction it would be a surety." He stepped toward her again. "If you stay married to him, it will sentence him to death. And I, for one, would happily see him come to his end flapping on the end of a rope," his smile was more like a sneer, "and you a widow." He stepped forward again, until he was just inches from her, and took her chin in his hand. "Are you willing to be the cause of his death, dear Katherine?"

She swallowed hard, staring back, unwilling to let him see how he intimidated her.

His eyes glinted. "No, I can see you are not." He brought his mouth to hover above hers. She could feel his hot breath on her lips. His fingers pressed into her jaw. She wanted to pull away, but knew he did this to torment her and that to react would invite further persecution.

He brushed his lips over hers then pulled away, dropping his hand.

"On the other hand, you could petition for a decree of nullity stating the marriage was not valid. If granted, the charges will be dropped and he could live." He looked her up and down boldly. "Is there any chance you did not consummate the union?"

Katherine flushedt.

He shook his head and his eyes went hard. "No, I thought not. Whether he lives or dies, you will be sorry for not saving yourself for me."

"I will never marry you," Katherine said, her voice strong.

"Ah, dear Katherine. I thought you understood. Your only grounds for annulment would be to acknowledge our marriage contract."

"I never agreed to marry you."

Finch straightened a ruffled cuff. "But I think you will agree to it now to save your lover's life."

He stepped back from her and took a folded paper from his inside pocket. "If you have any doubts about his regard for you, perchance you should read this." He held it out to her.

Unwillingly, she took the paper from Finch's hand. Addressed to her father, it was from Nicholas, and dated a few weeks prior. He offered to trade her and a lot of money for Ashfield. Each word, like a knife, pierced deep into her heart.

Where had he penned it? Salisbury? Devizes? She had known he had played her false, but to hold the proof in her hand was shattering. Since the beginning, he had toyed with her, telling her he protected her, yet he had used her instead.

"See you now the man you married? Know you now his true regard? He does not want you. But I do." Finch took the paper from her limp fingers. "Revenge, dear Katherine, can be most satisfying. Examine your heart. Perhaps you would wish to see him dead?"

The shaking began as soon as Finch left. Katherine stumbled through the house in a blur before finding herself out the kitchen door, and in the garden.

Alternating between anger and regret, she railed at her image of Nicholas with his twinkling blue eyes, and full-lipped smile.

How could he, as the Raven, seek to expose the true nature of others, yet so despicably conceal his own?

What an irritating duplicitous man!

But could she condemn him to death? Could she watch him pay the consequences of his actions without trying to aid him? Could she take revenge upon him for the harm he had done to her? Or, since she had saved his life once, was she now obligated to do what she could to preserve it?

Katherine let out a great heaving sigh and wiped her hands on the back of her apron, surprised to see them covered with dirt. Looking about, she discovered she was on her knees, a pile of weeds beside her. The dirt below the rosemary and sage bushes was now clear.

The door behind her opened, and Annie slid through it. The little girl plopped down next to her. Thumb in mouth, she put her other hand into Katherine's.

"Would you like me to show you how to tend the garden?" Katherine said to the sweet face beside her.

Annie nodded.

"You have to be able to tell the good plants from the bad plants," she said, thinking how nice it would be if she could do the same with people. She showed the girl which weeds to pull. They worked together until a good part of the herb garden was clear of most of the wild growth.

Katherine sat back on her haunches and brushed the dirt off her hands. Working in a garden always acted as a healing balm. While her hands had worked, she had come to a decision. In spite of what Nicholas had done, she could not be the instrument of his death, nor contribute to it.

She would have to get an annulment.

Then she would have to do whatever she could to escape marriage with Finch, which put her back where she started.

But this time, she would find an escape on her own.

Nicholas woke cold and in pain. Had he heard someone call his name?

Eyes still closed, he rolled onto his back. The chill hard floor provided no comfort to his battered body and he liked it that way. The pain was a constant reminder of the mistakes he had made; the lies he had spawned, the heart he had broken.

"Nicky!"

He heard it again. The voice called louder, sounding very much like Henry. Nicholas groaned. He did not want to see Henry. Henry would want to help him, and he did not deserve to be helped. He deserved to be left to die.

Except, if he was going to die, he would probably have done so by now. Instead, he already felt the subtle and unwelcome signs that his body was healing.

"There he is. I see him." Henry's voice rose above the din and chatter.

Nicholas opened an eye. He lay in a corner of the felon's ward. The other inhabitants were scattered about. They had ceased to pay him any mind once they had taken all he had of value. He'd offered no resistance as they took his boots, coat, and shirt. They'd not taken his breeches. Maybe there was some code of honor here at Newgate. Or maybe his breeches would have had to be torn to bits to get them past his fetters.

He inhaled a painful breath. At least one rib had been broken. Finch had probably meant to kill him. Nicholas wondered why he hadn't.

He remembered little of the fight, and wished to remember nothing before that. Especially not the hurt and indignation on Katherine's face when she had dropped his lucky piece on the ground. Now it was gone. He must have lost it sometime during the fight or here at Newgate. And it seemed his luck had gone with it.

"What a sorry sight ye be, but glad I am to have found you."

Nicholas turned his head and was hit by a wave of dizziness as he looked up a long pair of legs to see Henry smiling down at him.

"Not I," he croaked at his old steward.

"No." Henry shook his head. "You're goin' to have to face up to it, lad. You're not just responsible for yerself now. Ye have a wife."

Nicholas turned his face away.

"Get up, Nicky, or I'll get you up. I've paid your garnish and ye'll be movin' to a better cell. We'll clean ye up and get yer wounds tended. And then ye will figure out what ye're going to do next."

As he struggled to rise, Nicholas cursed the loyalty of friends.

Katherine watched as a familiar old coach came to a rickety stop before the Pemberton residence. As her father's stout figure emerged gracelessly from the vehicle, a feeling of tired resignation ran through her. Yet she could not help the slight swell in her heart when she saw his familiar form.

She should have known he would turn up sooner or later. She had truly hoped it would be later, after she had petitioned for the annulment. Yet his timing had been ever thus.

Had he come to take her home? Surely Finch had sent him.

The butler showed Gerald into the small sitting room. He popped up from his chair when she entered. "What is the meaning of this?" He held up a piece of paper.

"Hello, father," Katherine said. "It is so nice of you to come."

"Fiddle-sticks," he puffed. "Explain this."

Katherine took the paper from his hand. Her heart tumbled when she recognized Nicholas's signature at the bottom. Her stomach did a familiar lurch, and she sank into a nearby chair. Another letter? Would this be as damning as the first?

She took a deep breath and began to read. After a formal salutation, it announced the matter of their marriage and went on to reassure her father that Katherine would be provided for in the event of Nicholas's death. Nothing was said of Ashfield. It was dated four days prior, yet there was nothing to indicate where it had been composed.

Why had he written her father with these reassurances? Could it be he felt some remorse for what he had done?

She handed back the letter. "This is true."

"Truly married?" Gerald nodded. His voice went up several notes. "To an Earl?"

Katherine nodded.

He smiled broadly. "That is very well done of you."

Katherine almost smiled in return at his rare praise, but brushed it aside instead. "No, father. I am afraid 'tis not. You see, the marriage is a hoax, and he is an impostor."

Gerald's face fell. "I am afraid I do not understand. He is not an Earl...?"

"He is an Earl, but he did not say so, nor did he say that his family once owned Ashfield. He only married me to get it back."

Gerald shook his head. "You have got it wrong, gel. 'Tis an

impostor who says he is an Earl when he is not. What you have is a very fortunate situation."

"'Tis my misfortune. I will seek an annulment, so I may put this *situation*, as you call it, behind me."

"No, daughter. I could not allow that."

"Father, you have guided me all my life, as is your duty, I know. But in this you will not. I will do what is best for myself."

Her father's face went pink. He raised a pudgy finger and shook it at her as he spoke. "What of your family, Katherine? Care you naught for them, and their needs? Do not be a selfish girl."

Katherine flinched inwardly as she shook her head. "I but do what is right."

Her father ignored her and continued. "I understand Lord Ashton will face charges as the Raven. If this is true, and he is to suffer for what he has done, be sure that before aught happens to him, you carry his seed." He looked at her sternly. "Make a son of it."

❧

Two days later, James Pemberton returned from his business trip. The tall, heavyset man ushered Katherine into the small, very cluttered room he used as an office. He listened, a forefinger placed across his lips, occasionally running a hand through his wild untamed hair, as she told him what had transpired. As she finished, his perpetual vague look vanished, and his eyes focused on her with hawk-like tenacity.

He tapped his lips with his finger. "I have looked into this case. The charges against Lord Ashton are serious. *'All ravishments and willful taking away or marrying of any maid, widow or damsel against her will...'*" he quoted from memory, "are capital offenses. The charges against him as the Raven are equally serious. He is in a good deal of trouble and could be sentenced to hang."

"So I have been told." Katherine's voice caught. "But 'twould be a lie to say I married him against my will, for I did not. 'Twas not an abduction. Although I was quite mistaken in his motives and identity, I did go with him of my own free will."

James nodded. "Should you provide that testimony, the charges of abduction would be dropped, yet you would remain married to the man."

Katherine made a weak nod. "What of an annulment? Is there some way to secure a release from this marriage without my being forced to a marriage with Richard Finch?"

"Annulment could be granted on the basis of the prior contract, if it really exists. Did you pledge yourself to this man, Finch?"

"We had not said our espousals. Yet I believe the financial agreements were final." Katherine sighed. "But now my father would probably say he agreed to the marriage with Lord Ashton"—her heart beat painfully as she said the name— "because he is an Earl, not because it is true."

James tapped his finger against his lip. "No doubt Finch would bring testimony that your father had approved his suit. That could provide you with the annulment you seek, yet it would not prevent a subsequent marriage to Finch." He clapped his hands together. "All this conflicting testimony could keep matters tied up in the Courts of Chancery for quite some time. That would keep Lord Ashton alive until the matter was decided, and prevent your marriage to Finch indefinitely."

Katherine chewed her lip. She did not want the agony of a prolonged legal suit. Would that this had never happened. That she had never said 'yes' when Nicholas had said they would marry. That she'd never been coaxed into such impetuousness by a pair of twinkling blue eyes and a dashing white streak of hair.

"Is there no other recourse?" she asked.

"No other way to end the marriage, except to petition for an Act of Parliament, which is granted so rarely I would not recommend you even think of it." He sat back in his chair and his eyes went unfocused.

Katherine waited so long for him to continue, she thought he might have forgotten she was there.

At last, he spoke. "You could get a separation from Lord Ashton with a formal agreement for alimony. It is unlikely you could obtain this through the courts. You would have to get your husband to agree to this. Do you have any bargaining power with him?" He smiled and snapped his fingers. "You could agree to testify against the abduction in return for this separation."

Katherine shook her head. Negotiate with Nicholas? See him again?

"Think on it, cousin. You do not need to make any hasty decisions. The wheels of justice move slowly." James smiled. "By the way, I have heard news of your husband. He has been transferred to the Tower."

Katherine's heart dropped.

James took her hand and patted it. "That just means that his noble status has been discovered and secured the move. In fact, it will be much better for him in the Tower. It is quite common for prisoners in Newgate to die from disease before ever going to trial."

His eyes sharpened on her. "Once you have decided what you wish to do, I will be most happy to prepare whatever documents are required, or speak to whoever can most help us. I am sure Alicia has already made it clear you are welcome here for as long as you require. In fact, I can already see we would be hard pressed without you."

Katherine's heart eased, just a little.

Nicholas paced the small cell that had been his home for the sennight since Henry found him. A small, cold, barren place, yet better than he deserved.

Henry had first obtained a better room at Newgate, and two days later Nicholas had been transferred to the Tower. For this, he should be grateful, but he was not. He did not like the peace or the solitude. He did not appreciate the good food Henry brought him, or the warm clothing, although the bath had been nice.

His body still ached from the pounding he had received from Finch. But it did not hurt nearly as bad as his heart. He now knew that living without Katherine's love was like living without the sun. He missed her sweet presence with a pain that pierced through him far worse than the injury Finch had done. And he had no one but himself to blame.

He filled his hours with pacing. The motion satisfied his busy mind, and it helped his body heal. There was naught else to do in this room but to wait. Nicholas did not like waiting. He liked to take action. Because of this he had got himself into a tight spot he could not get himself out of.

His one hope was Katherine. She was the only one who could clear him of the charge of abduction. She had not done so yet. He would not blame her if she never did.

Katherine knelt over the chamber pot. Though her insides heaved, she doubted there could be anything left to come out. She eased herself up onto the mattress where her bedmate still slept and put a hand on her tender stomach. What she would give for a sprig of peppermint, or a cup of willow bark tea. Rolling onto her side, she decided to get a few more minutes rest before the household awoke and the demands of a new day were upon her.

When Katherine did not come down for the morning meal, Cousin Alicia came up to her. "'Tis clear we are already spoiled by your presence," she announced cheerfully as she entered the room. "The children were peevish at breakfast. Hal and Robbie declared the porridge too thin, and Anne would put nothing inside her mouth besides her thumb. Now what is it that ails you?" She swooped down on Katherine, a mild frown across her forehead.

"My stomach does not sit well." Katherine tried to get up, but the offending organ made a lurch, and she lay back down again. "It has been so for several days now, but this morning is the worst."

Alicia put a cool hand onto Katherine's forehead. "Have you missed your monthly courses?"

Katherine took a slow breath. "I have not bled since leaving Ashfield." She swallowed. "Yet it is not so terribly late."

Alicia took Katherine's hand between hers. "The amount of lateness may not necessarily signify. One day can be the same as many. Do you have tenderness of the breast?"

Katherine nodded. Her nipples had been so sensitive of late that she'd had to lace her stays very tight to keep them from rubbing the fabric of her shift. She had thought their tenderness, in fact the heightened sensitivity of all her woman's places, was due to her body's awakening.

"Although it is early to tell, it seems the answer is plain," Alicia pronounced. "'Tis very likely you are with child."

"But I cannot be!" Katherine cried. "I do not wish it."

Alicia smiled. "You are not the first, nor will you be the last woman, to feel so." She patted Katherine's hand. "You manage very well with my children; surely you would wish to have your own?"

"Were my life settled, I would wish it," Katherine exclaimed. "But 'tis not. 'Tis a horrible muddle and this will only make it worse, not better. How can I possibly get an annulment now?" She pulled her hand from Alicia's and jerked the bed sheet over her head. "I have made such a botch of my life," she said through the rough linen.

Alicia laughed and tugged the fabric off Katherine's face. "I would not worry on that, cousin. You will be amazed to find how long nine months can be. You will have time yet to make it right, and when you are feeling better you will no doubt see the way to do so," she sobered. "Yet, perhaps 'tis not too soon to consider what you will you say to your father—and to your husband."

Katherine blanched. "If he were to know, Father would be uncommon happy. But I would ask you to keep this between us for now."

Alicia nodded assent. "You must do as you think best," she said, and gave Katherine a gentle pat on the shoulder as she rose to leave the room.

Katherine sat up.

A baby.

She splayed her fingers across her belly. A new life grew there. One last gift from Nicholas.

Why would he not leave her alone? He haunted her dreams. He haunted her waking hours. And now, there would be a constant reminder of him growing inside her.

Prickles ran across the back of her nose.

What was she to do? Katherine raised a tired hand to her eyes, as if to block out the mistakes she had made. Now an annulment would be impossible.

The next afternoon, Katherine looked up from her gardening to see Jeremy coming her way. She had cut the herb bushes back, freed them from choking weeds and now applied her labors to pulling out the dead foliage that dotted the yard.

"My Lady," he called to her.

His bruises had faded, and he wore an air of confidence she had not seen before. In fact, he looked quite handsome.

She brushed off her hands, pleased his interruption gave her a respite from a recalcitrant shrub. Although dead, it was not giving up its hold on the earth easily.

"Please, call me Katherine," she reminded him. "Or if you must, say mistress as you once did."

"Aye, mistress," he smiled back at her. "I have come to tell you I am leaving."

Katherine's face fell. "I had thought you happy to be in London? Have you decided to return to Ashfield then?"

"Nay. I am hale now and can no longer occupy the invalid bed in the kitchen. 'Tis time for me to move on. I have taken lodging with Henry."

"How will you get on?"

"I have been running errands for gentlemen at coffee houses and the clerks of the courts of law." Jeremy looked at her with serious blue eyes. "Even though I go, I would come to you at any time you would need me."

"Jeremy, I shall miss you. You are the best friend I have now." Katherine took his hand in her dirty ones. "Your loyalty has meant so much to me."

"I will not be far, my Lady, I mean mistress," he amended at her frown. "But can I not call you Lady? 'Tis proper since *you-know-who* is an Earl."

Katherine sighed. "You can say his name to me now, Jeremy. And yes, 'tis proper but I do not like it. Although I had thought to sever our bond, it seems I cannot do that." She bit her bottom lip. "Something has changed."

"Please, mistress, if it would make you feel better, tell me your troubles."

Katherine made a faint smile, remembering when she had unburdened herself to Jeremy in the coach on the way to London. She nodded.

He followed her along a slate pathway to a stone bench set amongst bramble bushes where they sat down.

"I have been putting off a decision I do not wish to make. Now something has happened; I can wait no more." Katherine searched his face. He was the only man who demanded naught of her, yet gave in return.

"Tell me how I can help you, mistress."

"I cannot think how you could," she said. "But, if you listen to my woes, perhaps that will lighten my heart."

As she spoke, her heart did ease. She told him of the visit from Richard Finch, Nicholas's letters, her conversation with James, and then about the babe.

"A babe? How?" He blushed and shook his head. "No, I know how. You need not tell me that. 'Tis wonderful news."

"No, Jeremy, not good news at all." Katherine shook her head. "I can no longer get an annulment. And because I must stay married, Lord Ashton will be tried for my abduction. He could hang." Katherine let out a deep sigh.

"Could you testify on his behalf?"

"I would, but I do not think they would believe me because of the letter. I would be so much better off if I had not married him!"

"You cannot say that. If you were not married your baby would be a bastard." Jeremy spoke fervently. "A babe needs a father."

"A babe needs more than a liar and criminal for a father."

He took her hand. "If you knew what I do, you would never say such a thing, or even think of your babe growing up with the stain of bastardy. I know this because I am a bastard. I am more than your friend, Katherine." His eyes held great sadness and yearning. "I am your brother."

A shock ran up Katherine's spine. "Brother?" she whispered.

"I am your brother by half, a natural child. We share our father, not our mothers." A pained expression glanced across his face. "We do not truly share our father. He has never been mine. I would not have known who he is had not my mother died and sent me to him. Even though he is not such a father to be proud of, I would have liked for him to call me 'son'."

Katherine's heart caught. Gerald Welles had never treated Jeremy with any discernment, ignoring him with the same benign indifference he paid all the servants.

"Brother," she said the word louder this time. She searched his face, his eyes, his nose, for familial recognition. She now understood why he occasionally reminded her of Edward. She remembered Edward's voice in her dream: *There is Jeremy.*

"Brother," she said again with conviction. "I have ever been sad to have lost one, and now to have another gladdens my heart. That it be you, Jeremy, fills me with joy." She put her hands up to his face and ran her dirty fingers over his cheeks, traced his nose and his brow. "But why did you not tell me before?"

"I was not sure you would want to know it," he said. "And my mother made it very clear that it was a secret, not to be shared. Although our father took me in on her death, we never spoke of it."

"Of course I would want to know," Katherine chided him. "You must tell me of your life before you came to Ashfield. I wish to know all those things it was never proper to ask before— what you like and what you do not like." She searched his eyes.

"No one need find out what you have told me, although I do not think I can hide my happiness."

"If you knew what I do, you would never wish a child to grow up without its father's good name." Jeremy smiled and covered her hands with his as they rested on his cheeks. "I think you must tell Lord Ashton about the babe. And, for the sake of the babe, you must do everything you can to preserve the life of your husband."

"James suggested I ask Nicholas for a formal separation. I have not wanted to see him." She sighed, realizing that was not the truth at all. She wanted to see him desperately, and just as desperately was afraid that just a glimpse of his twinkling blue eyes would melt the wall of ice she had built around her heart. "I have not wanted to help him, but I will do what is right and declare I was not abducted. I hope the courts believe me."

Jeremy smiled. "I will stand by you and help you in any way you wish. Dear Katherine, I have always loved you for doing what is right."

Katherine prayed she did so now.

CHAPTER EIGHTEEN

Katherine examined the woman looking back at her in the small hand mirror. Dark circles framed her tired eyes. Lips drawn in a firm line made her look grim. She pinched a bit of color into her cheeks and tried relaxing her mouth into a smile, but it did not reach her eyes.

Today she would go to Nicholas, tell him about the baby and ask him for a formal separation and support. In return, she would testify that she had not been abducted.

She would not smile at him, or touch him, or suffer his touch, nor reveal her feelings to him in any way, for she had discovered she could not keep the ice around her heart. She yet loved the man, though she would not trust him again.

So, she would speak to him, urge him, if necessary, to do what was right and then go.

If only it would be so!

Katherine glared at herself in the mirror and put it down. She took a deep breath and squared her shoulders.

Jeremy accompanied her to the hackney-coach waiting outside. They rode in silence on the short trip through the narrow London streets to the great fortress. He paid the driver and helped her out. Assuming a brotherly air of protection, he steered her through the crowd of gawkers and hawkers that thronged in front of the barbican.

The scaffold on Tower Hill stood quiet. Set against gray skies with a chill wind blowing off the Thames, the scene filled her with foreboding. Katherine clasped her nervous hands together inside her warm cloak.

A Yeoman Warder allowed them entrance and led them on the long walk into the complex. Inside was a hotchpotch of buildings. A series of towers guarded the perimeter. Several large ravens strutted on the green. As they followed the guard across the inner ward past workers and soldiers, Katherine shivered and tightened her cloak.

Entering one of the stone towers, they climbed a dark narrow staircase. At the end of a short corridor, the jailer unlocked a door for them. "Visitors," he barked, and stepped aside.

Katherine took a deep breath to calm the butterflies in her stomach. She stepped forward, motioning Jeremy to follow, but he shook his head. She would be on her own for this interview. Raising her chin, she pulled herself to her full height and entered the room. The door swung shut behind her with a thud.

Nicholas turned from the narrow window. His eyes took a moment to adjust to the darkness of the room. Expecting Henry, he was surprised to see the outline of a woman in a familiar cloak. As she stepped toward him, his heart made a small elated leap.

"Katherine?" He walked toward her, hand outstretched.

But she did not raise her hand in return.

Sadly, he let his hand fall as he came to stand before her. He tried to search her face, but her head was set well inside her hood and tilted down. Only her nose and the firm line of her mouth were visible.

So it was not to be a friendly visit, but of course he knew that. He did not expect her to forgive him, and he had done nothing to make amends. Nicholas simply did not know what to do. He did not understand the feelings he had for Katherine, or her love for him. It paralyzed him, and left him afraid of losing the very thing he had lost. But whatever her reason for coming, he was glad to see her.

"Will you sit?" he asked, pointing to the room's one stool. Henry had offered to bring more furniture, but Nicholas had turned him down. Now he was sorry. He wanted to offer her more than a three-legged stool.

Katherine shook her head. "I am comfortable standing," she said, her voice as stiff as her body.

Nicholas nodded, wanting to see her eyes, willing her to raise her head so he could see if they were cold, hurt, or angry. Or— worse—if they showed no feeling at all. Tension mounting, he waited for her to speak.

"I am with child," she said, her gaze rising to his.

As their eyes connected and the meaning of her words settled into him, a hot flash ran through him.

A baby.

Nicholas swallowed. His legs were as unsteady as if he'd taken a blow to the stomach. Yearning pierced his heart, destroying it completely, yet at the same time leaving it whole and pounding fiercely in his chest. The small room seemed even smaller, the thick stone walls moving in by feet. Then he remembered to breathe, and joy flooded his veins, tempered by a great bolt of fear. "A child. *Our* child." His voice was thick with emotion. "I-I-am astonished. Though I should not be."

"I have come to ask you…" she paused, dropping her head down so he could not see her eyes again. "Nay, I have come to beseech you to grant me a formal separation, with an income for the baby and me."

Nicholas breathed deep enough to make his ribs ache. "Please, Katherine. Do sit. I find I must, and wish you would as well. This news and your request are most unexpected. You must give me a moment."

She inclined her head in assent and perched on the stool.

Nicholas took his seat on the bed. He ran a hand through his hair and shook his head. Could he be dreaming? Katherine had come to see him. She had brought him joyous news, and then dashed it just as fast. His heart constricted.

"I wish only well for you and the babe." Nicholas swallowed. "I want to be a part of my child's life—and yours—for as long as

I am still possessed of mine."

"No." Her lips pulled into a firm line. "You are out of my life and that of the baby. Should you not grant this separation, my only recourse is to annul our marriage. The charges against you for my abduction would be dropped, but I would be forced to wed Richard Finch, since the only grounds for annulment are to state there was a prior contract. This is unacceptable to me, and I would not do it if I had an alternative."

Nichols felt his blood rise. "I would not have you marry Finch. Not before, and not now. Nor would I allow that man to raise my child. It is out of the question."

She nodded, aware she had prevailed, and pulled her hood off. Her expression was taut, not triumphant, her eyes tired. Her hair had been pulled back tight, giving her the severe look of the Puritan Katherine he had met. Gone was *his* Katherine, the Katherine of the *Hawk and Pheasant,* the Katherine he dreamed about at night, and whose image came to him when he could not sleep.

The Katherine who sat before him was a Katherine unknown to him, hard and cold. For a moment, he wondered if it was because of the babe.

Then the shattering truth revealed itself.

He had done this. He had changed her, extinguished her warmth, turned her flesh into marble. Of all the crimes he had committed, this was the most heinous. He had destroyed her sweetness. He had killed her love.

"I would make a bargain with you," she said, her lips moving without a hint of kindness. "I will do what is right, if you do what is right. I will testify that you did not abduct me, if you sign the separation papers."

She proposed a trade he could in no way refuse. Once the charges for abduction were dropped, he had only the accusations against the Raven to face. Nicholas rubbed the wound from Finch's bullet—the injury that had brought them together and ended his misbegotten career as a highwayman.

Katherine once asked what would have happened if she had not found him in the cottage. It was a question he asked himself often these days. The more he had thought, the more he became convinced that they came together for a reason. Perhaps the reason was the baby.

He cleared his throat. "I spend my days in quiet solitude. I watch the river out my window and count barges as they go by. And I think. Was it fate that brought me here? Or did I arrive here of my own free will?"

Katherine pursed her lips and shook her head.

"I do not think to release myself from responsibility for my actions—especially to you, dear Katherine. I did treat you most unfairly. For that I am heartily sorry." He sighed. "I wonder this because as I stand to lose my life, I think about its purpose. Do you believe in fate?"

Katherine blinked and shook her head. For a moment, he thought that was her answer, but then she spoke. "Grandfather would say God foreordains all things. Even though 'tis blasphemy for me to say this, I have sometimes wondered if that can be true. How could God keep track of us all? And what is the point of our lives if 'tis predestined? And why would I think I have a choice if I do not?"

"I have been thinking the same. Yet, I have such a strong sense that fate brought us together. Did destiny guide you to me? Would I have survived without your good care? Is there some divine purpose in our meeting? Or was it merely a fortuitous event that you chanced upon me?" Nicholas sighed. "From the moment I saw you wore my lucky piece, I felt fortune had cast us together."

"Your what?"

"The Chinese coin you wore around your neck. 'Twas mine long ago when I lived at Ashfield."

Katherine shook her head. "I had not thought of that—your being a boy there. I suppose all those other bits that Edward and I found were yours as well?"

Nicholas nodded.

"And the initials? There are five of them. I thought 'twas for two people."

"No, they are mine: Nicholas Edward Henry Philip

Montford. I was four-years of age before I could keep them straight, seven before I was able to spell them."

Katherine looked him in the eye. "I do not think I have been lucky for you. As to whether fate or a thunderstorm brought us together, I think it matters naught. What matters is what will happen now."

Nicholas nodded. He had no choice. He had trapped himself. Should he survive, he could not have her. But he would not let anyone else have her either. Even were it not for the babe that grew in her, he would never sanction an annulment. The words came out painfully. "I will consent to the separation. I will sign an agreement that provides an income for you and the baby."

"Good. It is the best answer." Katherine stood up.

Nicholas rose with her.

She pulled the hood over her head. "I will send the papers. Once they are signed, I will provide my testimony. Richard Finch will not like that. He may try to discredit me. He has a letter you wrote to my father offering to trade me for Ashfield."

Nicholas winced. No wonder she hated him so. He should never have written that letter. The idea had been a stupid one to begin with.

"I did not mean to hurt you, Katherine. If I had it to do over again—"

"You would do it differently?" She shook her head. "I think not, Nicholas. I think you have made your own rules for too long, not having to consider the wishes of anyone but yourself. You cannot blame that on fate."

Katherine walked to the door and rapped on it twice.

From the other side a key rattled in the lock, and then the door heaved open.

"I bid you good day," she said, and swept out. The door closed behind her with a resounding clunk.

Nicholas stood quiet and still as the sound of footsteps echoed down the staircase with an awesome finality.

A queer ache spread through him. Panic seized his heart. He wanted to call her back and plead with her to stay, so he could warm her coldness and ease the responsibility he had left her to shoulder alone. Just one last time he wished to hear her say she loved him.

And he wished to tell her the same.

Could it be? Was this what love felt like?

He could not breathe. Pain radiated from his chest through his belly to his fingers and toes. Did love feel like a crushing blow?

Nicholas dropped to the stool where Katherine had sat, gripping his chest where his heart beat.

He had not been close enough to inhale her special fragrance. She had left naught behind—no keepsake for him to hold through the days and nights that spread before him. No promise she would return.

Nicholas lowered his head, suddenly too heavy for his body to bear. He would fulfill his part of the bargain whither or no she did hers.

A baby and heir. How proud and happy his father would have been, knowing his grandchild would have possession of the family lands. Nicholas should be happy too. Instead, he felt like his heart had been pulled from his chest and thrown into the icy Thames below.

Too late.

He had come to realize he loved her too late.

Katherine took a steadying breath. She smoothed her hands down her grey linen skirt, more to gain her composure than to straighten the fabric. Richard Finch had called twice in the past week. She had sent word both times that she was indisposed. But she could not do that indefinitely. Mustering her resolve, she stepped into the sitting room.

He looked her up and down. Without any preliminaries, he spoke, his voice cutting into her like a knife. "What is this I hear? Your father informs me you will not be getting an annulment."

The cloying perfume on his gloves evoked memories of their skirmish in the coach. Her stomach was so sensitive these days,

Katherine dropped onto a chair trying not to gag.

He came to stand before her, too close as always, his eyes glaring down at her, his periwig bobbing back and forth as he nodded impatiently, waiting for her answer.

She breathed in short gasps of air, trying to evade the pervading scent. "'Twould not be to my benefit to have an annulment, so I have decided not to." That was the truth, although not all of it. She had not told her father about the baby, nor would she tell Finch. They would have to remain ignorant of that change in her circumstances until her body no longer kept it secret.

Finch smirked. "I am surprised you have the courage to be the instrument of his death, dear Katherine."

"I shall be no such thing." She clasped her hands together in her lap as she struggled for composure.

"Have I not been clear? He will hang for your abduction."

Katherine looked away.

"Do you think to testify in his defense? Aha! That is your plan." He had the self-satisfied tone of a person who has just discovered someone else's secret. "With the evidence of the letter, the court will not believe you."

Katherine looked up at him. "'Tis the truth."

"Many an innocent man has gone to the gallows. I think the crowd likes it all the more when a man insists he is not guilty as the noose is placed around his neck and his life is ever so slowly wrung from him."

Katherine gasped. Her stomach lurched. She thought she might be sick.

"Once he is dead, we shall be wed." Finch nodded.

"We will not," she said taking in a lungful of air. "My father is in favor of my marriage. I think he would defend it in court."

"Do not forget, I have a letter to your father that is very telling. The court will not believe him; they will believe the letter. And," he drew the word out, "I am prepared to present witnesses that will attest to your abduction."

Katherine gasped. "There can be no witnesses. 'Twas not an abduction."

"Do not misjudge me, Katherine. I do what is necessary to get what is mine."

"I am not yours now, nor have I ever been."

The words were strong, but Katherine's stomach roiled.

Nicholas held the quill pen suspended over the inkwell, trying to gather his thoughts. He had composed the letter twice in his mind, but now that he was ready to commit pen to paper the words flew away.

He had gotten himself into much trouble these last weeks with letter writing. But this letter would be different. It would ease his mind, and safeguard that which he held most precious.

Stretching to ease the cramp between his shoulders, he dipped the pen into the ink and began to write.

To His Majesty the King of England, Scotland, France and Ireland,

I write to you from the Tower where I have been incarcerated and await trial for crimes as a highwayman and abduction of an heiress, as no doubt your ministers have informed you.

I humbly beg the King's mercy for another matter. I married a woman without your leave. Although my motives in befriending her were selfish, I have since come to love this woman. Because of my own foolishness, I have lost her. My greatest regret is that I came to know my heart too late. If it is my fate to pay for these crimes with my life, I will go to the gallows willingly, to avoid the worst punishment of all. I cannot live without her love.

Although I do not deserve it, I most humbly beg a boon from your Majesty. I leave behind a wife and child who may find themselves in need of a friend. Once you did call me that. It is my dearest wish you might consider them as such in my absence.

I remain your Majesty's most humble and obedient servant,
NEHPM The Earl of Ashton

Katherine spent the better part of the next two days in the garden trying to regain her sense of calm. This all scattered when she entered the kitchen to find Jeremy and Henry in hushed conversation. Henry stood when he saw her.

"Glad I am to see you, Lady Ashton."

Katherine nodded at the older man. In clean well-cut clothing, he looked almost dapper. "You look much improved."

"Aye, I am." Henry nodded, but did not smile. "If ye would grant me an audience, I would speak to ye about my master."

Katherine's heart dropped. Was it more bad news? "Let us talk in the garden."

They left Jeremy and went outside. The air was brisk, the sky grey. Katherine hoped it might rain. She could use a good drenching, to extinguish this fever that rushed through her every time she thought of Nicholas.

Katherine bid Henry be seated with her on the stone bench. She braced herself. "Is there news?"

"Aye. The trial is near. From what I hear, Finch is putting together a great deal of evidence."

Katherine nodded. She had expected this.

"What's worse, Nicky has decided to raise no defense. He says he will leave the outcome to fate. 'Tis a foolish notion of his, yet I cannot shake the man."

"'Twas not fate that made this mess. 'Twas Nicholas himself."

Henry nodded. "And I would agree w' you on that. But he thinks his fate is tied to you. I do not understand this. Mayhap you do."

"I will provide testimony that I was not abducted. I told him I would. I see not what that has to do with fate."

Henry sighed. "I need ye to help him because I no longer can. When ye agreed to marry him, 'twas in your pledge ye would take care of him. Are you good for your word?"

Katherine looked down, lamenting the nature of a pledge to cause untold grief. Henry was right. Even though she'd not known enough about the man she married, she had pushed away that worry. Some responsibility for their misbegotten marriage was hers. They would not have wed had she said 'no.'

Katherine chewed her lip. She didn't like it, but he might be right.

"Let me tell you about my master. I would speak to you about the things he would not. Nicky had a hard life as a lad. His mother died when he was eight. When he was eleven, he and his father exiled to Holland. I went with 'em. Times were tough there, they were, and the old Earl saw the bottom of many bottles."

Nicholas had told her some of this, but had painted a much merrier picture than the one Henry presented.

Henry continued. "It was hard on the lad watching his father kill himself slowly like that and not be able to prevent it. They lived in dreadful surroundings, one step off the street. Nicky fell to petty thieving to feed the two of them. When his Da lay dying, he made the boy promise to get the family estate back, and force the Puritans to pay for what they had done to him. Of course, the lad agreed."

Katherine nodded, remembering Nicholas's fevered ramblings when she'd found him in the cottage. That explained the Raven. An inventive and ineffective revenge, it still made a certain kind of sense. What would the old Earl have thought of Nicholas's method? She could only think Nicholas's father had something more conventional in mind.

"Then what happened?"

"The next years, Nicky floated from one place to the next, living off French and Spanish nobles, fellow Englishmen in exile, harlots and thieves. He became a man. A man without a home, without a family. And he came to believe that getting back his family lands would make everything right. And, of course, in trying to make it all right, he made it all wrong. He should never have done what he did to you. From the first, he should have told you his true name. He hasna the wisdom he needs to go with his guile, so he made a big mess of it. But he did one very right thing in all of this."

Henry looked her straight in the eye. "He found you: his

match. The other part that would make him whole. He rescued you from your home, and took you off on a wee adventure. Now 'tis for you, in return, to rescue him. You must teach him what honor is, because it's not fulfilling a promise a young boy should have never had to make. It is fulfilling the promise he made to you in that church, e'en though we could barely understand it."

Katherine looked away. She had made a promise too. Now that promise cut into her heart, but could she truly turn away from it and feel she was doing the right thing?

"In you, he must see the courage to love and be loved. He's a man that does not easily know his own heart. He had it twisted when he was young—to lose his mother and then see his Da die like that." Henry shook his head and scratched his chin. "I can not speak more plain. You are his last chance. He needs yer help, m'lady."

Katherine chewed her lip. "I had thought providing testimony was all I could do. Now you make me think I have been looking at it wrong. You give me answers to questions I did not know I had." She sighed. "My heart is heavy."

"Look inside yer heart, milady. Listen to what it says. Do not turn it away from yer husband, or yerself." Henry rose, nodding to her.

Katherine barely saw him leave the garden. She stayed behind, her mind reeling. Could she have been so full of her own pain, she not seen Nicholas's? She shook her head. If Nicholas truly had not meant to hurt her, he had a lot to learn. But how would he ever learn if he did not have the chance?

Had it been fate that had brought her to him?

If it was fate, then it was not just his fate. It was her fate as well.

Katherine chewed her lower lip. More importantly, how much longer could she ignore the love for him she still held in her heart?

CHAPTER NINETEEN

"How about the pink?" Alicia held an elegant silk-gauze mantua up to Katherine and examined it against her with a critical eye. "No," she shook her head, and tossed it onto her bed. "It does not suit your coloring, nor mine either," she sighed.

Katherine looked at the garment longingly. It reminded her a bit of the dress Nicholas had bought her. Yet, the color did not suit her mood. "Perhaps something bit darker? A nice brown?"

Alicia raised her eyebrows. "Brown will never do. At court, you must wear something gay. Let us see." She burrowed through her wardrobe and pulled out another dress. "What about this?"

Katherine's breath caught. Dark satin shimmered in the light, catching emerald highlights on a forest green. The gown was beautiful, and cut simply as well, without ruffles or flounces, just a bit of ecru lace at the cuffs and neckline. She held it up to herself. Other than its length, it would fit. She caught Alicia's approving eye.

"I think that will do very nicely," her cousin said. "It is a bit tight on me, and somewhat out of fashion, but 'tis simple as I know you like, and it suits you very well."

Katherine ran her fingers across the cool, smooth fabric before trying it on.

Alicia marked the new hemline. That evening when they sat in the small sitting room before the cheery fire, the two women sewed the hem and made some other small adjustments to the fit.

"You will need a bit of jewelry," Alicia said.

"I have never worn jewelry," Katherine protested.

"Nevertheless, you cannot see the King without wearing a bit of flash and sparkle. We can take a look through my jewelry case tomorrow before you leave." Alicia reached into her skirt and pulled something from an inside pocket. "You might wish to wear this." She held her hand out to Katherine, and then opened it to reveal the Chinese coin on the fine gold chain.

Katherine gasped. "My coin! But how did you get it?"

Alicia dropped the trinket into Katherine's hand. "One of the boys found it in the street after the fight. It was Jeremy who told me it belonged to you. I think your husband must have lost it during the scuffle."

Husband.

Katherine's heart made an aching thump as the word echoed through her, reverberating down to the hand holding the coin. On the morrow, she would say that word to the King, avowing she had married of her own free will. She would tell him the evidence against Nicholas was a sham, and plead the King's mercy for a man who did not love her.

Even if Nicholas would do nothing to change his fate, she could not leave it so. She would fight for him, because she loved him still. She could not change that. Nor could she rid herself of the pain from wanting her husband to love her, with a love that was stronger and more passionate than a pledge made to a sick dying father. A love above all else.

Katherine's fingers closed over the Chinese coin.

They entered Whitehall through the Great Gate. Katherine repressed a nervous gasp as a footman helped her out of the coach. Opulently dressed courtiers mingled about, some out for a stroll of St. James Park. Others, apparently on business, walked with a more purposeful air.

The very simplicity of her borrowed gown, with just Alicia's pearl necklace and emerald brooch for decoration, seemed to attract comment. Katherine straightened her shoulders and raised her chin. The curls at the side of her face bounced against her cheeks.

"You are sure he got the letter? He will come?"

"Yea, sister. I handed it to him. He read it, and said he would be here. I still do not know why you wanted him to come."

Proving Jeremy right, Richard Finch separated from the crowd and came to meet them. He looked more resplendent than she had ever seen him, not a hair out of place on his periwig. Like a fine bird, his clothing was bright, colorful, and rich. He reached for her hand, but she clutched Jeremy's arm, and moved a step closer to her brother.

"What is he doing here?" Finch glared at Jeremy.

"I have invited him to accompany me, as I invited you," said Katherine, trying not to let her nervousness creep into her voice.

Before Finch could reply, James Pemberton came puffing up and Katherine made the introductions. James gave her a vague but heartening smile, and took the group inside the nearest building. They walked through corridors, rooms, and galleries, each more splendid than the last. Chandeliers glittered on high gilded ceilings. Beribboned courtiers stood about in clusters. Katherine felt more conspicuous than she could ever remember, but she pulled herself as tall as she could and forced her lips into a smile as they entered an enormous room. The buzz of voices echoed off the high painted ceilings.

"Ah, there he is," James spoke into her ear, and nodded his head toward a cluster of people at one end. Katherine peered in that direction but could not see above the tall plumed hats of the men, nor around the wide sleeves of the ladies.

They made their way through the crush of people, into what seemed like an unofficial line, waiting their turn to meet with the King. A lump rose in Katherine's throat. She told herself if she held her hands together, no one would be able to see them shake.

At last, they arrived before the great man. Katherine made a deep curtsey, surprised at her calm before the most powerful man in the realm. Her eyes rose over a magnificent peacock blue brocaded waistcoat, lace ruffed shirt, to dark curly hair framing a swarthy complexion, full lips, and dark but twinkling eyes. She felt a glimmer of familiarity and sensed, all around them, curious eyes and ears.

"Sire," said James, raising his portly girth from a bow. "We are grateful for this brief audience."

Charles smiled upon the assembled group. "I have heard there is some issue about Lord Ashton and an abduction?"

"Yes, your Majesty," Finch spoke. He made a courtiers bow. "'Tis shocking. I have a letter written by this rogue, a ransom note, bartering Mistress Welles for her property."

Charles turned an appraising eye upon Katherine. "We are sorely distressed that one whom we did call friend has caused you such anguish. Shall we punish Lord Ashton for the trouble he has caused?"

Katherine could barely speak for the anxiety that rose up from her very feet and flooded through her body. "Your Majesty," she said, lifting her eyes up to his for but a moment, "'twas not an abduction or a kidnapping for I went of my own free will."

Finch made a sharp indrawn breath.

"I sense a gentle heart within you," said the King. "But if Lord Ashton has caused you harm, then harm should come to him."

"Majesty," Katherine met his eyes again. He gazed down upon her with a warm curiosity, and she felt emboldened to continue. "I cannot say he has not caused me harm, for my heart is sorely wounded. Yet, I cannot see him punished for the wrong offense. I do not think there is a law against breaking a woman's heart."

Charles reached a bejeweled hand to her chin, and raised it up with a long finger. He gave her a sad smile, and then a sparkle lit his eyes.

"'Od's fish, Madam. Did you bring your cat? But then my spaniels are not here, so I think you would not give me such a merry chase as you did last time we met."

Katherine's eyes grew wide. Now she knew where she had seen him. Running after half a dozen yapping dogs! And then she broke into a smile, recalling the comical expression on his face when she and Montford had taken off down the hall.

The King nodded. "I do believe you went with him willingly. Else you could have left him when I saw you."

"Yea, Sire, it is so. Although he kept me ignorant of his true name and motive, I did seek his aid to leave my home before I could be married to my neighbor." She nodded at Finch.

"You did not consent to that match?"

"I wished completely to avoid it."

Charles took his hand from Katherine's chin and she swallowed. He turned his attention to Finch.

"What say you to this new accusation? Did you seek to wed this woman without her consent?"

"'Twas her father's wish that we wed," Finch sputtered. "It had been arranged, the settlements agreed upon."

"And did you not seek to woo her?"

"Yea, Majesty. I did most heartily."

"Yet, I wonder, did you not perhaps seek to woo her property more than her heart, and thereby miss the mark?" Charles chuckled at his own joke. "You will find that ladies are wont to be agreeable when you are more congenial." He turned dismissively from Finch back to Katherine.

"So I must punish the rogue for breaking your heart," he brought a hand to his chin and paused, thinking. "Shall it be transportation? Death? What say you, Lady Ashton?"

"Sire, my husband is a prankster, as I think you already know."

"Indeed, his latest mischief vexes me sorely."

"I find it so myself," Katherine agreed. "Yet, I plead for clemency. His crimes as the Raven were meant as a jest. He caused embarrassment, but not harm. Although he should have his hand slapped, twould be a pity to see it cut off."

"And Ashfield? What say you to that? He had petitioned for its return."

"Ashfield belongs to my father. I never wished to be heiress to it. My mother provided me with an adequate dowry, and my brother Edward was to inherit, but he died." She took a deep breath. "My other brother, Jeremy," she tipped her head at him, "should be the one to inherit, as is proper for a son."

Gasps and indrawn breaths accompanied Katherine's pronouncement, and she was dimly aware of heads turning toward them. Nearby, voices quieted. Jeremy's face turned noticeably white as he looked around their immediate circle.

Finch's mouth twisted in grievous displeasure. "It cannot be true," he said, "and if so, has no merit." He turned to James. "The boy is clearly a bastard, and bastards do not inherit."

"There is no doubt in my heart," Katherine spoke up. "Jeremy is my brother. And although he was not to speak of it, there was no such restraint put on me."

James coughed. "A *filius nullius* has no legal right to inherit. Yet, it might be possible, should your majesty see fit to allow it, as there is no entail on the property."

"*You* cannot have Ashfield!" Finch advanced on Jeremy.

Jeremy did not move. His eyes sparkled, whether with tears, anger, amusement, or some combination of the three, Katherine could not tell. "I will do what is best for Lady Ashton," he said. "And for my family."

"You have no right! No right at all! The property was to come to me. 'Twas arranged—"

"Yet it did not," Charles's commanding voice cut in. "Now the Lady is wed. As to the disposition of the property, I will have to think on't." He nodded and turned to Katherine. "You are a woman of brave mettle, and uncommon pretty as well. I have always found it most difficult to disappoint an attractive woman, and in your case, since I see your heart is firmly affixed elsewhere, I believe I have a fancy to play cupid. In your heart, do you still wish your husband's love? Would you like to find out if 'tis there?"

Katherine nodded, unable to break his gaze.

Charles raised an eyebrow. "Are you also willing to find out if 'tis not?"

Katherine took a deep breath, and then nodded. Yes, she had the courage.

The King tilted his head back in a flourish of feathers, as his broad-brimmed hat made an elegant sweep. He tapped his walking stick on the wood floor. The room quieted. "Come back on the morrow, and we will discover Lord Ashton's true regard."

Katherine's heart caught, and she curtseyed.

That night Nicholas was transported by barge from the Tower to the Gatehouse at Whitehall. Instead of the trial he had expected, soon he would face his King. Would Charles find it in his heart to pardon Nicholas's indiscretions, or would the King see that justice was sure and swift? As an Earl, would he be given the honor of a quick beheading with a sword, or would he hang from a gibbet as a common highwayman?

And what of Katherine? Would Nicholas ever have a chance to tell her he loved her?

He had met with his man of business. The papers that would protect her and the babe and assure their future were drawn up.

If he had it all to do again, he would do it different.

At least, he hoped so.

A resplendent royal messenger arrived at the Pemberton household next morning bearing a message for Katherine and causing quite a stir. The butler even straightened his periwig before answering the door. Robbie and Hal spent the next two hours marching around the house with scraps of paper, handing them to the housemaid, the cook, and Alicia, until she told them "enough" in that tone that sent them scurrying outdoors.

The note contained two words: *Three O'clock.*

Katherine could not eat or concentrate. In fact, she excused herself from overseeing even the simplest household chores. Dressing took much longer than usual. Alicia styled her hair, adding again the pin curls at the side of Katherine's face and applying a bit of color to her lips.

Katherine's stomach made a painful lurch every time she thought of Nicholas, and though she tried, she could not stop thoughts of him from appearing every few minutes.

The cousins embraced, and then Katherine was off.

Jeremy accompanied her in the Pemberton coach. He had said little to her since she had announced the truth of his parentage.

"Do you mind that I did say you are my brother?"

"I know not what to think," he said. "I am proud that you would wish it known. Yet, I cannot think our father will be pleased. And our neighbor was truly displeased. 'Tis kind of you to think of Ashfield for me, Katherine, but I do not think 'twould be right for me to inherit the property."

"'Twere it entailed, I would not be in line to inherit." Katherine sighed. "Truly, I do not wish to see the place again."

Jeremy made a tense smile.

They spoke no more on the long trip to Whitehall. The clickety-clack of the wheels, and the pounding of Katherine's heart combined to heighten her alarm. By the time they arrived, she was in a state of near panic. Taking a steadying breath, she allowed Jeremy to help her out of the vehicle.

An unsmiling footman bade Jeremy stay behind. After an appraising look at Katherine, the servant led her through a labyrinth of back corridors and staircases to a small room. With a knowing smile, he closed the door, leaving her to wait.

Did he think her one of the Kings sweethearts? Katherine repressed a snort at the outrageous thought.

What would the King tell her? Would he really appear, or would he send Nicholas alone?

It did no good to wonder. He would come or he would not. The King said he would help her discover the truth, and perhaps that truth would help her heart to mend.

Katherine lifted her chin and looked around the room. Scientific books stood on the shelves, many in Latin. Several tables were scattered about, containing all sorts of devices and models. Katherine had no idea of their use. Some looked fanciful, others complicated. One, made of metal and glass, looked so delicate she could not imagine what it could be used for. A pile of charts and drawings topped another table.

"Do you know what that is?"

Katherine jumped. She had not heard the King enter. Now he stood just behind her.

She shook her head.

"Hazard a guess, Lady Ashton."

It seemed to contain an eyepiece, and looked vaguely similar to the strange object she and Jeremy had found in Nicholas's cloak. "Maybe it is for looking at things," she said.

"Indeed, you are right." Charles clapped a hand on her shoulder. "It is for looking at things that are very small, and making them bigger. Oft times, when we are able to see the finer parts of an object, we can understand it better."

Katherine nodded.

"Science is very good for that," the King continued, "for showing us how a thing truly works, helping us become acquainted with the fine details. But though it can show us how a heart beats, it cannot show us why a heart beats, nor for whom the heart beats."

He walked her across the room. "Shall we find out about Lord Ashton, the knave who called himself my friend, and who called himself the Raven to you?"

"Yes, sire. I am well ready to know his heart."

A footman, who must have been standing just outside, entered, and Charles bid him get Nicholas. The King showed her where to stand in a concealed spot behind a curtain, masking an open door at the top of a staircase. There would be plenty of room for her. Now, Katherine could see how the King had been able to enter the room without her knowing.

❧

"My liege," Nicholas said, making a deep courtly bow.

"You may rise," Charles said. "I bid you be seated."

Nicholas sat in a chair. This was a good sign. It appeared they would talk, rather than the King talk and Nicholas listen.

"How long have we known each other?" asked the King.

Nicholas knew Charles remembered as well as he when they first met, but supposed the King wished to make a point.

"Was it not twelve or thirteen years past we met in Paris?"

"Yes, I believe that is so. You provided aid to me freely when others would do so only if I made them promises. For that, Nicky, I have always had a particular fondness for you. Yet, certain recent events try my patience." Charles gave him a stern look. "You have taken a wife under most peculiar circumstances, without obtaining consent of her father, or, more importantly, consent of your King. Furthermore, your wife did not know who you were when you married her. Can this be true? And you perpetrated this deception to gain control of her lands, which I do recall belonged to your family before they were forfeit by that villain, Cromwell. Was there not an interview some two months past, when you petitioned me for return of those lands? And then…" Charles tapped his lip with a bejeweled finger. "I believe I have not seen your face again until this very moment."

Nicholas squirmed.

"And now I assume you seek my pardon, which I am wont to give you, Nicky, as you did stand by me when others did not." The King rose and walked to the window. "I ask you this, my old friend, were it in my power to grant you either the woman you took as wife, or Ashfield, but not both, which would you have?"

Nicholas thoughts went back to that day long ago, to the young boy listening through silent tears as his father, infirm and old before his time, beseeched him to right the wrongs done to the family. At his father's bidding, he'd placed his hand on the family bible and vowed to get back what was rightfully theirs. Just a lad of sixteen, he'd thought himself to be a man. But now, Nicholas knew he'd just been a boy who had carried a man's responsibilities, and thought himself to be making a man's pledge.

He had never wanted Ashfield for himself. He'd made his own life out of the ashes of his father's life. He would not know what to do with Ashfield if he had it.

Nicholas had wanted revenge. And he had got it. But the revenge had been on him. He now knew his heart's desire, and he'd lost it due to his own foolishness.

He had made a man's pledge to Katherine in the church. Although he had done it for the wrong reasons, he now knew the right one: he loved her.

Nicholas silently begged his father's forgiveness before speaking. "I would choose Katherine over all things. She is my destiny and my desire. I find that now I have lost her, she is all I ever truly wanted. I should have known when she discovered me ill and nursed me to health that I needed her with a fierceness I have never felt for anyone or anything before."

Charles eyes softened. He rose and walked across the room.

Nicholas continued. "By my rash actions, I know I have lost her. I know you cannot give her back to me. Katherine is a woman who knows her own heart. 'Tis quite clear to me that if I did once have it, 'tis gone now."

"Are you certain of that, Nicky?" Charles pulled back a curtain to reveal a woman.

Nicholas stood up in protest. Had one of the King's mistresses listened to his heartfelt avowal? Then she moved, and a jolt of recognition hit him.

Katherine.

Yet, this was not a Katherine he had ever seen before. This Katherine wore a fancy gown, with lace and frills, and her hair had been dressed in the current fashion.

"Katherine?"

She nodded, and the curls on the side of her face bobbled back and forth.

"I did not recognize you. The clothes...the hair..." He went to her and took a curl into his hand, letting it wrap around his finger.

She looked up at him. "Clothes do not the person make.

Perhaps 'tis time for you to see me for who I truly am."

He knew that to be true. He had forever been misjudging this woman. In her, he had found strength of purpose and love he had never known.

"My liege," he looked over Katherine's shoulder. "Do I have your permission?"

Charles nodded.

Nicholas took Katherine into his arms and gave her stiff form a powerful hug. "I have long known that I need you," he said. "But it is just recently that I have come to understand that I love you."

He looked down into her beautiful brown eyes, full of wariness, but not love. Clearly, he had not done enough to win her back.

But he was on the right road.

"The two of you must regale me with your adventures," the King interrupted. "But now that you have reunited, 'tis time for us to resolve other matters that are before us."

Nicholas loosened his hold on his wife.

"It is now established to my mind, and the courts will easily be persuaded, that an abduction did not occur. Yet, I am afraid there are still some very serious charges against the man who called himself the Raven."

A different footman led Nicholas and Katherine down the stairs, through the warren of stairways and corridors. They passed through hallway after hallway until they came to the Gatehouse.

Katherine felt no sense of triumph. No sense of elation or completeness coursed through her veins. While Nicholas might think all was fixed, she was sorely vexed.

Once alone, they faced each other. Nicholas smiled and held out his arms to her.

Katherine crossed her arms over her chest. "Do you think that by telling the King you love me everything is fine?" She tapped her foot. "Methinks you should have more to say."

Nicholas put up a hand. "Whoa, dear wife. 'Tis plain any thoughts I had on that matter were mistaken." He ran a hand through his hair. "I know I have much to atone for. And although I have spent these days in jail, have confessed my heart before my liege, have lost any claim to the lands of my family, I must still make amends with the woman who has discovered my heart."

He came to her and put his hands on her shoulders, despite her uninviting stance. "I have not had much love in my life. It is not a feeling I understand. So it has taken me some time to realize that these feelings I have for you—of happiness when I am with you, of emptiness when you are gone, of my need to protect you, and the desire I have for you, not just for the pleasure I find in your body, but for your gentle yet firm presence and good sense—I now know these feelings are love." His voice broke as his eyes reached into hers, touching her in that place he had hurt so badly.

Katherine softened.

"I would wish you love me too. I know you said so before. But I could understand, after my actions, that any good feelings you once had for me are now gone. I have played you false, my dearest Katherine, and I can only hope that you have it in your power to forgive, and that there is room in your tender heart for me."

His eyes pled for her love and understanding.

Katherine looked away. "'Twould be more convincing had you given up something that belonged to you, Nicholas. Ashfield was never yours. 'Twas your father's, then my father's."

"I gave up the dream of Ashfield, Katherine. 'Twas bigger than the real Ashfield. And a bigger loss as well."

"You confessed your love to the King, yet you have not said it to me," she said.

"He was the first to ask," said Nicholas.

A glance showed Katherine the twinkle she so loved to see in his eyes.

"I'truth," he said, "I did not know my own heart until the

door shut behind you at the Tower, and I heard your footsteps echo down the hall as you walked away. But I feared it was too late. I had not thought to see you again. I thought it best to leave things as they were, with you hating me for what I had done. Especially since I had no reason to hope I would be forgiven for my crimes. My future is still cloudy. I can only think because you are here you must harbor some good feelings for me."

He went down on one knee before her. "I do hereby vow, my dearest Lady Ashton, that I love you with my whole heart and body, and I shall never lie to you again. Never."

Katherine smiled down at him. "Rise, Lord Ashton, and know my love for you has never left. Although at times I wished it, I could not make it go."

Nicholas rose and took her into his arms. Molding to each other they kissed, a magical kiss of fire, desire, and joy.

The next afternoon, a footman brought the lovers to the crowded banquet hall. Even when Katherine saw Richard Finch scowling at her from across the room, her rosy glow did not leave. Jeremy stood with James Pemberton and smiled at her. To her surprise, Gerald Welles was there as well, looking like a country squire clearly out of place in such magnificent surroundings.

She held Nicholas's hand, savoring every moment, knowing that their brief happiness could be shattered or cemented by the outcome of this next interview.

At last, they were summoned. A footman brought all of them to an inner chamber.

King Charles smiled as they entered, but he did not bid them be seated. He addressed Nicholas. "Ravens are bothersome birds, loud and messy. There have been some at the tower for quite some time now. I did once try to rid the place of them. Do you know what I was told?"

"No, sire."

"I was told that as long as there are ravens at the tower, the

Monarchy will stand." The King nodded at Nicholas. "Do you say you are this Raven? This outlaw as you have been accused?"

"Sire, once there was an outlaw Raven, but he is no more. Any ravens at the tower from this point on, I hope will only be birds. I vow to you, I will always do what is in my power to keep your crown safe."

"I trust what you say is true, Nicholas Montford, for I have come to a decision.

"First," Charles said, "since taking a woman against her will and marrying or defiling her is a felony, you will forfeit any claims to Ashfield." The King turned to James. "Although I have been assured he did not truly take her against her will, I have no doubts that had the young lady known his true identity, she would never have gone with him." Charles eyed the group and seemed satisfied by the looks on everyone's faces. His gaze came to rest on Katherine and he smiled. "So perhaps ignorance was good in this case.

"Secondly, for the crimes of the Raven, Lord Ashton will be encouraged to emigrate to America. With seven other Lords, he will be appointed a Joint Proprietor of the Province of Carolina." He winked at Katherine. "I am sure that your husband's pluck, good humor, and inventive strategies will prove a boon in developing this territory.

"Third, since it is customary in our land for sons to inherit from fathers, Jeremy Welles, though *filius nullius,* will take his place as heir to the property called Ashfield."

Gerald sputtered.

Charles continued. "Fourth, since Lord Ashton, has no use for his title, he will lose it. I hereby rescind the letters of patent, and bestow the title onto the young lad here,"

Jeremy's eyes almost popped out of his head. Everyone turned to him. Gerald raised his hand to his heart. Finch had turned white with shock.

"In that way, it will stay with the property, and he will make himself worthy of it." Charles smiled at Jeremy. "Nicky can retain the title of Baron Eddington, which he was before his father passed, a title which I understand he *has* been willing to use."

"Finally, I charge Lady Eddington to accompany her husband to the New World. I give her the assignment of reporting directly to me should Nicky be up to any mischief!"

EPILOGUE

Province of Carolina
November, 1664

Nicholas Montford, newly appointed Lord Proprietor, dodged low hanging tree branches as he moved quickly through the woods. Blood congealed on his left arm.

At a rustle in the brush behind him, he glanced over his shoulder, ready to draw his pistol if need be. But it was just the wolf—*his* wolf Katherine called it—that was ever guarding his rear. Or perhaps today, tantalized by the smell of blood, it would not let its prey out of sight.

Nicholas planted each foot firmly on the blanket of brown pine needles that coated the forest floor. Each crunch released their pungent aroma to mingle with the crisp morning air.

At last he made the clearing that held his home.

Their home. The small wooden cottage he fully intended to replace with a brick mansion once the materials arrived from England. One day his boots would tread upon a finely tended lawn with topiary, but for now he dashed across a hard dirt glade before hurdling the steps to the cabin's entrance.

He burst into the small main room. Katherine looked up from the table where she was writing with a smile that fell away when she saw his arm.

Nicholas hastened to reassure her. "I have brought you something."

Katherine rose and took a step toward him. She looked closely and frowned. "Our dinner?"

"No. At least I think 'tis not dinner yet." Nicholas uncurled his arm and held out the quivering bundle of brown fur and blood. "I think it can be fixed. That is, I think *you* can fix it."

Katherine could not gainsay him. She took the rabbit and turned it on its back. It stopped shuddering and went limp in her arms.

Nicolas watched with dismay. "Is it dead then?"

"'Tis just a rabbit trick." She ran her fingers lightly over the blood-covered bunny, examining its eyes, nose, and paws. "Ah. I see. It's lost a claw. So much blood from such a small wound. I wonder how that happened."

Nicholas looked out the door at the wolf hovering at the woods edge. "Perhaps because it tried to climb a tree."

A slow smile spread its way across Katherine's face, and their eyes met, both surely remembering when another small furry animal climbed up a tree.

"Rabbits don't climb trees," said Katherine.

"They try to if a large gray wolf is chasing them."

"First a wolf and now a rabbit. You bring home many pets when what we really need is a cat—perhaps two. I was just writing this to Alicia, asking her to send them from Montford's recent litter once they are old enough to travel." She examined the bloody paw again. "'T'will not be serious unless it putrefies. I will need to clean and bandage it. Since 'tis washday, Lizzie has started to heat the water. I need you to fetch some and clean rags, too."

"I am to get water and rags?" Nicholas tried to look stern, but failed miserably as he always did with Katherine. "I do not understand this. Did not the clergyman say *you* were to obey *me*?"

"'Twas hard to understand the man so I am not surprised you misheard. 'Twas *you* who vowed to obey *me*. Do not forget, our liege did say I am to inform him if you are up to mischief." She looked at him with such natural coquetry his blood ran hot. "Clearly it is our King's desire for you to obey me."

Nicholas laughed. "Then I shall happily do your bidding and get water and rags before you come up with any more difficult tasks."

From a nearby cradle came the unmistakable sound of a baby wakening. Katherine and Nicholas looked at each other with conspiratorial panic. Once Elizabeth Mary Margaret Isabella Montford woke up, there would be no question of who would be obeying whom. They were both already her devoted servants.

Katherine peeked into the cradle while Nicolas tiptoed from the room to the outlaying kitchen and laundry.

When he returned, it was to see Katherine with the babe at her breast. The little mouth suckled the globe of Katherine's creamy skin; the head of honey colored curls bobbed up and down, her hand grasped the Chinese coin hanging on the chain around Katherine's neck.

It was a vision so sweet it brought tears to his eyes, and he had to blink them away. He remembered Katherine on their first night in London trying to explain how a person could cry from happiness. He now knew how that could be.

Just as he knew he was the luckiest man to have found Katherine—rather, to have been found *by* her. She had saved his life. She had changed his life. She had given him the best reason to live by gifting him with her love.

What's more, she had taught him that love once gifted becomes evermore stronger when it is gifted back.

ABOUT THE AUTHOR

Gina pounded out her first story on an old Royal typewriter when she was eight. For most of her adult life she worked in television counting backwards and telling people what to do. Now she lives in Central California with her personal hero and a cat, and spends her time writing books.

Visit Gina at www.ginablack.net

COMING SOON!

THE UNSUITABLE EARL

In the spring of 1665...

After rising from stable boy to the Earl of Ashton, all Jeremy Welles wants from life is to eat, drink, be merry, and forget he's been elevated into a position he's eminently unequal to. But then he meets Lady Eliza Stanfield...

Strong willed and spoiled, Lady Eliza has no intention of ever marrying. So when she finds herself being courted by the awkward and unassuming Earl of Ashton, she sees an opportunity she can exploit—an unsuitable suitor—one she can use as a shield against her parents and their prospects.

Then the plague breaks out, and the Stanfields flee London to their country estate, bringing Jeremy and other nobles in their tow. Away from the constant party that has been his life, will Jeremy find himself happier and more welcome in the stables or the drawing room? And will Eliza allow her heart to be captured, and herself to be tamed, by the unsuitable young Earl of Ashton?

Paperback copies of Gina's books can be found at
http://www.greatbirdbooks.com

www.ingramcontent.com/pod-product-compliance
Lightning Source LLC
Chambersburg PA
CBHW030115180626
46812CB00002B/425